What the readers say about *The Declaration*

'To anyone who's a fan of *Divergent* by Veronica Roth, *The Hunger Games* series or Richelle Mead's *Vampire Academy* series, this is a must-read'

'One of the best realised dystopian visions I have read in a long time'

'This is a disturbing novel with a shocking ending and will stay with you long after you close the book and the sequel, *The Resistance*, is even better'

What the papers say:

'A darkly disturbing and intriguing tale'
Financial Times

'A well-imagined and endlessly thought-provoking story'
Sunday Telegraph

'Should be on everyone's reading list because it has you clinging on for dear life around every twist and turn'
Sunday Express

The Legacy

The
Legacy

GEMMA MALLEY

BLOOMSBURY
LONDON NEW DELHI NEW YORK SYDNEY

Bloomsbury Publishing, London, New Delhi, New York and Sydney

First published in Great Britain in September 2010 by Bloomsbury Publishing Plc
50 Bedford Square, London, WC1B 3DP

This paperback edition published in November 2012

A CIP catalogue record for this book is available from the British Library

ISBN 978 1 4088 3689 7

Typeset by Dorchester Typesetting
Printed and bound in Great Britain by CPI Group (UK) Ltd, Croydon CR0 4YY

1 3 5 7 9 10 8 6 4 2

www.bloomsbury.com

For my sisters, Maddy and Abigail

Prologue

Albert Fern stared down at his hands, which were trembling. He could feel small beads of sweat collecting in the crevices of his forehead, lines etched over the years from concentration which provided him with a face that looked older than his seventy years. Seventy years, he found himself thinking. It had gone by so quickly, much of it spent in this very lab, the place he loved the best, searching for answers, for breakthroughs, for . . .

He wiped his forehead with the sleeve of his lab coat. There was no doubt about it – he'd done the test twenty times and still the same result was forcing itself on him. He had the cure, the cure for cancer, the cure that would save his daughter's life, and yet with it came something else. Something incredible. Something terrifying.

Carefully, the professor put down the syringe he'd been holding in his hands, removed his gloves and pulled off his protective goggles. He took a few steps backwards, as though attempting to escape from his creation while at the same time feeling unable to look anywhere else. The Holy Grail. That's what it was. He wiped his hands on his lab coat; immediately more sweat appeared on them.

The door behind him opened suddenly, and he started, jumping rather more violently than was perhaps to be expected. Nervously, he turned round, his forehead furrowing.

His assistant looked at him, his eyebrows raised in a way that made Albert uncomfortable. 'So, did you do it? Did it work again?'

Albert said nothing, but his eyes spoke for him. The corners of his assistant's mouth crept upwards. 'It did, didn't it? You've done it. Jesus, Albert, do you realise what we've got here?'

Albert noticed the 'we' and let it go. 'Perhaps. But perhaps . . .' His voice trailed off. He wasn't ready to articulate the truth, wasn't yet ready to face the realisation that only a few metres away lay the answer to the question that mankind had been asking since it developed the power of speech. He was in shock, in awe – the discovery made him hot yet at the same time froze his blood.

'Albert?' His assistant walked slowly towards him. The man who'd been at his side for the past few years, the man Albert still didn't trust. 'Albert,' he was saying uncertainly, 'what's wrong? Did something go wrong?'

Albert shook his head, then nodded, then shook his head again. 'Nothing went wrong,' he whispered.

The young man's face lit up. 'Albert, you know what this means, don't you? We have the world in our hands. We've achieved what no one else has.'

Again, the 'we'. Albert nodded uneasily. 'Richard,' he said carefully, 'invention is not always good. Sometimes our inventions are too powerful for us to control. Splitting the atom, for instance. Ernest Rutherford couldn't know what was to follow, and yet we all associate him with the atom bomb.'

'The atom bomb killed people,' Richard said, rolling his eyes dismissively in the way only young men could, Albert thought to himself. 'This is about saving lives. Prolonging lives.'

'But indefinitely?' Albert asked quietly. 'Do you know what that would mean? Have you understood the ramifications? It would change the world completely. It would change humankind completely. We would become demigods.'

'We've been through this a thousand times,' Richard snorted impatiently, scanning Albert's desk then looking up when he felt Albert's eyes on him. 'It's just an excuse for prevarication because you're weak, Albert. Stop worrying. Stop feeling like you're responsible for every possible repercussion of what you've created. You're not.'

'But I am,' Albert said.

'No, you're not. And anyway, why shouldn't humans become gods? Isn't it the inevitable next step?

All because of you, Albert. All because of you.' He picked up a test tube and shook it. 'What we have here is the most beautiful thing I've ever seen,' he said, his voice almost a whisper. 'It's incredible. It's wonderful. And you did it. Think of the glory.'

Albert frowned and shook his head. 'I don't want glory,' he said quietly. 'I don't even know that I want this . . . to be responsible . . . to have created such a potential monster . . .'

'Not a monster,' Richard said quickly. 'You've just been working too hard, Albert. You should take a break.'

'A break?' Albert looked at him incredulously. 'You think I can take a break now?'

'Yes,' Richard said, walking towards him, calmer suddenly, and putting his hands on Albert's shoulders. 'You've saved Elizabeth's life. You've done it. Now just give me the formula and you can get some rest.'

He'd saved her life. Albert felt his heart thud in his chest. That was how this whole enterprise had started. The search for the cure for cancer, Elizabeth's cancer, which had ravaged her body, turned her against him. His beautiful daughter, virtually a stranger to him. This had been something he'd been able to do for her. Not enough – never enough – but something.

Albert looked at Richard, taking in his angular chin, his ambitious eyes, his stiff posture. His daughter's husband. His son-in-law. He had to remind himself of this fact on a regular basis – to Albert, he was always just 'his assistant', the young man who had refused to take no for an answer, who had appeared one day, fresh-faced from university, telling Albert without any irony that he knew Albert would make the right decision and hire him. Then, as though determined to force himself into every crevice of Albert's life, Richard had turned his attentions on his boss's daughter. Undeterred by Elizabeth's failing health, he had wooed her, swept her off her feet and married her. She'd even had a child while in remission, before the cancer took hold again, more violently this time.

Albert studied Richard for a few seconds. He often wondered what had induced Elizabeth to fall in love with this man, with his loud voice and complete belief in himself, so different from him. Then again, he mused, perhaps that *was* the reason.

'So, the formula,' Richard said. 'Let's get it patented right away.'

'Patented?' Albert asked vaguely, still thinking about his daughter, about his granddaughter. Elizabeth had banned him from visiting a month ago, when Albert had first had doubts about the beast he feared he was creating. Richard had conveyed the message soberly and apologetically. She was getting worse, he'd told him; she needed the cure and she needed it soon, and she would not allow a man who had the power in his hands to cure her illness to see his granddaughter. After all, if she died at his hands then she would lose Maggie. Why should he have what she couldn't? It had been blackmail; Albert recognised that, but still he acquiesced, throwing himself into his work, watched closely by Richard. And now . . . now . . .

'I haven't seen Elizabeth for so long,' he said tentatively. 'If I could talk to her . . .'

'Yes, of course,' Richard said seriously. 'But Elizabeth will want to know that the drugs are in production, won't she? That the formulation is being created and tested. Give me the formula. I'll tell her the wonderful news and I know she'll want to see you straight away. Just think, once Elizabeth starts taking the drugs you'll have all eternity to make things up with her. Think of all the time you two can spend together.'

Albert felt a sad little smile creep across his face. His assistant spoke of eternity so lightly, as though it were a good thing, an adventure, not the horror it really was. But that was the optimism of youth. Such self-belief. Such conviction.

'You don't think perhaps we're making a huge mistake?' he asked quietly. 'The vista of eternal life has corrupted men throughout the ages.'

'The vista, but not the reality,' his assistant said, a trace of impatience in his voice. 'Albert, it would be morally wrong to hold this back. People have a right to know. Science can't be selfish – you taught me that.'

Albert swallowed uncomfortably. He wanted time to think, time to reflect, to weigh up his options, to review the evidence, to consider the implications. And yet there was no time. Not for his daughter, at any rate.

'Why don't you at least show me how it works?' his assistant said, then, 'Please, Albert?'

Albert thought for a moment. Until now he'd held back from sharing with Richard any more than was absolutely necessary, fearing that his over-enthusiasm, his obvious desire for glory, might tempt him to interfere. Then he nodded. The truth was that he wanted someone else to see the beauty of what he'd created, even if he wasn't ready to share the means yet. He gave Richard the goggles, led him to the microscope.

Carefully, Richard leant down. 'What am I looking at?'

'The cell on the right.'

'What about it? It's old. It's ravaged.'

'Indeed,' Albert said. 'You can tell by the colour, by its lack of vibrancy. Now watch.' He took out a syringe and carefully inserted a drop of liquid into the cell. Immediately the cell began to renew; ragged edges became smooth again, its inside became luminescent once more. Albert watched his assistant's face take on an expression of wonderment, watched his eyes open, his hair stand on end.

'It's incredible,' Richard breathed. 'Albert, it's the most extraordinary thing I've ever seen.' He stood up, turning to Albert with utter admiration plastered across his face. 'You've made old cells young again. No one else has come close to this. Albert, you're a genius!'

'Not a genius.' Albert felt himself redden slightly with pleasure. It was rather an achievement, he conceded. Quite a coup. The scientific community would be all over him. He'd have papers published, he'd give talks all around the world. He closed his eyes, allowing himself to imagine his future – what was left of it. Then he laughed lightly. His future was as long as he wanted it to be. That was the whole point.

'Yes,' Richard was saying under his breath, 'a genius. Think of the power. Whoever holds the key to this drug holds the key to the whole world.'

The smile that had made its way on to Albert's face disappeared abruptly; his face darkened. 'I don't want power, Richard. Renewal is not about power or politics or –'

'Renewal?' Richard's eyebrows shot up. 'That's what you call the drug? I love it. Renewal. Does what it says on the tin.'

'Renewal is the process,' Albert said, frowning slightly. 'The drug does not exist, Richard. It has no name.' He breathed heavily, the battle that had taken hold inside his head weeks ago when he realised he was on the brink of this discovery not abating. Science versus humanity. The scientist within him was at a fever pitch of excitement; the man was terrified of what he'd created.

'Not yet,' Richard said. 'But it will, and soon. Actually, perhaps you're right – perhaps Renewal isn't quite right. Maybe something that suggests extension instead of replacement. I'll get the marketing lot on to it right away.'

'Wait.' Albert banged his hands down firmly. 'Richard, you have to stop. I am not ready. I . . .' His voice broke off. He didn't know how to end the sentence.

'You'll never be ready, Albert. But think of your daughter. Think of all the people dying needlessly, painfully, leaving others behind, vulnerable . . . Give me the formula, Albert. Give it to me and then you don't have to worry any more.'

'You think it will be that easy?' Albert asked, raising an eyebrow.

'Yes, because it will be out of your hands,' Richard said, moving closer. 'Let the government worry about the rights and wrongs, Albert. You've done your bit now. Give yourself a pat on the back and relax a bit.'

Albert looked at him for a moment. He had a point. Decisions about such things were the government's domain. He was a scientist, not an ethicist. Slowly, he handed over the syringe.

'This is it? Just this?' Richard's eyes were shining.

Albert nodded. 'In its purest form, yes. It can be made into tablets too, if that's what people want. If that's what the government . . .'

But Richard wasn't listening to him; he was staring at the syringe in rapture, his mouth open, his eyes gleaming.

'It's beautiful,' he murmured. 'It's so beautiful. The

elixir of eternal life.' He looked up at Albert suddenly. 'It is eternal, right?'

Albert nodded, the scientist taking over, forcing a smile on to his lips, pride into his voice. 'It seems that organs renew indefinitely, yes. Of course that doesn't mean eternity. One has to factor in Nature's ability to change and morph.'

'Indefinitely,' Richard whispered. 'Oh, Albert, you did it. Now, the formula. What is it exactly?'

Albert opened his mouth to speak, then stopped. It was Richard's eyes – the glint he'd seen a few times over the past few weeks. There was something about it that made him anxious. He put his left hand over his right, turning the ring on his finger – something he always did when he was nervous, but which today somehow had more significance.

'The formula,' Richard said, more insistently this time. 'Write it down for me, Albert. I'll take care of everything, don't you worry.'

'Write it down? No, no, it's far too complex . . .' Albert said, stalling for time. He looked at his watch – it was late, too late. There would be no one else in the building now.

'Then show me your notes. Show me where the workings are.'

Albert shook his head. His paranoia was surfacing again. 'Not now, Richard. Tomorrow. You're right – I need a rest. I'll go home now. Tomorrow we'll look at this again . . .'

'Not tomorrow,' Richard said, his tone changing

slightly. 'Now, Albert. I know you've been deliberately keeping the formula from me, hiding your paperwork. But now is the time to share, do you understand?'

Albert looked at him uncertainly. He heard the threat in Richard's voice, knew that he was meant to have heard it.

'Tomorrow,' he said. 'I need some rest. We'll discuss this tomorrow.'

'No, Albert, you'll give it to me today,' Richard said darkly.

Albert's eyes widened. 'What did you say?'

Richard was looking at him menacingly. 'I said, give me the formula now, Albert. Otherwise you'll regret it.

'Are you threatening me?'

'If I was?' Richard asked.

Albert looked at him steadily. He wasn't afraid, he realised – a fact that surprised him. In some strange way he'd been expecting this moment, ever since Richard had arrived in his laboratory. 'If you were, I would tell you that there is no use,' he said quietly. 'I will not give you the formula, Richard, and without it you have nothing.'

Richard digested this. 'I have this,' he said thoughtfully, holding up the syringe. 'I'm sure some of your colleagues can work out the formulation.'

Albert held Richard's gaze for a few seconds, then he shrugged. 'Perhaps they could copy it, yes. But it won't be the same. Richard, is it not enough to cure cancer? To cure your wife, my daughter? Is that not enough glory for you?'

Richard's eyes widened, then he laughed. 'You're never going to give me the formula, are you, old man?'

Albert shook his head. 'No.'

'Then you might as well know Elizabeth is dead,' Richard continued. 'Has been for weeks.'

Albert felt his stomach clench. 'What did you say?'

'She died. The cancer killed her. That's why I told you she didn't want to see you any more. Couldn't have your only motivation for creating this drug disappearing, could I? So anyway, no, curing cancer is not enough. Eternal life. That will be my legacy.'

'Your legacy?'

Richard smiled. 'Actually, not a legacy. You have to die to have a legacy, and I don't intend to. Not now.' He took out his phone and pressed a button. 'Derek? Yes. Now would be good, thank you.'

He looked back at Albert. 'You're sure you won't give me the formula? You insist on making things hard on yourself?'

'Richard, don't do this,' Albert said urgently. 'This is too big, too important. You'll fail. Eventually you'll fail. Nature will win.'

'I will win,' Richard corrected him. 'You see,' he said, holding up the syringe and looking at it lovingly, 'you are the past, Albert, and I am the future.'

The door to the lab opened and a man Albert vaguely recognised appeared. One of the security

12

guards on the door, he thought.

'Ah, Derek,' Richard said warmly.

Albert stared in disbelief as Derek walked towards him and grabbed his arms. 'You need to come with me,' he said flatly.

'Come with you? No,' Albert said, stepping backwards. 'Richard, this is madness. You can't do this.'

'Oh, but I can,' Richard said, walking away. 'I tried to give you a chance, Albert, but I knew you'd blow it. Just can't take the pressure, it seems. Scientists rarely can. Goodbye, Albert.'

'No! Get your hands off me,' Albert said, struggling against Derek, who was holding him in a vice-like grip as Richard watched him detachedly.

'There's no point, Albert,' Richard said. 'I've got what I need. I've got the drug and by the end of the day I'll have the formula too.'

'Wait!' Albert yelped. 'Wait – you don't have anything. Richard, you can't do this. Without the exact formula you know nothing. It won't work. It can't work.'

'Then give me the formula,' Richard said.

Albert shook his head. 'Never. The circle of life must be protected,' he gasped. 'Without it you have nothing.'

'The circle of life?' Richard asked, rolling his eyes. He snapped his fingers at Derek. 'Take him,' he ordered. 'I'm tired of this conversation. I have what I need.' He picked up his phone and dialled a number.

Derek, meanwhile, took a rag out of his pocket and

forced it into Albert's mouth so that he could hardly breathe. 'Now, about this new company,' Albert heard Richard say as he was dragged from the room. 'I was thinking I'd call it Pincent Pharma.'

Chapter One

Richard Pincent paused, his face grim. Taking a deep breath, he pulled open the door in front of him and walked into the cold, dank room. It used to be a store cupboard – now it had become an autopsy suite and the smell of death hung in the air. Death. The very word made Richard shiver, made his mouth curl upwards in revulsion. Death and illness, his old adversaries – he had beaten them once before and he would beat them again.

Dr Thomas, one of his longest-serving scientists, was standing over a corpse, his forehead creased into a frown, a bright light shining overhead.

He looked up; he seemed uncomfortable. 'I'm afraid it's bad news,' he said, turning his gaze back to the body – or what was left of it. The skin was tight against the bones, as though every ounce of moisture had left the body; the eyes were wide, staring. Richard wished Dr Thomas had closed them – he

15

would have done it himself if the very idea didn't make him retch. Instead he looked directly at the scientist, trying his best to hide any flicker of fear that his own eyes might betray.

'Bad news?' The ominous feeling of dread flooded through him. 'I don't want bad news. I thought I made that clear.'

Dr Thomas sighed and stood upright, wiping his forehead with his sleeve and taking off the plastic gloves that encased his hands. 'I don't know what else to say, Mr Pincent. I don't know how many more bodies I can cut open when I'm faced with the same conclusion every time.'

Richard stared at him angrily. 'The same conclusion? Are you sure?' His voice caught as he spoke and he cleared his throat loudly.

'Yes.'

There was silence for a few minutes as they both digested this prognosis.

'You're wrong,' Richard said eventually, his voice defiant.

'Mr Pincent, sir.' The tension was audible in Dr Thomas's voice. 'Just because you want something to be the case does not make it so. I have cut open several bodies now, and I'm telling you that I have found the same thing in all of them . . .' His voice trailed off as he saw the expression on Richard's face and realised that he had stepped over the line.

Richard held his gaze for a few seconds then dropped it. He looked at the corpse. Number 7. They had been arriving every day since the beginning of the week when a Catcher had collapsed and his worried colleague had taken him to the doctor, suspecting food poisoning – the only possible illness in a world where Longevity had made illness and disease things of the past. By the time they had reached the doctor's surgery, however, the man was dead. Hillary Wright, the Secretary General of the Authorities, had been alerted immediately and had had the foresight to arrange for the situation to be tidied up quickly. Excuses were made and the body was brought to Pincent Pharma for analysis.

'I'm sorry,' Dr Thomas said carefully. 'I didn't mean to be negative.'

'No?' Richard's voice was flat, angry.

The doctor cleared his throat. 'No,' he said. 'But the facts remain. This virus is deadly. Longevity can't seem to . . . can't seem to fight it, sir.'

'Longevity can't fight it?' Richard repeated slowly. 'It cannot fight a mere virus?' He felt sickened. It wasn't true; it couldn't be true. Longevity fought every disease, every infection, every bacterium. It kept the world young, it fought off death, it bestowed the gift of eternal life on humanity. It also made Great Britain the most powerful country in the world. Like Libya in the late twenty-first century with its oil, or Rome in the first century with its armies, no one dared to cross its government, no one dared to challenge its demands. 'You're wrong,' he continued. 'Longevity fights everything. It's invincible.'

'Of course it is,' Dr Thomas said tentatively. 'But perhaps . . .'

'Perhaps what?' Richard's eyes narrowed.

Dr Thomas wiped his forehead again. 'Perhaps . . .' he said again, his voice tentative. 'It's just a theory, but . . .'

'But what? Spit it out, man,' Richard barked impatiently.

'Perhaps the virus has mutated. Perhaps it has found a way to . . . a way of . . .' Small beads of sweat continued to appear on Dr Thomas's forehead in spite of his attempts to wipe them away. He took a deep breath. 'Of beating Longevity,' he said finally, his eyes widening at the enormity of his words.

'Beating Longevity?' Richard looked at him uncertainly. 'What exactly are you suggesting?'

'I'm suggesting that we have a big problem,' Dr Thomas said, his voice cracking. 'I'm saying that if Longevity can't fight this virus, then . . . then . . .' He took a deep breath. 'Then we're all going to die.'

Richard nodded, digesting this. 'Die,' he said thoughtfully. Then he shook his head. 'Impossible. Longevity is invincible. You know that. Everyone knows that. Our society is built on that reassuring fact, Doctor. I am the most powerful man in the world because of that fact. There is no virus that Longevity can't destroy. Man is immune to illness, to ageing, to death. There must be another explanation.'

'No,' Dr Thomas said, shaking his head. 'No, Richard, you're wrong.'

'I'm wrong?' Richard looked with interest at the scientist he had known for so long, the man who had served him faithfully for decades, never questioning him, barely even daring to look him in the eyes. Until now. 'That's a bold accusation.'

Dr Thomas sighed heavily. 'I'm sorry, sir. I didn't mean – it's just that the enormity of this – if I'm right, what it means for me, for you, for everyone . . .' He was sweating heavily now. Richard looked away in distaste.

'If you're right,' he growled. 'So at least you'll admit there is a chance that you're wrong. And may I suggest that this chance is a very big one. You are not a brilliant scientist, Doctor. You did not invent Longevity; you did not invent anything. You simply research things I ask you to and give me your findings. So please excuse me if I don't take your proclamation of the end of the world too seriously. Or even at all seriously.'

'But if this virus is left to spread there's going to be an epidemic,' Dr Thomas said, wringing his hands desperately. 'Longevity has suppressed our immune systems – we don't have need for them. A virus like this could kill millions. Hundreds of millions.' His face twisted uncomfortably.

'And that's it? That's all you have for me?' Richard's eyes narrowed angrily.

Dr Thomas cleared his throat. 'I wondered if maybe we should consider Old Medicine,' he said cautiously. 'If we go back through the files, tweak one or two old drugs, I'm sure we can come up with something that might help. Antivirals. Even antibiotics, for secondary infections. The incubating period for this virus is five months. If we could develop a vaccine, perhaps, then we could –'

'Old Medicine? Old drugs?' Richard cut in angrily, his face creased with incredulity. 'You want us to go back to the Dark Ages when each disease had to be treated separately, when it was a fight just to keep people alive?' He could feel the vein in his neck throbbing angrily.

'No. I mean yes. I mean, we have to do something, don't we?' He was agitated; Richard could see the fear in his face as he spoke.

'And then what? We wait for the next virus to take hold?' Richard could hear the stress in his own voice and forced himself to take control.

Dr Thomas looked up. 'I don't know,' he said quietly, his shoulders slumping. I'm just looking for answers like everyone else. I don't want to die, Mr Pincent. I don't want my family to die. I don't . . .'

He didn't finish the sentence; instead he started to sob quietly, pathetically.

Richard turned away, searching for anything to look at other than Dr Thomas and the body laid out on the slab. But there were no windows to relieve his sudden claustrophobia – nothing but grey walls. This was a room, like others around it, that had been used variously over the years as a torture chamber, a prison, a hiding place. It swallowed its inhabitants whole, rarely returning them to the land of the living.

'You appear to have lost faith,' he said eventually.

Dr Thomas looked at him uncomfortably. 'I haven't lost faith. I just think we need to warn people. We need to do something before more bodies arrive here in the dead of night. We need the Authorities to know. They need to make plans.'

Richard looked thoughtful for a moment.

'You think we should tell people? Is that it?'

'Longevity cannot fight this virus,' Dr Thomas said determinedly. 'Think of the implications, Richard. It is going to spread. Spread unhindered. It will become an epidemic, a pandemic. It will kill everyone in its wake. It will –'

'Stop!' Richard shouted, holding his hand up. Then, without warning, he rounded on Dr Thomas, gripping him by the shoulders. 'You spend your days in labs, enjoying the benefits of Longevity, being paid by me for years to improve Longevity, to perfect the formula, to keep Pincent Pharma at the top, and now you turn round and you tell me that we need to dig graves? The only reason anyone is alive is because of me, because of my drugs. The world owes me everything. You owe me everything. And the threat of some virus that doesn't even exist as far as I know is enough to make you predict the end of the world?'

Dr Thomas went pale, then cleared his throat again. 'We owe you everything because you promised us we would live for ever. If you cannot keep that promise . . .' His voice was trembling, but there was steel in it.

Richard closed his eyes briefly then looked back at the quivering doctor. He would not listen. He could not listen. Longevity would triumph, because the alternative was too terrifying.

'Enough of this,' he said curtly. 'You will continue to conduct autopsies until we have different conclusions. Do you understand?'

'But that's impossible. There are no other conclusions I can draw.'

Dr Thomas was looking Richard in the eye and it unsettled him. Years ago, people used to say that death was the great leveller. Richard disagreed – it was *fear* of death that made men forget themselves.

'I see,' he said. 'Well, in that case I'm sorry.'

'Sorry?' Dr Thomas looked at him hopefully.

'Yes, I'm sorry,' Richard said, nodding his head slowly. Then, in one deft movement, he took out a pistol and fired it. Dr Thomas looked at him in surprise, then slumped to the floor, blood oozing from his chest. 'Sorry,' Richard continued, 'that you've given me yet another body to dispose of. Sorry that I've lost one of my best scientists.'

He took out his phone. Dr Thomas was dead, but his words, his worries, were still hanging in the air like dust. Richard felt as if he was choking on them.

'Derek? It's me. I need you down in the basement.'

'Of course.'

Richard put his phone back in his pocket, then

22

leant against the wall. He didn't have to wait long. Derek Samuels, his head of security, appeared minutes later. From his expression Richard deduced that he was not shocked by the sight of his former colleague now lying lifeless on the floor.

Immediately, Richard felt relief flood through him; immediately he felt the familiar reassurance of Derek's businesslike voice and demeanour. Derek Samuels was the only man Richard could trust to be entirely unemotional, to focus on the job, to show no interest in the rights, wrongs, ifs or buts. If he had a conscience, he hid it well. Richard suspected that he enjoyed his role as enforcer, enjoyed the power he yielded, enjoyed the suffering he caused. Richard had had no idea all those years ago just what a companion Derek would turn out to be when he offered him £5,000 to do him a favour, to take care of someone for him, to help him get rid of a problem.

'So Thomas didn't find the answer you were looking for then?' Derek asked, his tone as businesslike as usual.

Richard shook his head and sighed. He suddenly felt very tired.

'No,' he replied wearily. 'He said it was a virus that had mutated, that had discovered how to get past Longevity. He said it's going to be an epidemic. He said we're all going to die.' He attempted a laugh, but it rang hollow.

'Ah,' Derek said grimly, as he lifted the body into a plastic bag and started to clean up the mess. 'I see.'

Richard found himself watching Derek in admiration as he methodically got to work. The one man who never let him down, whose long life had been dedicated to smoothing the path for him, dealing with his enemies, protecting him from his friends.

'I don't know what to do,' he said, his voice so quiet it was barely audible. 'What shall I do, Derek?'

Derek looked up and frowned. Then he turned back to the blood on the floor and continued to clean it. 'Have you still got any of the original formula left?' he asked matter-of-factly.

'The original formula?' Richard's brow furrowed. 'No. Well, a drop, perhaps. But we copied it exactly. You don't think . . .'

'I don't think anything,' Derek said. 'It was just a question.'

'Yes,' Richard said, his mind racing. 'But a good question. An important question. You think that it's the copying that's the problem? You think that the copies of copies are no longer as powerful as the original?'

Derek shrugged lightly. 'I wouldn't know about science, sir – that's your domain. But photocopies – they're not originals, are they?'

'No, no they're not,' Richard said, beginning to pace. 'But we don't have the formula. We never found it. All we have is copies. It's all we've ever had.'

'We never found it back then, but that doesn't mean it isn't out there somewhere,' Derek said as he attended to the body, wrapping it up as though it were simply an animal carcass going to market. 'He'll have written it down somewhere. Must have done.'

'We've searched,' Richard said uncertainly. 'We've searched everywhere.'

'We searched a bit,' Derek conceded, 'but you had the stuff itself. Your scientists copied it OK, didn't they? We didn't think we needed the formula. We stopped looking.'

'We stopped looking.' Richard nodded, his eyes lighting up.

'So now we start again,' Derek said, standing up and inspecting the floor, which was now spotless.

Richard breathed out, his shoulders relaxing slightly. They would find the formula. The formula would solve everything. No mutated virus. No pandemic. No end to everything he had spent his life building up. Everything would be back to normal. Everything would be restored.

'Thank you, Derek. I knew I could depend on you.' Richard allowed himself to exhale, then he looked at Derek meaningfully and left the room, making his way briskly back to his office, away from the bowels of Pincent Pharma to the light, airy spaces above.

Chapter Two

Anna sat bolt upright, her heart thudding in her chest, sweat pouring from her forehead. It was pitch black, but without hesitation she jumped out of bed and ran towards Molly's room. Quietly she inched open the door, then dropped to her knees at the foot of her daughter's makeshift cot. Allowing her breathing to return to normal, Anna watched her beautiful baby sleep. Just four months old, her little hands were curled into fists, her chest gently rising and falling with each breath, her lips pursed, her eyebrows furrowed as though concentrating as hard as she possibly could on sleeping. Molly was fine. Of course she was fine. It was just a dream, a nightmare. Just like all the others.

Every so often Molly would sigh and reach for some non-existent object. Her thumb would find her mouth, she would roll over and then, as sleep embraced her once more, the thumb would drop out again. Anna knew this little routine better than anything else in the world. Every night for weeks she had watched it, reassured that her worst fears were only that and no one was stealing her baby, not in the real world.

From the day she was born, Molly had represented so much to Anna. It was as though her own happiness and peace of mind were to be found within that tiny body. Molly was more precious to her than she'd been prepared for – she would have slept on the floor by the cot every night if Peter had let her. He'd told her she had to move on, told her that she was safe now, that Molly was safe, that she didn't need to fear any more, that she should sleep contentedly.

But it was sleep itself that awoke all Anna's fears. The dreams that filled her mind as soon as she drifted into semi-consciousness were filled with Catchers trying to snatch Molly and Ben, Anna's three-year-old brother, away from her. Their innocence of the world they had been born into, their lack of awareness of just how precious their lives were, made Anna as protective as a lioness. Like her own mother, she would die for them – she understood why now.

Anna hadn't known much innocence in her life. Taken by the Catchers to Grange Hall when she was very little, she'd grown up under the wrath of Mrs Pincent. Only when Peter had arrived two years before had she learnt that she wasn't evil, wasn't a Burden on Mother Nature, that it was wrong to make her work tirelessly to pay for the sins of her parents. Now she was Legal, but even that didn't offer much protection, not when her very existence was such a threat to the Authorities, not when Richard Pincent wanted her and Peter dead, out of the picture.

But the Underground were keeping them safe. She knew that. During the day, she reminded herself regularly, there was nothing to worry about. As Peter said all the time, they were going to be fine. The Underground had found them somewhere to live, somewhere no one could find them. They were self-sufficient, more or less; they were protected. Everything was fine. At last, everything in Anna's life was OK.

Quietly, Anna padded over to the chest of drawers where a pile of Molly's ironed clothes lay. She picked them up and, one by one, put them away. Order reassured her – she'd spent most of her life trying to achieve it.

But at night the demons came – the terrible monsters who wanted to steal her children away, wanted to imprison them as she had been imprisoned, wanted them to hate her, wanted them to know a life without love, without laughter, without her.

Anna had spent her childhood in Grange Hall. A Surplus Hall, it was a prison for children born illegally to parents who had signed the Declaration – a piece of paper that most signed too young to understand that in return for eternal life they would never bear children. Peter had been a Surplus too, but he hadn't been discovered by the Catchers; instead he had been passed around Underground supporters for most of his life, hidden in attics, never knowing whether he'd be in the same place the next day or whether he'd be moved again. It was only when he was taken in by Anna's real parents that he'd seen what family was all about and it was their love that had driven him to hand himself in to the Catchers and get himself sent to Grange Hall so that he could help her to escape.

And now he knew no fear. Anna loved that and feared it in equal measure; loved his strength, his courage, his ability to laugh when she expressed her worries to him in a way that didn't belittle them but made them obsolete. *I am here*, he would say to her. *No one will ever hurt you again.* But she even saw his fearlessness as a threat; she worried about his restlessness, his need to be fighting someone, something. Feared that the strength within him would eventually take him from her. From the children.

The clothes folded away, Anna sat down next to the cot and listened to Molly's rhythmic breathing. All was quiet. Her loved ones were near her, were sleeping, were going nowhere.

'Anna?' She looked up with a start to see Peter standing in the doorway, looking at her quizzically. 'What are you doing?'

She blushed. 'Nothing.'

'You're watching her sleep again, aren't you?'

Anna bit her lip. 'I just . . .' She sighed. 'I had another nightmare.'

'Don't tell me,' Peter whispered. 'Catchers?'

She met his eyes – they were twinkling kindly.

'Not Catchers this time,' she said, slowly standing

up and moving towards him. 'I dreamt about Sheila.'

'Sheila?' Peter frowned. 'What did you dream?'

Anna closed her eyes for a moment. Sheila, her friend from Grange Hall. Was friend the right word? Sheila had been her shadow. Younger than Anna, she had turned to her for protection which Anna had reluctantly given. Sheila wasn't strong like Anna; she had got into trouble with the other girls, with the House Matron Mrs Pincent, with everyone. Like a ghost with her pale, translucent skin and pale orange hair, Sheila had been so fragile, and yet there had been a steely quality to her, a refusal to accept her Surplus status, a determination that her parents had wanted her, that she didn't belong in Grange Hall. And it had turned out that she was right. They'd only found that out later, after Anna had escaped with Peter, leaving Sheila behind. After Sheila had been taken to Pincent Pharma, experimented on, used . . .

Anna shuddered at the memory. 'I dreamt . . .' She exhaled slowly, her breath visible in the cold night air. 'I dreamt that she was angry with me. Because I hadn't believed her. Because I'd told her she was a Surplus. I dreamt that she took Molly away to serve me right, to show me what it was like.' Tears started to stream down her cheeks and Peter pulled her into him, out into the corridor. Then he closed Molly's door behind them.

'Sheila wouldn't do that,' he said gently, stroking Anna's hair.

'It was my fault she ended up at Pincent Pharma,'

Anna said, her voice hoarse. 'She asked me to take her with me. I didn't. I left her behind.'

'You had to,' Peter said sternly. 'And she's fine now anyway. She's with Pip and Jude in London. There's nothing to feel guilty about. Nothing.'

'I looked after her. In Grange Hall,' Anna whispered. 'When I left . . .'

'When you left you were brave and strong and courageous. You saved my life. Stop this, Anna. Stop finding problems where there aren't any.' Peter's voice was sterner now. 'No one's going to take Molly away. Not Sheila, not the Catchers, no one.'

'I know,' Anna said, wiping her eyes and shaking herself. She looked up at Peter earnestly. 'I know that. I don't know why I keep having these horrible dreams . . .'

'Because you're not working hard enough during the day,' Peter said, a mischievous glint suddenly appearing in his eye – the glint he employed whenever Anna worked herself up. 'I dug up all those potatoes yesterday and you just sat and watched.'

'I didn't!' Anna protested earnestly, even though she knew he wasn't entirely serious. 'I dug up carrots. And scrubbed the potatoes. And –'

'I'm teasing,' Peter grinned. 'Look, the dreams will stop eventually. But no more creeping around at night. You need your sleep and so do I. OK?'

'You think she's OK? Sheila, I mean. You think she's happy in London?'

'I think she's very happy. I also think she's her own

31

person now. She's not your responsibility. Not any more.'

'You're right.' Anna nodded.

'Of course I am.' Peter grinned. He took her hand and Anna squeezed it, allowing him to lead her back to their bedroom. And if she had a sense of fore-boding, a feeling that something terrible was going to happen soon, very soon, she suppressed it. Peter was right – she had to learn to trust, she told herself. She had to learn to be hopeful.

Jude's hand was shaking. It wasn't nerves – at least he told himself it wasn't. It was his cramped position which was causing his muscles to spasm, to rebel, to quiver indignantly. He took a deep breath and returned to the wires in front of him, painstakingly making connections, checking and double-checking. He was ready to upload the film, ready to show the world what he'd just seen. He looked at his watch – 4 a.m. Looking around him one more time to make certain that he hadn't been followed, that the dark shadows beneath him were just that and not a gather-ing army of Pincent guards ready to pounce, he held his breath and pressed the blue button on his hand-held computer. Upload. He heard a familiar whirring, the comforting sound of the device flicking into action. And then, for the first time in three hours, he allowed himself to relax slightly.

It had been his idea, filming the raids on Pincent Pharma. After all, they had been going on for years and nothing had ever happened – a few batches of Longevity had been destroyed but Pincent Pharma had just made more. In the battle of David and Goliath, Jude had pointed out to Pip, Goliath wasn't just winning, he was triumphant, arrogant. They were barely making a dent. But Jude knew technology – knew how to harness it, how to make it work for him. And so he'd persuaded Pip to let him help. Initially they'd just tracked the raids through the Authorities' network of CCTV cameras so that Pip, Jude or anyone else who wanted to, could watch the Underground soldiers bring the Pincent lorries to a halt and destroy the Longevity drugs within them. It had made everyone feel better, made them feel part of it, more entrenched in the rebellion. And then Jude realised that if more people saw the attacks, they too would feel part of the rebellion or, if not, at least they'd know it was happening. At least the Authorities and Pincent Pharma couldn't deny it any more.

He pulled himself up and shook out his aching muscles, trying not to wince. He hated being reminded of his physical weaknesses, of his slim frame, his pale skin. He was nearly seventeen but still looked like a boy, not a man. Every time he glanced in the mirror he cringed at his reflection. He wanted to be strong, powerful, but instead felt like the runt of the litter, the also-ran. Peter, his half-brother, was the action hero who'd broken into a Surplus Hall to save Anna. Jude . . . Jude was just a techie.

He heard something, a noise, and ducked down again, his heart beating rapidly. Someone was here. Who? Had he been followed? Still, silent, he crouched and waited. Then, hearing nothing more, he relaxed slightly. He'd probably imagined it. After all, he was always careful. Peter was the brave, impetuous one; Jude was the planner, the organiser. In short, the boring one, he thought wryly.

He'd never thought of himself as boring before he'd met his brother; before he'd met Pip and joined the Underground, the resistance movement that had been set up to fight Pincent Pharma, Longevity and all it meant for humanity. He'd been a White Knight in his previous life on the Outside – a computer whiz who worked for good, identifying weaknesses in companies' networks and offering to fix them. He did it for a price, of course, but there were others who simply took advantage of weaknesses to steal, to spy, to cause havoc. Jude had always seen himself as a benevolent protector; he'd liked that image, liked the kick he'd got every time he contacted a major corporation to let them know that he'd just hacked into their network and could, if he wanted to, empty their bank account. In return for his work he demanded a fee big enough to keep him going for a few weeks, sometimes a few months. And then he'd reward himself by going on to MyWorld. It might only have existed on his computer, but it often felt more real than the world outside. In the real world there were no young people, but MyWorld was full of them. And in MyWorld Jude was a genuine hero, popular with everyone.

The truth was, life without it had taken some getting used to.

'Come on, come on,' he muttered under his breath as the digital film slowly uploaded. It frustrated Jude that connectivity had, in recent months, got slower not faster. Like everything these days, things were getting worse all the time. Falling energy supply, falling water supply – he'd heard that in the south-west people had been forced to start queuing for water at the municipal well. Drought had meant that food was being rationed too, and not even under the pretext of identicard choices either. But at least they could queue up openly. At least they weren't like him, hiding in a grungy, barely habitable building where sometimes food didn't materialise for days at a time.

The Underground. The Resistance Movement. Jude had known of its existence all his life, but only in shadowy references. It encouraged people to have children when the world was already full – too full. It believed that Longevity drugs were wrong when Longevity had cured the world of disease, had cured man of ageing. Jude, a Legal child (certain senior Authorities' positions came with the perk of having a child), had been brought up to loathe the Underground and all it stood for. But as he'd grown older, as he'd hankered after company, after anyone his own age to play with, his father's arguments in favour of Longevity had seemed less compelling. And when, just two years ago, his father, Stephen, had been murdered by Margaret Pincent, his first wife, and the truth about how Jude's legality had been snatched from his half-brother Peter was revealed, he'd realised that nothing was as it seemed. Peter, Margaret's son and Stephen's second son, had been born just two months after Jude, but Jude's birth had rendered him a Surplus. So while Jude had been brought up in an affluent household, Peter had been hidden in attics, in cellars, forced to move from place to place.

No wonder Peter was the hero, Jude thought as he watched the download bar, drumming his fingers on his thigh. And no wonder Pip hadn't wanted Jude to join the Underground. He was a thief; his very birth had robbed Peter of his rightful legality.

Jude shook himself and turned back to his device. Any minute now Authorities police could turn up. He had selected this place carefully – a disused factory under demolition orders, its walls and structure condemned and barbed-wire fences preventing entry. But still, that wouldn't stop a guard or policeman if they suspected what he was doing here. And if they caught him . . . He shivered. It didn't bear thinking about. Ever since he'd thrown his lot in with Pip and Peter, ever since he'd made the decision to join the Underground, he'd been on the Most Wanted list. If he so much as tried to use a credit card he'd be tracked, traced, caught and imprisoned or worse. The Underground might not offer much in the way of hospitality, but at least it protected him, kept him safe.

He looked around cautiously then, with a sigh of relief, saw that the job was done. Quickly he pulled the wires apart, jumped down and started to sprint away.

But as he ran through a door and what had once been a fully functioning staircase, Jude was stopped in his tracks by the sound he'd heard before. He looked around and carefully sank back into the shadows, his heart beating in his chest – from the running or from fear, he wasn't sure. And then he heard it again. A gasping, wheezing noise. It didn't sound like enemy guards. It wasn't like anything Jude had ever encountered before.

Hesitantly, he crept along the wall, being careful to stay hidden in the shadows. He was on a platform, a corridor that was now missing both of its walls. Beneath him were two platforms just like this one; beyond the gap where the other wall had been was a five-metre drop down to the central floor where disused machines sat redundant, rusting like sunken ships.

The wheezing was getting louder. Jude thought again about running, but he couldn't – he had to know if he'd been followed, had to know what or who was making this sound. It could be a trap, but that was unlikely. Free food would have been a better trap than the sound of someone gasping for air. Free food, if it was good, would almost be worth walking into a trap for. Pausing briefly to contemplate his concave stomach, Jude shook himself and continued edging towards the sound. He turned the corner; the sound was louder and yet he still couldn't see anything. Frowning, he moved away from the wall to look down at the central floor, but still he could see nothing. It sounded like an animal, he realised with growing relief. It wasn't human. Probably a dog. He listened carefully; it was coming from directly under him. Dropping down to the floor, Jude inched to the edge of the platform and lowered his head over the side, craning to see the wounded animal making the now frantic noise. And then he felt the blood drain from his face and felt his hands go clammy, because it wasn't a dog. It wasn't an animal of any sort. It was a woman.

She was sitting clutching her throat, her skin tight around her hands, around her face, and she looked as though someone was strangling her, as though they were pulling at an invisible cord round her neck, because she was choking and her eyes were bulging and staring wildly, her hands scratching at the air above her head as though it might save her. But Jude could see no one pulling the invisible cord; the woman was alone. Without thinking he turned, gripping the floor he'd been standing on with his hands, lowering himself down to the platform where she sat. She saw him, but she could barely bring herself to look at him.

'Water!' she gasped.

Jude took out his precious water bottle and after only the briefest of pauses offered it to her. She tried to grab it but her arms were flailing hopelessly. Carefully, he poured some of the water into her mouth. She nodded frantically and he poured the rest in, but as the liquid slipped down her throat, she wailed agonisingly.

'What? What is it?' Jude asked anxiously, but the woman wasn't looking at him, she was clutching her throat again.

'Water!' she said again.

'It's finished,' Jude said. 'What's wrong with you? What happened?'

'Thirsty,' the woman said, her eyes glinting now. 'Water.'

Jude edged back, his eyes wide, his heart thudding loudly. 'I don't have any more water.'

The woman nodded, as though finally understanding what he was saying. Then, without warning, she mustered her strength and launched herself at him, taking him by surprise and toppling him to the ground.

'Water,' she screeched. 'Water!'

Her hands were clawing at his neck and then her elbow was pressing into his windpipe and he couldn't breathe. He tried to push her off but she seemed to be imbued with incredible strength – the strength of desperation, he found himself thinking – and everything started to go black. And then, without warning, the pressure disappeared. He gasped for air, choking for oxygen, rolling over on to his front, pulling himself up to all fours. The woman had fallen away from him; she was on the ground now. His throat still hurting, Jude stared at her angrily, fearfully, but then he recoiled. Her skin was drying up. Not just her skin – her whole body. Right in front of him. It looked like every ounce of moisture was literally being sucked out of her. She lifted her head and looked at him, her eyes huge, her eyelids receding – like a skeleton, Jude found himself thinking. And then, with one last shriek, she fell back and was silent.

Jude didn't move for a minute. Shock and fear made him stay completely still as his brain tried to process what he'd seen, tried to make sense of it. Then, tentatively, he pulled himself up. His neck still felt sore, his breathing was still laboured as he crawled towards the woman. He didn't get all the way there – he couldn't bring himself to. Her skin had become blackened; her mouth and eyes were open, large circles that invited him to look deep inside. Instead he looked around – he wanted a tape of this, needed to know where to find the images. But there were no cameras here. He kicked himself. Of course there weren't any cameras – he'd chosen the place because of it. He stood up on shaky legs, considered bringing the woman with him to the Underground headquarters, then rejected the idea immediately on grounds of safety and practicality. At least that was what he told himself. But the real reason was his revulsion, his terror, his desire to leave this place as soon as humanly possible and never come back.

Taking one last look at the woman, he turned and ran to the back entrance of the building. Once outside, he threw up violently, then continued his journey back to the Underground.

Chapter Three

Jude dealt with the Underground security checks as quickly as he could before bursting through the door. It was still early, but hours were not important here and meetings were regularly held in the dead of night. Pip, as far as Jude could tell, rarely slept and even when he did, he would wake and be ready for action within seconds of something happening.

'Pip!' he called urgently. 'Pip, where are you?'

'Jude?' Pip appeared in a doorway, his expression unreadable, but Jude knew that he would disapprove of such an outburst. Pip, who had set up the Underground hundreds of years ago and had steered it ever since, was a man of few words and those he uttered were well thought out, ordered, carefully chosen. He favoured caution over passion, reason over gut feeling. He and Jude could not have been more different from each other.

'Pip, you've got to hear this. I've just come from the processing plant. The disused one up near Euston . . .'

'Yes, Jude. I've seen the footage you uploaded. Congratulations on another success.' He spoke softly.

Pip, the enigmatic, unofficial leader of the Underground movement – the rebel group set up to fight Longevity, to fight the Declaration, to fight Pincent Pharma and everything that it stood for – rarely raised his voice; it meant that he never sounded enthusiastic, never sounded proud or sufficiently surprised by anything. It was the most frustrating voice Jude had ever come across.

'Not that,' he said hurriedly. 'Something else. Something . . .' His face screwed up inadvertently at what he was about to say. 'I just saw someone die. It was hideous.' He regretted his use of language immediately – it felt clumsy, dismissive. But he didn't know what else to say, how else to describe what he'd seen. He'd long got over his terror, his disgust; on the way back to the Underground he'd shaken himself down, told himself not to be so pathetic. But now, rather than coming across as brave, he felt slightly foolish. After all, he'd seen people die before – Underground soldiers, killed by Pincent Pharma's henchmen. It was just that this was different. The woman seemed . . . ill. It was a word from history, a concept that had seemed abstract somehow. Until now, that is. Now it felt very real and very horrible. He saw Pip raise an eyebrow and he reddened slightly. 'It was a woman. She was gasping, like really gasping for breath, and she wanted some water so I gave her some, and then she just . . .' He felt his legs weakening beneath him as the impact of the sight hit him once more. He could feel Pip watching him; he wanted to impress him, wanted his admiration. But instead he could see sympathy, worry. His shoulders fell despondently. 'She shrivelled up,' he said, disappointed with himself. 'She died, right there.'

Sheila appeared next to him, wide-eyed, and pulled out a chair for him; he felt the usual flutter of longing that filled his chest every time he saw her and sat down.

'She died? So she was an Opt Out?' Sheila asked. Opt Outs were the people who opted out of the Declaration, who chose to forgo Longevity drugs in order to have children. They were few and far between and regarded with suspicion by Legals – who would want to get old and be open to disease when Longevity tablets could protect you? Who would want to have a child when the world was now almost entirely childless?

'She was alone?' Pip cut in before Jude could answer; he was looking at him intently now.

Jude nodded.

'And no one saw you?' Pip continued.

'No. I mean, I didn't see anyone. I was careful – coming back here, I mean.'

'Good. Sheila, would you be so kind as to make Jude a cup of tea? And then, Jude, I would like you to tell me exactly what happened. Every detail, everything you can remember. Can you do that?'

Jude nodded.

'Tea?' Sheila asked, her face screwing up indignantly. 'But there's no tea left. We don't get more until

44

this afternoon and –'

'And I was hoping that you might be resourceful and find some,' Pip said, his eyes twinkling slightly.

Sheila's eyes narrowed and Jude felt his protective urges kick in as he realised that Pip had discovered her little collection of tea bags, of biscuits, of anything else she'd been able to secrete. She couldn't help herself – Jude knew that, and didn't blame her for it. She'd grown up with nothing to call her own. Jude, who'd been brought up with plentiful supplies of everything except love, didn't begrudge her more than her share of anything – he'd have given her the shirt off his back if she'd asked for it.

'I don't need tea,' he said quickly. 'Really, I –'

'Yes you do,' Sheila said quietly. 'I think actually there might be one tea bag left. I'll go and look.'

She disappeared into the kitchen and Jude forced himself to look back at Pip.

'Are you OK?' the leader of the Underground asked, sitting down next to him. Jude nodded.

'I'm fine,' he said, in his mind's eye seeing Sheila taking one of her treasured tea bags out from wherever she'd hidden it.

'It must have been a shock.'

'I'm fine,' Jude insisted. 'I'm not a complete weakling, you know.'

His tone was more sarcastic than he'd intended and he saw Pip frown slightly.

'I don't consider you to be a weakling at all,' he said after a short pause. 'Tell me what you saw, Jude.

45

Don't leave anything out.'

Jude sat back in his chair and told Pip everything – about the raid, the cameras, uploading the film, hearing the gasping and finding the woman. Pip listened attentively, nodding every so often, his face serious.

'Her skin was blackened?'

'She looked almost like she'd been burnt,' Jude agreed, shuddering slightly. 'She looked like a skeleton.'

Pip nodded, deep in thought. Then he looked at Jude, his eyes, which had clouded over, suddenly bright and clear.

'What do you think was wrong with her?' Jude asked him searchingly. 'Do you think it was something to do with Pincent Pharma?'

'I think it seems likely,' Pip said gently.

'So let's find out. I'll get in there somehow, find out what's going on.' He looked at Pip hopefully. Just a year before, Peter had gone to work for Pincent Pharma, pretending that he wanted to work for his grandfather, Richard Pincent, pretending that he had severed all links with the Underground. Pip had trusted him to spy for him, to uncover the vile secrets that Richard Pincent had been hiding. Peter had been a hero; even now everyone spoke his name almost with a whisper. Jude longed to have a similar chance to prove himself, to show himself worthy.

But Pip was shaking his head. 'No, Jude,' he said, standing up. 'You must stay here. There is much to do.'

'Like what?' Jude asked defensively. 'I can spy too.

I got into Pincent Pharma last time. I can do it again. Just give me a chance to –'

'No,' Pip said again. 'I need you here. I need you to study.'

'To study?' Jude sighed irritably, his eyes resting on the pile of books Pip had given him to read: political biographies, history books, books on survival, on disasters, books on leadership, books on plumbing . . . They both knew that reading books wasn't going to achieve anything. Pip just didn't rate him, didn't believe in him. And, Jude thought heavily, maybe he was right.

'Studying is very important,' Pip said seriously, moving towards Jude. He raised his hand and for a moment Jude thought he was going to put it on his shoulder, but then he appeared to change his mind and instead brought it back down to his side.

Jude didn't say anything; a thud of disappointment was threatening to bring tears to his eyes, choking his voice. Yet more evidence that he was no hero, he thought desperately.

Sheila appeared with a cup of tea and handed it to Jude, who took it miserably.

'Thank you, Jude. That has been most illuminating,' Pip said, standing up, not noticing – or perhaps not choosing to notice – the look of irritation on Sheila's face as she realised she'd missed everything. 'And now there is a great deal to do.'

'Like what?' Jude asked suddenly, his usual defence of sarcasm finally kicking in. He took a slurp of the hot drink and felt it warm his insides.

Pip frowned. 'I'm sorry?' he said.

'You said there's a great deal to do. I just wondered what that is,' Jude said, looking Pip right in the eye.

Pip took a deep breath. 'Jude,' he said quietly, 'have you read that book there?' He was pointing to an old, battered book; the spine was missing but Jude knew it was full of short stories. Stories aimed at children, not young adults like him.

'Yes,' he said tersely. 'It's full of fairy tales.'

'Not fairy tales,' Pip corrected him. 'Fables. You should read it sometime. Particularly the story about the mouse and the lion.'

'The mouse and the lion?' Jude asked wearily. Yet another diversion.

'The lion catches the mouse and is going to kill him, but the mouse hops on to his tail and the lion chases it and chases it, not even noticing when the mouse hops off and escapes.'

'Right,' Jude said flatly. If Peter were here, Pip wouldn't be talking about lions and mice. If Peter were here, he'd be in the thick of the action. 'Right. Thanks. Sounds like a great story.'

'It is, Jude. As I said, you should read it sometime.' Then, quickly, Pip walked out of the room, leaving Jude shaking his head in frustration.

Sheila caught his gaze and rolled her eyes. 'There is,' she said solemnly, doing a very good impression of Pip, 'a great deal to do.'

Jude sighed, then allowed himself a little smile.

'Many, many important things, he dead-panned, taking another sip of hot tea.

'So she really died?' Sheila asked, removing his cup from him and taking a sip herself. 'In front of you?'

Jude nodded.

'Eeeuuughh!'

'Yeah,' Jude said, raising an eyebrow and managing a grin. 'You'd have fainted for sure, or run screaming from the place.'

'Would not,' Sheila said defiantly.

'Yes you would,' Jude said, warming to his theme and taking his cup back. 'You would have been hopeless.'

'You ran in here pretty quickly,' Sheila said airily. 'And I'm sure I heard screaming just before you arrived.'

'No you didn't,' Jude said gruffly, his sense of humour evaporating suddenly. If Pip thought he was weak, that was bad enough. But Sheila? That he couldn't bear.

Sheila looked at him archly. 'Well, you were scared.'

'I wasn't,' Jude said, turning away angrily. 'I wasn't scared, OK?'

Sheila didn't say anything for a few seconds, then slowly she walked over to Jude and sat down on the arm of his chair. 'I would have been terrified,' she said in a quiet voice.

'Would you?' Jude asked searchingly. 'Really?'

'Really,' Sheila said. 'Unless you were there. Then I wouldn't have been scared at all.'

Jude felt himself getting warm. 'You . . . you wouldn't?'

'No,' Sheila said firmly. 'You saved me from Pincent Pharma.' She turned to look at him, and Jude saw a flicker of real emotion in her eyes. 'I know that you'd protect me,' she whispered. 'You always protect me.'

'And I always will,' he said, wrapping his arm around her and hugging her tightly into him. He wasn't a hero, he knew that, but he could be Sheila's hero if she'd let him.

'So do you think it was Richard Pincent who killed that woman?' Sheila continued, the anxiety audible in her voice. 'Like he was going to kill me?'

Jude tightened his grip around her. 'I don't know,' he said grimly. 'But don't worry, he's not going to get away with it.'

'He will though,' Sheila said, biting her lip. 'I mean, he always does. The Underground is never going to win, is it? So what's the point?'

'The point is,' Jude said gently, reminding himself that Sheila's life had been tough, that it wasn't her fault she said the things she did, 'we have to keep fighting. The more young people there are, the more opposition there will be to the Authorities and Pincent Pharma.'

'But the Declaration makes sense,' Sheila said, her brow furrowing. 'There are too many people as it is. We don't have enough water. You told me that the rivers are drying up in Africa. We don't have enough energy, or food, or anything. I don't want more people. I want *fewer* people.'

Jude shook his head firmly. 'It's not that simple,' he said.

'Isn't it?' Sheila asked searchingly.

'No,' Jude said, his brow furrowing. 'The world needs young people. It's not fair to stop new people just so that old people can keep on living. It's not . . .' He trailed off; he couldn't think straight. All he could think about was Sheila's proximity to him, and the strange sensations shooting around his body – like fear, only . . . different. She turned to look at him, and he reddened. 'Don't you . . . have chores to be getting on with?' he asked, his voice breaking awkwardly as he spoke.

He regretted the words as soon as they'd left his mouth, but it was too late. Sheila raised her eyebrows, stole a final sip of tea from Jude's cup, then flounced out, leaving him on his own. Sighing inwardly he looked up, allowing his eyes to travel around the room.

It was a small space, one of a handful of rooms that made up the Underground headquarters. Today's headquarters, at any rate. Rumour had it they were moving again soon. And by rumour, Jude meant Sheila had told him, which meant it had approximately a fifty per cent chance of being true. Sheila liked to know everything, and if she didn't know something she'd make it up rather than admit her lack of knowledge. According to Sheila, Pip told someone just the other day that they'd be somewhere else by the end of the week, and since today was Thursday, that didn't leave many more days to up sticks and leave.

He pulled himself up and walked over to the table that he used as a desk, then sat down in his chair and put his feet on the table, like he used to when he'd lived in his own house, with his own rules. It seemed a very long time ago. Almost a lifetime ago.

In reality it had just been a few months since he and Sheila had moved in as permanent residents. A few months since Pip had deemed them both too high risk to be based anywhere else. They both knew, had seen first hand, the sordid activities taking place at Pincent Pharma, and Richard Pincent had promised to track them down and kill them in memos that Jude had hacked into.

It had made him feel important back then. Now – well, now he wasn't so sure that Sheila didn't have a point. It wasn't the Underground per se. Jude was fully on board with the whole anti-Pincent thing. He couldn't not be, not really, not seeing as how hardly anyone his age existed any more and those that had been born had been rounded up and shipped off to Surplus Halls. He knew Pip was right, knew that the Declaration – those bits of paper that people signed promising not to procreate just so they could take Longevity – was fundamentally flawed, that a world full of old people completely sucked, even if the people didn't *look* old. And he knew that Richard

Pincent was the most evil man in the whole world. No one hated him more than Jude – no one.

But he'd kind of thought the Underground would be more like an army than a . . . a . . . He searched for the right word and failed. He'd thought the Underground would be different, a hive of activity, full of soldiers, brave men and women talking about the revolution to come, making plans and carrying them out. Instead, there were hardly any people there for one thing – people came in for procedures or, occasionally, for meetings, but no one ever stopped to make conversation and you weren't meant to look at anyone too closely because it was risky, because the idea was that people could hardly identify any other supporters if they were caught, if Richard Pincent or the Authorities got hold of them. The only people there permanently were Jude, Sheila, Pip, and one or two guards. Jude had seen more drama when he'd lived in a small close in South London.

Suddenly it hit him. A family, that's what the Underground was like – a slightly dysfunctional family. Pip had taken on the parental role, generally disapproving of and criticising everything while being convinced that everything he did was right and the best possible way to do things. Peter and Anna were the golden children. Sheila was the youngest, indulged child. And Jude? He was the let-down, the misfit, the 'troublesome' one. Sometimes he wasn't even sure he was in the family at all.

Shaking his head wearily, Jude turned on his

computer. There was no point thinking about it really; he'd never be Peter, would never be held in the same esteem. And in the meantime another Pincent lorry was being ambushed that afternoon and he needed to track it. It soon appeared on his screen and he watched for an hour or so then, bored, looked over at Sheila who had appeared again on the other side of the room a few minutes earlier and was leaning against the wall, broom in hand, daydreaming. He knew she was waiting for him to call her over.

'Fancy a game, Princess?' Princess was his nickname for her – he told her it was because she behaved like one, because she was so difficult and demanding, but really it was because the first time he'd seen her, he thought she looked like a princess in a fairy tale, frozen, scared, waiting for someone to rescue her. He'd seen her when he'd hacked into the Pincent Pharma network, when he'd realised that Pincent Pharma was more than just a pharmaceutical company – it was a prison, a torture chamber. That was when he'd given up everything he'd taken for granted all his life and wormed his way into Pincent Pharma to rescue her, to save his princess from the dark forces at play in the bowels of that odious place. That was where he'd finally met Pip and Peter and together they had made the shocking discovery that Surpluses were being shipped in and used for their stem cells to make Longevity+, the wonder drug that would treat the external signs of ageing as well as the internal renewal process.

That had been the end of Jude's existence as a Legal citizen – from then on, he'd needed Underground protection. But the truth was, Legality wasn't all it was cracked up to be, not when you were the only Legal person your age in what felt like the whole city or possibly the whole country.

'No thank you,' Sheila said haughtily, immediately starting to push her broom around the floor. 'I've actually got a lot of things to do.'

Jude grinned. 'But we both know you're not going to do them.'

Sheila folded her arms defensively. 'I am. I'm not a layabout like you.' She turned and swept some dust out of the corner, then swept it back again. He watched in amusement, but didn't say anything. Sheila had grown up in a Surplus Hall. She never tired of telling anyone who'd listen that she wasn't a Surplus, that her parents had Opted Out of the Declaration, forgoing Longevity so they could have her, but even so she'd still ended up being taken by the Catchers and trained to be a Valuable Asset, a housekeeper or other servant. Except it seemed that wasn't what Valuable Assets were after all. At Pincent Pharma, she'd discovered that Richard Pincent needed them for . . . other things.

'Suit yourself.'

'I will. And if I were you I'd read some of those books Pip gave you. You're lucky to be here, Jude.'

'So what – I should make myself more valuable?'

Again he regretted the words as soon as they were spoken. When they'd first been taken in by the Underground Sheila had made a big deal about the housekeeping skills she'd learned at Grange Hall, about how valuable she'd be to everyone. But the Underground tended to choose derelict and uninhabitable buildings for its premises, and it wasn't that easy being a housekeeper in a place that was full of dust and where no one really seemed to care if the floors were clean or not. It soon turned out that Sheila wasn't that great at cleaning anyway, nor at cooking, unless charred food was your idea of haute cuisine. Which meant that she spent most of her time trailing around the place, a slightly defensive look on her face. Jude could relate to that; he felt like he was continually trying to defend his position, his value, his usefulness.

'I was *rescued*,' Sheila said, evidently deciding that attack was the best form of defence. 'I was in a Surplus Hall because the Catchers stole me from my parents. You're . . . well, you were just living in a house, weren't you? I mean, you don't really need to be here at all.'

Jude took a deep breath. Always the same digs, the same pointed comments, as if life was a competition and if Sheila didn't attempt to put him down at least three times a day she'd somehow be losing in the game of life. Trouble was, she'd already lost so many times and Jude knew it. A life spent at Grange Hall, her first taste of the world outside being strapped to a bed in Unit X, Pincent Pharma's dirty little secret.

Sheila had never been on her own but he knew she'd been lonely – desperately lonely. She'd been very hazy about her friends at Grange Hall, but she sometimes told him stories about the vicious games they played there, the bullying and the punishments regularly dished out, which made Jude ache when he thought about it. He would forgive Sheila anything because of what she'd been through – her biting comments, her twisted morality, the way she watched him quietly then skulked into the shadows the moment he turned round.

'Not like me,' she continued. 'I mean, I was Legal too, but the Catchers stole me from my grandparents and my parents couldn't find me again.'

She shot Jude a meaningful look and he sighed inwardly. She'd told him this story a million times. More than a million. And last week, stupidly, *stupidly*, in a moment of weakness he'd agreed to see if he could track her parents down for her. Even though Pip had made it clear that he didn't want him to. Even though Sheila had been told not to look for her parents under any circumstances.

'Palmer, their name was,' Sheila said, looking at him cautiously. 'In Surrey . . .'

'Palmer. Right,' Jude said awkwardly, noticing a piece of paper in front of him, a list of names and addresses. He sighed. 'OK. Look, Sheila, maybe I did a little bit of digging. The thing is . . .' he said, biting his lip.

Sheila looked up at him excitedly. 'Yes? The thing is

what? You've found them? Oh, tell me, Jude. Please. I know Pip doesn't want me to find them, but you have to tell me. You have to –'

She was interrupted by Pip himself walking into the room suddenly. 'Sheila,' he said, 'we have a nurse along the corridor who could do with some help, if you'd be so kind.' Jude looked up in surprise; he hadn't noticed him, didn't know how long he'd been standing there.

'Have you found out what happened? What was wrong with that woman?' he asked hopefully, but Pip didn't answer; instead he looked at Sheila pointedly.

She opened her mouth as though to protest, then, catching Pip's immovable expression, shrugged heavily and wandered down the corridor.

'So?' Jude asked when she'd gone.

'Sheila has had a difficult life, wouldn't you say?' Pip remarked, walking towards him.

Jude nodded warily. He'd learned to watch what he said to Pip, who had a way of twisting his words, making him seem to agree to things he'd had no intention of agreeing with.

'She hasn't seen her parents for years, I believe.'

'Not since she was about four, I think,' Jude said.

'And now, for the first time in her life she is comparatively safe. She has you, and she has the protection of the Underground.'

'That's right,' Jude agreed.

'So you think that it is a good idea, now, to muddy things, to distract her with thoughts of her parents?'

Jude frowned. 'But I –'

'No buts, Jude. And now there is a lorry that requires tracking and I think it deserves all your focus.'

'I am focused.' Jude could feel his mouth fixed in an angry grimace. Did Pip not trust him at all?

'No, Jude, you are not focused. If you were focused, you'd have noticed that the lorry has been stopped.'

Jude's eyes widened and he enlarged the SpyNet software screen, which was hijacking Pincent Pharma's own CCTV system in order to track the progress of Pincent Pharma lorries now heading into an Underground ambush. 'Shit!' he said. The lorry was on its side in the middle of the road. One lone car swerved to avoid it, but kept on driving. 'Shit! I'm sorry, I . . .'

He turned to Pip, who smiled gently and pointed back at the screen. Jude nodded, swivelled round and watched as men dressed in khaki jumped out in front of the lorry, pulling out the driver, forcing the back open. Jude felt the familiar surge of adrenalin as he watched the scene unfold – David against Goliath, Good against Evil.

The doors were open now and Jude's eyes were on the driver who was on the ground, two men holding him down. He looked agitated, fearful – he was shouting something. The Underground men were dragging large boxes out of the lorry; they didn't look like the usual boxes carrying Longevity drugs. Not that it mattered – they would be torched anyway, destroyed. The Underground would leave its message loud and clear on the side of the road.

But as he watched the boxes being prised open Jude frowned, the lines between his eyes deepening. Something wasn't right. The boxes weren't cardboard, they were made of wood. The men were improvising, making tools from their guns in order to break into them. And then one was opened and Jude's jaw dropped, and his hand moved towards his mouth, clamped over it, his eyes widening, his pulse quickening, a dark foreboding rising up within him.

He looked up at Pip in alarm. 'They're not drugs,' he said, watching bodies tumble out of the containers – dead bodies, black, shrivelled-up bodies. The men were jumping back as they took in the horror that lay in front of them. Some were running away, others were prodding the bodies to see if they were alive.

'No,' Pip agreed, his gaze fixed to the screen, his clear blue eyes clouded suddenly. 'No, they're not.'

'They're like the woman,' Jude gasped, fear gripping at his chest like strong, icy hands.

'The woman? She looked like that?' Pip asked, his voice urgent and low.

Jude nodded. 'Exactly the same,' he said breathlessly.

Pip didn't say anything; he just kept looking right ahead at the screen.

'Pip?' Jude turned to him anxiously. 'What does this mean? What happened to them?'

'A very good question,' Pip said gravely.

'It's Pincent Pharma, isn't it?' Jude said through gritted teeth. 'I'm going to upload this on to the Web. Tell the newsfeeds. People have to see this.'

Pip turned to him, his eyes cloudy, and shook his head. 'No, Jude. Now is not the time to act. Now is the time to wait.'

'Wait? For what?' Jude asked incredulously. 'Stop pushing me away. I can help. We should be broadcasting this. We should be using this to let the world know that Pincent Pharma is corrupt, that it's killing people! Let me be part of the fight, Pip. Please.' He looked up hopefully, desperately, his eyes passionate, his fists clenched. And for a moment, he thought Pip was going to say yes; for a moment, Pip looked like he was really considering it.

But then he felt himself crash down to earth as Pip shook his head. 'A broadcast isn't necessary or desirable, Jude. News of this will get out eventually, I assure you.' He got up and started to walk away.

'That's it? That's all you're going to say?' Jude asked desperately. 'What do I say to the men? What do I do?' He looked down miserably at his handheld device. 'Do you even realise what I've got here? Are you even aware that I worked for months on this communications network? That it's unrivalled as far as I know? Do you care that I don't just film attacks; that because of me, you or I can speak directly to the leaders of the soldiers, send for back-up, give orders when dead bodies spill out of lorries instead of drugs?

Do you?'

He stared at Pip defiantly, angrily.

Pip looked back at him, then nodded. 'Of course I know, Jude,' he said quietly. 'Tens, maybe hundreds of lives have been saved because of what you have done.'

Jude started in surprise. Pip had never so much as said thank you for the network, never seemed to show any interest in it. 'So what do I tell them to do?' he asked.

'You tell them to go home,' Pip said quietly. 'And then you track the lorries back through their journeys. I want to know where they came from and where they stopped on their way. Can you do that, Jude?'

'Track lorries? Sure, I can do that,' Jude said heavily, turning back to the images and feeling his blood turn cold at the sight of them. 'I can do whatever you want.'

Chapter Four

Richard stood at the window of his large office, looking at but barely seeing the panoramic view of
London, the symbol of all his power and success. He
felt ill, felt tired, felt . . . scared.

Power and success. Already it felt as if they were
evaporating. He walked over to his desk and gripped
it. Slowly he breathed, in, out, in, out. He would find
an answer. He always found an answer.

But even as he told himself everything would
resolve itself, he found his mind flooded with doubt.
For so long he had buried all thoughts of Albert Fern,
of his protestations as Derek led him to his death.
*'You don't have anything, Richard . . . Without the
exact formula you know nothing . . . The circle of life
must be protected . . .'*

Richard shuddered. How he hated his former boss,
his former father-in-law, the man who had treated
him with such contempt, forcing him to undertake
menial tasks in the laboratory when it had been clear
he was meant for greater things. But Richard had had
the last laugh. It had been an article he'd happened

upon while at university that had convinced him he should go and work for Albert – an interview in which Professor Fern had made an offhand remark about his pursuit of the cure for cancer, saying that he feared they would cure ageing before they cured every strain of that terrible disease. He'd done his research and from what he'd read, Albert had seemed to be the real deal. So Richard had waited for an opening, for a job to come up in his laboratory. And when it had, he'd been ready.

Everything had gone to plan too. More to plan than Richard had allowed himself to dream. Except . . .

He moved towards his large leather chair and sat down heavily, then pulled out from his top drawer the papers he'd stolen from Albert's desk on the day of his death – meaningless scribbles, equations and streams of letters that even the most brilliant scientists had been unable to interpret. All Richard could hear in his head was Albert's taunts about the circle of life. The circle of life? What was it?

Angrily, he let the papers fall from his hands back on to the desk. Several times over the years he'd almost thrown them away – they were meaningless drivel and he hadn't needed them. Despite Albert's protestations, his team of scientists had been able to recreate Longevity, as he'd named it, from the professor's original sample. The drug had sailed through all testing and trials and had taken the world by storm, and Albert Fern had been recast in the history books as a genius who had died of natural causes before his great discovery had been accepted, adopted and legalised.

Richard knew that the scientific community would never have accepted the story that he himself had invented the drug, and Albert's 'sad and untimely' death allowed the drug's genesis to be fabricated, manipulated and, most importantly, kept as opaque as possible. Meanwhile, he had taken his place at the helm of the most powerful company in the whole world. But now . . . now . . . now he needed the formula, needed to understand Albert's scribbles. But instead of helping him, they were as impenetrable as ever. He could almost feel Albert mocking him from beyond the grave.

Richard brought his fist down on the desk so hard that the papers jumped up in the air. 'What is the bloody circle of life?' he shouted. 'Is it the formula? Where is it? Where is it? You bastard! You bloody sanctimonious, conniving bastard!'

Even as he shouted, he knew he had to stop this momentary lapse of control. Anger would solve nothing. But this was anger that had been building up for years – anger and fear that one day Albert's words would come back and haunt him. Richard always liked to have all ends tied up; it was why he had told Derek to dispose of Albert rather than lock him up somewhere. Neat ends enabled you to move forward. Opponents, problems – they had to be dealt with efficiently, not left to fester. And he had succeeded too, except for the formula. However much he had told himself that he didn't need it, that an exact copy was perfectly adequate – more than adequate – he had always suspected, known even, that this ragged end, this unfinished business would come back and haunt him. When Dr Thomas had been blathering about viruses mutating, Richard had dismissed him immediately. He knew what the problem was. Derek knew too. He suspected that they'd both been half expecting it for years.

He had to think. He had to think hard. He would find a way forward – he always did. And in doing so, he would turn the situation to his advantage. There was always an opportunity in crisis, however desperate things seemed.

His phone started to ring and he looked at it with loathing – it would be Hillary Wright, head of the Authorities, haranguing him for more information, for explanations. Dead bodies were not easily hidden in a world where no one died; illness was not easily explained away when Longevity stopped even the tiniest of infections from taking hold. As he'd predicted, the number of deaths was growing – single figures had become double and now there were hundreds of corpses piling up at Pincent Pharma, buried in hastily dug shallow pits. Pincent guards were taking them when they were ill, before anyone could witness the horror, the blackened corpses. Thankfully, living forever had meant that most marriages had broken up – a lifetime's commitment was now rather too long for most to stomach. With no children any more the vast majority of people lived alone, making it much easier for the Authorities police to take them away in the middle of the night and bring them to Pincent Pharma to die and to be examined.

Richard ignored the phone. Hillary could wait, he decided. She would have to – he had to think, had to find a way through the maze. So far he had evaded her questions, lied to her when necessary. He would not admit there was a problem until he also had the solution. He needed the formula; that was the quest. But how? It was like a puzzle, a game, only one with terrible consequences if he lost. Could he dig up Albert's body? Bring him back to life? Torture him into revealing the exact formula?

Nice idea, he thought wryly.

But no. There had to be another way.

He stared again at Albert's notes. Impenetrable scribblings, little doodles around the page – he'd got his best scientists to work tirelessly in an attempt to interpret them, but to no avail. The formula could not be concealed within their pages; it must be hidden somewhere else. But where? Richard had ransacked Albert's house, his car, his office – everywhere. He'd examined everything – after his death and then again a few weeks ago when one death had turned into five and he'd realised that something was wrong.

Sighing, he scrunched up one of the pieces of paper and threw it across the room. But as he did so, his eyes were drawn to something on the page beneath – an image he'd seen somewhere before. A picture of a flower. He'd dismissed it as a doodle, but now . . . He knew he had seen it somewhere else. Where? He didn't know. He closed his eyes, tried to picture the place he'd seen it, but . . . nothing. Then he opened his eyes again. Underneath the drawing, in tiny letters, was written, over and over again, 'The circle of life. The circle of life. Must be protected.'

There was a knock at the door and Derek walked in, silent as always. 'I wondered if there had been any . . . progress,' he said.

Richard looked up and shook his head miserably. 'The circle of life,' he said, sighing. 'All I have is this stupid drawing and his scribblings about the circle of life.'

Derek looked thoughtful. 'That's what he was shouting when I took him away,' he said.

'The circle of life? But what was he talking about? Did it have anything to do with the formula?' Richard asked uncertainly.

Derek didn't say anything for a moment, then he walked back towards the door. 'You'll find it, sir,' he said quietly. 'I know you will.'

Richard sighed heavily. 'The one person who believes in me,' he said. 'I wish I had your confidence. Thank you, Derek.'

'Thank you, sir,' Derek said smoothly, and left the room.

Jude looked around cautiously to check that no one was watching him, but he needn't have worried; as always, Pip was nowhere to be seen and Sheila was lying sprawled over some cushions reading a romantic novel that one of the supporters had donated a few weeks ago.

Quickly he looked back at his computer and adjusted the sound levels so that no one but him would hear what the cameras were picking up. Pip might not think he was as clever or brave as Peter, but Peter wouldn't be able to do this, Jude thought to himself, adrenalin coursing through his veins.

He could feel a light film of sweat cover his body which, bearing in mind the temperature of the Underground, had nothing to do with heat. He was scared. Excited. His neck muscles were tense, his eyes wide, because he'd done the impossible – done what no one else had even attempted. He might not be a hero in Pip's eyes, but Sheila believed in him and that had given him the idea. He'd got into the Pincent Pharma security system, which wasn't in itself terribly challenging – he'd been doing that before he'd even met Pip. Network security had been his bread and butter in the Outside world and there was nothing he didn't know about firewalls and chinks that let him go wherever he wanted. But now things were different. Now he'd made the leap into the most protected area in Pincent Pharma. Now he was seeing what no one else could see.

He hadn't expected to get into Richard Pincent's camera system on his first attempt, though. He hadn't expected to be sitting here a few hours later watching him up close.

Silently Jude watched as Richard stared at some handwritten notes in front of him. Then, hearing someone approaching, he quickly turned the volume down even further and got ready to minimise the screen. But it wasn't Pip, it was Sheila. He considered minimising the screen anyway, but he didn't want to. Not now. Not when he was this close.

As Sheila approached, her eyes widened like saucers. 'That's . . .' she said anxiously.

Jude nodded. 'Shhh,' he whispered and Sheila sank silently into the chair next to him, her face white.

'He keeps looking at that picture,' Jude said under his breath. 'And muttering about the circle of life.'

Sheila looked at him worriedly and he put his arm around her. 'Don't worry. You're safe here.' She leant into him and as usual he felt his chest lurch.

'What's the circle of life?' she asked under her breath.

'I don't know. But I think this image has got something to do with it. Look.' He zoomed in on the flower. 'I've seen it before,' he said. 'I know I have. But I can't remember where.'

Sheila looked at it carefully. 'And why is he looking at it?'

Jude looked at her for a few seconds, then looked around again to check no one else was near. 'I don't know,' he said cautiously. 'I mean . . . I don't think Richard Pincent knows either, to be honest. But he keeps staring at it and he was shouting before, asking

70

what it was.'

'Does Pip know you're doing this?' Sheila asked, frowning.

Jude shook his head.

She appeared to digest this for a second, then she leant forward. 'Richard Pincent's got a very nice room,' she breathed. 'Big windows. And it looks really warm.'

Jude nodded. 'Yeah, well, when you're Richard Pincent I guess the normal rules don't apply.'

Sheila nodded. Then she looked at Jude intently. 'The other day. You were going to tell me about my parents. Will you tell me now?'

Jude looked down. 'Your parents? It was nothing. I didn't find anything – that's all I wanted to tell you.'

'Really?' Sheila asked suspiciously.

'Really,' Jude said, not meeting her eyes.

'That's a shame. Because I know what it is. The picture, I mean.'

Jude raised an eyebrow. 'The picture Richard's looking at? How?'

'I just do,' Sheila said with a little shrug.

'So tell me,' Jude said, raising an eyebrow.

She turned to look at him; she was so close he was sure she could feel his heart thudding in his chest and wished it would calm down a bit. 'I'll only tell you if you promise to find my parents. Properly find them.'

She was staring at Jude intently and he felt himself getting hot. Pip wouldn't be happy about it, but then again Pip was never that happy. And after all, this was Sheila they were talking about. She probably didn't know anything. She was just making stuff up as usual.

'OK,' he said.

'You promise? You cross your heart and hope to die?'

'What?' Jude screwed up his face. 'Why would I do that?'

'It was in a book I read,' Sheila said earnestly. 'You have to say it. That means I know you're telling the truth.'

'Fine,' Jude said with a little grin. 'I cross my heart and hope to die. So? What is it? If you really do know.'

'Of course I know,' Sheila said lightly. She got up and stood behind Jude. 'Zoom in on it again,' she said.

Jude did what he was told.

Then she nodded happily. 'Don't you recognise the pattern?' she asked.

Jude stared at it. 'I do. I think I do, anyway. But I can't . . . I don't know where it's from.'

'I do,' Sheila said. 'It's Peter's ring.'

'Peter's ring?' Jude looked at her uncertainly and turned back to the computer. Then he breathed out loudly. 'You're right. It's the image on Peter's ring. How did you know that?'

'I notice stuff,' Sheila said. 'So, are you going to start looking for my parents? Look for all the Palmers in London. Look now.'

'I will,' Jude said vaguely, but his mind was already

72

racing. Peter's ring. The circle of life. Why was Richard staring at it? What did he want it for? He would find out. He would discover what was going on, and Pip would look at him anew, and he would be the hero suddenly, he would be the Resistance conqueror. Not Peter. Not any more.

'Well, go on then,' Sheila persisted.

Jude looked at her distractedly.

'My parents,' she said, her lip quivering slightly. 'You promised, Jude. You promised.'

Jude sighed inwardly. 'Sheila, stop looking for your parents, OK? Just give it up. Parents aren't that great anyway – I hated mine most of the time.'

Sheila stared at him angrily. 'I don't want to give it up,' she said hotly. 'You promised you'd find them. You promised.'

'I know,' Jude said uncomfortably, reddening as he spoke. He could see Pip standing in the doorway watching them; he was out of earshot, but Jude still couldn't risk telling Sheila what he knew about her parents. It had been stupid to promise that he would. 'But it's not that easy.'

'No,' Sheila said tightly. 'I guess it isn't. I guess it isn't sensible relying on other people either, is it, Jude? When all they ever do is let you down.'

She stood up and ran from the room, pushing past Pip who looked at Jude with a bemused expression.

'I'd never let you down,' Jude said miserably, his voice catching slightly as he turned towards her. But it was too late – she couldn't hear him. And he hardly believed himself anyway.

Chapter Five

Anna chopped tomatoes for the picnic, every so often glancing down at the pile of cushions heaped on the floor, on top of which lay Molly. 'Beautiful,' she murmured. Molly was the most beautiful creature in the whole wide world – Anna could stare at her for hours with no awareness of time ticking by. Her daughter. Her Molly.

'Are you ready?' Peter swept into the kitchen, stooping down to grab Molly and bringing her to his chest. Molly's eyes opened for a second, her arms shooting up in a startled reflex before she nestled her head into his shoulder and resumed her nap. Anna turned back to the tomatoes.

'Five minutes,' she lied, knowing that the picnic wouldn't be ready for at least ten, but knowing also that with Molly in his arms Peter, usually impatient, would not notice if five minutes became ten or even fifteen. Time, for Anna, was the real luxury of their freedom. On her wrist Embedded Time, the watch etched into her own skin, reminded her constantly of her days at Grange Hall where every minute was accounted for. There it was drummed into her, into all the Surpluses, that time was not theirs – that it belonged to Legals, just as they did. But she covered it up these days with long sleeves and even when she caught a glimpse of it, it no longer caused her heart to beat faster. She owned her own time now. If the picnic was late, it didn't matter. Nothing mattered except their little family unit, their safety.

She glanced back to where Molly had been lying, her imprint still visible in the cushion. She opened her mouth to say something, to tell Peter about the letter waiting for him, the letter that she had stuffed under the cushion minutes before he had appeared. Then she closed it again. She knew what he'd say. The letter would blacken his mood.

'And how's my little Molly?' Peter was grinning, kissing his daughter on the nose, causing her eyes to open again sleepily. She gurgled and Anna turned back to the kitchen worktop, her heart thudding in her chest. She knew who the letter was from, knew exactly what it would say. And she also knew that Peter wouldn't read it, that he would dismiss it with an angry stare, tell Anna she could open it if she wanted to but that he didn't want to know the contents, that he had no interest in the letter or its sender, that he had no mother, whatever she thought.

And he was right; she knew that sometimes. But she also knew that you couldn't just deny something and be done with it. Peter's mother was Mrs Pincent, Anna's overbearing tormentor, a woman who she still sometimes imagined watching over her, criticising her. A woman who she still somehow felt a desperate need to please; a woman whose pain she couldn't help sharing in her darker moments. To live without knowing Molly? Without knowing Ben? Terrifying.

'She's trying to sleep,' Anna said, forcing her mind back to the present, as Peter threw Molly gently in the air.

'Sleep's for wimps,' Peter retorted. 'Anyway, I think she wants to play. Don't you, Molly?'

Molly produced a big smile which Peter pointed to triumphantly. 'See?' he grinned. 'I told you.'

Anna nodded and forced a smile. To tell Peter would risk ruining the day. Not to tell him would mean that she would be carrying a secret around with her. And secrets, Anna knew, were mini-betrayals. She had kept her escape secret from Sheila, leaving her vulnerable friend exposed to the wrath of Mrs Pincent and everyone else at Grange Hall, leaving her to be abducted by Richard Pincent, used to further his scientific ends. She had kept a secret before, for a woman she'd thought was her friend but who'd turned out to be a Catcher, who'd had her arrested and nearly had Molly destroyed in the process. Secrets were never good. They were supposed to protect people, but they never did. They always made things worse.

'Peter,' she said tentatively, 'you got a letter this morning.'

He looked at her for a second and immediately the

joy left his eyes and they took on the steely look that made her nervous even though he never directed it at her. 'Another letter?' he said, his voice light and apparently unconcerned. 'Well, you know what you can do with it.'

'She's going to keep writing,' Anna said, her throat drying up as she spoke. 'Couldn't you –'

'Couldn't I what?' Peter rounded on her. 'Write back to the woman who made your life a living hell? Who tried to kill me? She's evil, Anna. I want nothing to do with her.'

Anna nodded. 'I know,' she whispered. 'But she's your mother.' She couldn't explain to Peter how enormous that fact was to her. Her own mother had been a virtual stranger to her; she'd met her briefly, loved her, only to have her snatched away again. And now she was a mother herself and it made her feel both stronger and more vulnerable than she'd ever thought possible.

Peter shook his head. 'She isn't my mother,' he said tersely. 'I have no mother.' Then he sighed. 'How are her letters even finding the Underground? That's what I don't get.'

'One of the inmates . . .' Anna said tentatively, not wanting to risk angering Peter further with her in-depth knowledge of Mrs Pincent's previous letters. 'An Underground supporter.'

'What? They just give away the contact mechanism to Richard Pincent's daughter?' Peter asked sarcastically.

'I don't know,' Anna said quietly.

Peter digested this. 'You want me to write back, don't you?' he said eventually. 'I don't know what hold that woman's got over you, but you want me to write to her and tell her I forgive her. You want that twisted psychopath masquerading as a human being to have some peace before she falls apart and dies.' His eyes were boring into Anna's but she stayed silent. Then he shook his head. 'Well, I won't. I want her to die unhappy, Anna. I want her to die crying out in her misery because of what she's done.'

Anna stepped backwards. Her eyes were brimming with tears and she didn't know why. She wasn't crying for Mrs Pincent. She couldn't be. Herself then? She didn't know. She shook herself. It didn't matter. Peter was right – Mrs Pincent was evil. She didn't have a hold over her. Did she? 'Fine, I'll go and wake Ben,' Anna said, wiping her hands on her apron.

'You do that. And I'm going to check my messages. From people I actually want to write to,' Peter muttered.

As Anna left the room she could hear him switching on the computer and frowned involuntarily. Perhaps Mrs Pincent had some strange draw for her; perhaps she thought of her old House Matron from time to time. But Peter's own weakness was a far more physical and constant presence in their life and far more time-consuming – it was his computer. The machine was their conduit to the outside world – to Jude, Peter's half-brother, and the Underground. To Peter, the computer was his connection, his lifeline; to Anna it represented only the uncomfortable knowledge that their rural idyll in the Underground safe house would not last for ever. Peter would hunch over it whenever he got the chance, sending messages, downloading news programmes, searching for information on Longevity drugs, on Pincent Pharma, on all the things he hated. Anna understood, but that didn't mean she didn't sometimes entertain thoughts of smashing the computer and cutting them off completely.

Ben was awake in his makeshift cot when she walked into his room, pulling himself up to a standing position, a huge smile plastered on his face.

'Mama Nanna!' he said excitedly as Anna approached, his name for her a result of many attempts at explaining that Anna was like his mother but really his sister, and that he could call her Anna or Mama, or . . . 'Mama Nanna up now. Nanna up.'

Obediently, Anna lifted him out of the cot; he wrapped his little arms around her neck briefly, then wriggled his way on to the floor. Anna guided him down the corridor to the kitchen, then opened the door and ushered him through.

'Teter,' Ben said, toddling in the direction of the kitchen, of Peter. 'Teter play,' he said, nodding to himself as though deciding that this was a reasonable and sensible expectation. Anna loved that – loved his innocence, his lack of awareness that if anyone saw him they would call the Catchers. Children did not exist in a world that had become the preserve of the old; there was no place for them, no infrastructure, no welcome.

New life only emphasised the futility and endlessness of old life, Anna thought. That was why people were scared of children, she told herself. That was why people betrayed them and called the Authorities. And that was why she kept Ben and Molly hidden, why she would not leave this house, this land, whose isolation provided them with the freedom and independence they would find nowhere else.

'Teter!' Ben's eyes opened wide with pleasure as he saw Peter sitting at the computer, and he ran over immediately. Molly was asleep on Peter's shoulder, Anna noticed with a wry smile. 'Teter play. Teter play now.'

But instead of turning round and giving Ben a hug and a smile of welcome, tousling his hair, Peter remained still. Frowning, Anna moved towards him; he was staring at the computer screen, his brow furrowed.

'Peter?' she chided. 'Peter, Ben wants to play.'

'Not now.' His voice was tense and Anna noticed that his shoulders were tight.

'What?' she asked, her heart immediately thudding in her chest. 'What's happened?' Possible catastrophes rushed through her head: Jude was dead. Pip was dead. The Underground had collapsed. Richard Pincent had found them. The Catchers were coming. Everything was over. 'Is it something terrible?' She scooped Ben up in her arms, her eyes moving anxiously towards Molly. 'Peter, tell me what's happened.'

Slowly, Peter looked up. Then he shook himself. 'Nothing. Nothing at all. I was just reading a message from Jude.'

'What did he say?' Anna said, her throat constricting and an ominous foreboding taking hold of her. *It's started. I knew something terrible was on the horizon and now it's here.* 'Is something wrong?'

'Not wrong,' Peter said cautiously. 'Not in so many words. He just said to stay alert.'

'We're always alert,' Anna said, looking around worriedly. 'We only go out for two hours a day and we never leave a trail and –'

'And we're going to be fine,' Peter said, getting up and walking towards her. 'Like I said, it wasn't a warning. It was probably just a reminder.'

'A reminder,' Anna said, biting her lip. 'Are you sure?'

Peter pulled her towards him. 'Anna, we're safe here. You know we are. No one can find us and even if they did I'd protect you.'

'You promise?' Anna asked tentatively.

'I promise,' Peter said, kissing the top of her head distractedly as his eyes returned to the computer screen. 'Although I wish I knew what was going on. I'm sick of being treated like a convalescing child up here in the middle of nowhere.'

There was something about the way he said it that made Anna's stomach clench. A few times recently she had found Peter pacing up and down, a look in his eyes that she recognised, that she feared. Eyes that darted around, thinking, noticing, planning. 'I don't mind not knowing,' she said quickly. 'It's a small price to pay.' She looked over at the children then back at Peter; he nodded immediately.

'You're right,' he said quickly. 'Of course you're right.'

And she *was* right, Anna thought to herself defiantly. They'd earned their freedom, earned this new life.

'We're happy here,' she said, not sure why. 'We're happy here. Aren't we?'

Peter looked at her for a second or two, then grinned. 'Of course we are, Anna. We're very happy. So, picnic?'

She handed Ben back to him and moved over to the kitchen counter. 'Picnic,' she agreed.

'Nic nic,' Ben said immediately, taking Peter's hand and leading him towards the kitchen door. 'Nic nic playtime.'

Chapter Six

Jake Gardner hauled himself out of bed and walked slowly and painfully to the bathroom. Ignoring the female voice warning him not to use more water than was absolutely necessary and reminding him that cold water was more bracing and healthful than warm, he turned the hot tap on full, perching on the side as his bathtub – a luxury he was glad he'd refused to give up in spite of high taxes, warning letters and threats to have it removed – filled up. He was shivering, his face hot, his skin an odd yellowish colour – although he'd spent so long looking at it, trying to establish what the problem was, that he'd forgotten how it usually appeared. The thirst was new. He felt as though his body had been starved of water. A fever, he'd thought, then dismissed the idea. Impossible. Ridiculous.

Jake knew all about disease. He worked with it day in, day out at the poultry production centre. But people were not chickens. The rules for humans were different. There was no such thing as human disease. There would be another explanation. Maybe he'd exerted himself more than necessary recently.

He eased himself into the bath, sighing with happiness as the warmth enveloped him even as his teeth still chattered.

A plague on your people. He remembered the line from somewhere – he couldn't recall where. Plague. Pestilence. Things man brought upon himself, he found himself thinking. But these were crazed thoughts. There were no plagues now; there were no gods now either. No higher powers – except of course the Authorities. Was this a punishment for refusing to throw out his bath? Was this his penance for being wasteful?

He shook himself. His mind wasn't his own – racing, darting, seeing things where they weren't, like a dream where things were movable, where the usual laws of physics didn't apply. If only he wasn't so cold. If only he could warm his bones up somehow.

Cull them. If disease is left it will spread, infect the entire barn. You've got to get them early. He imagined himself as a chicken, running from his keeper, stumbling, his large body too heavy for his pockmarked legs, colliding with other chickens, knowing that it was futile, that he was going to die, going to be taken . . .

No, I'm human. Humans don't get ill. Longevity. Did I take my Longevity? Yes. Yes, I took it. Take more. Yes, I'll take more. Now. The water was still warm; he didn't want to leave its embrace. *Afterwards. I'll take them afterwards.* He hadn't been

84

to work today. Nor yesterday. Had he been missed? What were people saying? He must go in tomorrow. He just needed some sleep. It was fatigue, plain and simple. Or perhaps he'd been bitten by some insect. He looked down at his body and felt his mouth fall open in shock. It seemed to be shrinking, wasting away before his eyes, the skin tightening around his bones as though the water, his blood, his flesh, was leaking out. No, the light must be playing tricks on him. He shook himself, then looked back, but was met by the same horrific image, his skin being sucked into his bones, blackening, shrivelling up. He was hallucinating. He had to be. But the pain – the pain was excruciating, his windpipe was constricting, he needed air, needed water, needed . . .

He hadn't heard the front door open and looked up in shock and surprise when two men walked into his bathroom, his mouth open but no words coming out of it. He felt like a fish, gasping for oxygen, splashing fruitlessly in the water.

The men looked at him, their lips curled in disgust – the same look Jake knew he wore when picking out chickens, grabbing them by the legs and breaking their necks in one seamless movement.

'I'm not diseased,' he garbled. 'It's cold. I needed to warm up. I . . .'

The men looked at each other, shared a raised eyebrow, a wry smile. Then one produced a metal stick and dropped it in the water. Immediately Jake's eyes opened wide and his body began to shake violently, his lungs expressing air in a loud howl of pain, until there was no more air, until the current had done its work.

Silently, the men emptied the bath of water, checked the body was safe to move, then wrapped it up and took it down to the lorry.

'You're a fast learner,' Jude said appraisingly as Sheila deftly navigated her way through the Underground security network to pick up a message in its inbox. Sheila shrugged but inside she was glowing.

It was a few days later and, in order to make up for his broken promise, Jude had finally agreed to teach her how to use the computer. It had been a struggle – Jude's computer meant more to him than anything and every time she hit the wrong key she'd seen him wince. But he hadn't known how closely she'd been watching him all this time; hadn't known that she'd already picked up a lot. All she'd needed was the opportunity to touch the thing.

'Yes, I am,' Sheila agreed with a little smile. She turned to Jude and studied his face briefly – a face that looked so like Peter's except for the eyes. Peter's eyes were intense, restless, always darting around. Jude's were calm. In spite of her anger with him over not finding her parents, his eyes reassured her, they instilled confidence. She felt safe when he was around. She didn't know why he always got so defensive about himself, why he always seemed to think that he was in competition with Peter. In her opinion Jude would win hands down. Peter was the sort of person who got you into trouble; Jude was the sort of person who got you out of it.

Her brow creased in concentration she stared at the screen, trying to remember the next sequence – the sequence that would enable her to reply to the message. In spite of her protestations that computers were incredibly dull – protestations that were the result of her defences kicking in because she'd known so little about them, protestations that she kept up so that no one would suspect her intense interest – Sheila had jumped at the chance to use one for herself. She knew that Jude's computer was a treasure box of information; through it she could communicate with anyone she wanted to, find out anything and everything. She'd watched him carefully for months, learning how to unlock its secrets, how to make it work for her. The fact of the matter was that she had a plan, a dangerous plan – one that still brought her out in goosebumps every time she thought about it. She knew Jude wouldn't understand, would try to stop her if he got a chance, and this was the one thing that nearly made her change her mind several times a day.

But she knew she had to do it. Jude might put up with the Underground, with its dank rooms and its meagre food supply, but Sheila had her sights set on a better life. She knew that this was not her destiny, that this life was not meant for her. She might have been labelled a Surplus, like Anna, but she knew that she wasn't. She remembered her parents; remembered being told by them that she was Legal, that she was very special. She remembered the night she'd been taken too – she'd been at her grandparents'. Someone had called the Catchers and Grandma hadn't had the paperwork. She remembered Grandma's screams, remembered being taken by a man who smelt dirty and coarse . . . and then began the life that she should never have led. A childhood spent in Grange Hall, waiting for her parents to come, dreaming of the Outside, of a land of plenty where everything was warm and soft, where food was always available, where she could lie on a sofa daydreaming to her heart's content.

When she'd finally been rescued – not from Grange Hall but from Pincent Pharma, where she'd been sent to be a Valuable Asset – she'd thought that escape would lead her to a better life, not to the Underground. It was hardly any different from Grange Hall here – small grey rooms, chores, rules. There was no cruelty here, she wasn't ill-treated on a daily basis and encouraged to hate herself, but still, it wasn't the world she'd been waiting for – it didn't even come close. She wanted her old bedroom, wanted the softness of her mother's embrace, wanted all the food in the world and all the love to boot.

She turned to Jude with a little smile. 'If you didn't look over my shoulder all the time I'd learn far more quickly,' she said.

Jude shook his head. 'That's my computer you're on. No one uses my computer without me there.'

Sheila frowned. 'You mean you don't trust me?'

'I mean this computer has too much on it. It's too important. If you make a mistake, press the wrong button –'

'I won't,' Sheila insisted. 'You always get annoyed that Pip doesn't trust you, but you're just as bad.'

'I'm not,' Jude said, his eyes widening. 'This is different. This is . . .'

He trailed off uncertainly.

'See?' Sheila said triumphantly. 'You're just as bad as him.'

'No I'm not,' Jude said forcefully. 'Fine.' He stood up gingerly, looking as though he was fighting a magnetic pull to move away. 'Fine. I'll leave you alone for a few minutes. You know not to touch that button? And if you're unsure about anything, anything at all –'

'I'll ask you, ' Sheila promised. She held her breath and waited until Jude was far enough away, until she was sure he wouldn't be able to see what she was doing. Then, her heart fluttering, she began to navigate through his files, doing exactly what she'd watched him do. Soon everything she'd ever wanted would be hers. She was going to look after herself from now on. She was going to be just fine.

Chapter Seven

Anna stared at the piece of paper in front of her then grabbed it, screwed it up into a little ball and threw it in the bin. She looked up at the ceiling, searching for something, but she didn't know what. It wasn't inspiration she needed, it was more than that. It was the answer to the question that had been pressing at her for weeks, months: should she write back to her old House Matron? Should she put Mrs Pincent out of her misery? Would she be letting Peter down? Would it be an act of weakness or strength?

She sighed. Life in Grange Hall used to be so full of certainties: right, wrong; good, bad; useful, waste of space . . . Now nothing was clear. Peter didn't seem to mind that – he had his own principles, his own guiding beliefs that were, as far as Anna could tell, a mixture of the Underground doctrine and his own gut feeling about things. Anna, though, struggled daily. It wasn't just being on the Outside either – it was motherhood. Often she felt more driven by fear for her children than by rational thought; she wasn't sure any more where she stopped and her desire to protect them began. As for Mrs Pincent – she was an ogre, Anna knew that. But she had also thought that her child had been murdered; she had suffered intolerably. Did that not affect her guilt? At the same time, unaware that Peter was her long-lost son, Mrs Pincent would have had him put down like an animal if they hadn't escaped. Perhaps she deserved nothing but her own misery to keep her company until her inevitable death.

Then again, to hear from Anna would not give Mrs Pincent any pleasure. Not when she heard the truth from her pen – that Peter would not acknowledge her existence. Anna would simply be telling her the facts. It would stop Mrs Pincent writing, stop her hoping for a response from her son that would never come.

Surely even a monster deserved that?

Anna exhaled slowly. Peter had said she could. He'd said, 'Write to her yourself if you want.' Had he meant it? She couldn't ask. To ask would be to revisit, to awaken Peter's anger again. Every time the Pincent name cropped up his eyes would darken, his neck would tense.

She would do it, Anna decided suddenly. She would write so that there would be no more letters, no more reminders. It was for Peter that she was doing it, not for Mrs Pincent – not for the woman whose twisted, manipulative regime was the nearest thing to parenting that Anna had known during her incarceration in the Surplus Hall.

Slowly, she took out another sheet of paper and began to write.

The wind was battering Pincent Pharma, doing its best to unhinge drainpipes, to uproot the signage surrounding it. Hailstones swept past its windows, forcing people off the street, but at least the hail might melt, might provide a little moisture for the parched land below. It was summer, but the seasons meant little any more and the days were cold, dark and rainless. The landscape was not the same one that Richard Pincent had known as a child, but then again the world was not the same either. Doom-mongers had been warning of the end of the world for as long as he could remember and he had always brazened it out, carrying on just as he liked. His room, after all, was warm, secure and sterile and kept at a constant temperature, triple glazing ensuring that any sound or gust of wind was kept safely on the outside rather than encroaching on the sanctity of his workspace. He loved the control he felt every time he closed his window, shutting Nature out, proving yet again that he reigned supreme over his empire.

People used to speak of Nature as if it were a good thing, as though 'natural' conferred upon something a worth, a value. The truth, Richard knew, was that Nature was a tyrant who killed and maimed without a thought, to whom survival of the fittest wasn't an ideology but a requirement. Nature did not favour the weak; Nature took no prisoners. If Nature hadn't been Richard's sworn enemy he might even have felt some kind of respect. Like knows like, he thought to himself from time to time.

'Richard, are you listening to me?'

He looked over at Hillary Wright and for a moment was tempted to tell the truth: that he hadn't slept in days, that he was terrified, that nothing was under control, that for the first time in his life he didn't know what to do. Instead he forced a smile. She had no idea, and if he told her the truth what good would it do? His own scientists didn't even get it; they might not argue openly with him but he knew that their view was the same as Thomas's – that it was the virus that had mutated, not Longevity. But Richard knew they were wrong; he felt it in his bones. This was Albert Fern's legacy, the ticking bomb that he had left behind. Richard would find the combination – he would triumph just as he always had. But to explain this to Hillary? Hopeless. She was a bureaucrat, not a politician – the Authorities had long given up on the notion of democracy since voting numbers had virtually evaporated and the same politicians had stood year after year. Now everything was run by civil servants who wrote lists and policy documents that organised and managed with tick boxes and regulations. Hillary knew how to chair a meeting, how to run the country in an ordered way, but she had no vision, no imagination. She thought that a few people had become ill after taking their Longevity incorrectly. And still she was reacting as though this were a major national crisis. If she knew the truth she would implode. Far safer to keep it from her.

'I'm sorry, Hillary. Please go on,' he said.

'I had finished,' she said pointedly. 'I was waiting for you to say something.'

Richard nodded slowly, his default action when caught on the hop.

'What would you suggest, Hillary?' he said, playing for time. For weeks now he had avoided this meeting, brushing her off with the line that a rogue virus was only affecting a very few people, that those affected were being examined and treated, that Pincent guards were taking those affected in the night so as to prevent any further panic. And she'd believed him – why wouldn't she? But the few bodies had become many, and those who had seen the Pincent vans taking their loved ones away had started to demand answers. Conspiracy theories were beginning to spread up and down the country.

And now Hillary wanted answers. Wanted reassurance. She sat forward in her chair. 'It can't go on, Richard,' she said, pursing her lips. 'The virus has spread. To America, to China, to the rest of Europe. People are dying, Richard. I've just been on the phone to Saudi. They say that bodies are stacking up.'

'They are exaggerating,' Richard said, his hand moving to his collar, which suddenly felt very tight. 'I told you, if people take their drugs correctly . . .'

Hillary looked at him furiously. 'They say it has affected people on the correct dosage. You said the virus wouldn't spread, Richard. You said it would be contained. A few people taking their drugs incorrectly, you told me. *A few people.*'

Richard took a deep breath, tried to calm himself. The bodies. The vile, twisted bodies, their faces full of horror even in death. They filled his dreams and their stench seemed to follow him wherever he went. They were mocking him. Taunting him. *You lied to us. You said we would live for ever. We didn't. You won't either.* 'They are lying,' he said, his voice strangled.

'No.' Hillary shook her head. 'I have been sent photographs. Dried-up bodies. Horrible. Too horrible.' She shuddered. 'I need to know what's going on, Richard. We already have protesters on the streets over water rationing. If people get wind of this, if they think that Longevity can't protect them –'

'It can protect them,' Richard said forcefully, banging his hand down on his desk suddenly. 'It has always protected them. Shut the protests down. Put more police on the streets.'

'It's not as simple as that,' Hillary said tightly.

'Of course it is,' Richard said.

'Hundreds of people are missing, Richard.' She looked at him searchingly. 'Taken away in the middle of the night. Hundreds. I told you weeks ago that we needed to communicate more with their families, their friends.'

'Families? No one has families any more, Hillary,' Richard said irritably. 'No one cares about anyone else any more. You know that. We have communicated, anyway – we have told people what they need to know when they need to know it.'

'You mean you have told people nothing,' Hillary said stiffly.

'What else would you have us do?' Richard stared at her insolently. 'We're getting to the bodies as soon as their identicards reveal their temperature rising. Would you have us spend our time instead counselling next-door neighbours and writing long letters to their estranged sisters and brothers?'

'No, Richard, I would have you get rid of the problem,' Hillary said. 'They're calling them the Missing. People want to know what's going on. *I* want to know what's going on. What do we tell the newsfeeds? That Longevity is safe? That no one is getting ill? They're beginning to report on the missing people. We're losing control here and you have given me no answers.'

Richard stood up heavily; he needed height over Hillary. He felt tired. So tired.

Hillary looked back at him boldly; he could see in her eyes that she suspected the balance of power was up for grabs. 'Do I need to bring in scientists from other countries?' she asked pointedly. 'Do The Authorities need to take over Pincent Pharma?'

His eyes narrowed; he could feel adrenalin course through his veins. How dare she! How dare she question him! 'Don't you dare,' he said angrily.

'Then I need answers. Proper answers. Do your

drugs not work, Richard?' She was looking at him triumphantly, mockingly. She had no idea, Richard realised, how close she was to the truth.

'Of course the drugs work,' he lied.

'I know they work,' she said exasperatedly, 'but you must tell me the truth. I don't buy your story of a virus, Richard. Longevity protects us from viruses – we all know that. What's really going on? Are the conspiracy theories true? Are you testing new drugs on an unsuspecting public?'

If only, Richard thought. If only it were that simple. He closed his eyes. When you are weak, attack – it is the best defence. That had always been his mantra. So why now, when he needed it, was he lost? Why could he not see what to say, what to do? Even Hillary could see his weakness – he was exposed, vulnerable. He needed his armour, needed to wrest control. He thought frantically. Then suddenly, like a dove appearing over Noah's ark, an idea occurred to him – an idea that would get Hillary off his case, that would give him time. It was brilliant. He smiled to himself. He felt his energy returning.

Grimly, Richard leant towards Hillary, his eyes serious. 'You really want to know what happened? Why people are ill? Why they might be dying in other countries?'

'I really want to know,' Hillary said, her eyes wide with expectation.

Richard stood up and sighed for dramatic effect. It was a bold lie that he was going to tell, and one that could backfire spectacularly – but only if managed badly, and Richard never managed anything badly. Slowly he turned to Hillary, his expression serious. 'You're right. There is no virus.'

Hillary nodded victoriously. 'As I suspected. Go on,' she ordered him.

Richard paused for dramatic effect before continuing. Then he took a deep breath. 'There was a contamination,' he said, his voice low. 'The Underground . . . They contaminated a batch of Longevity.'

Hillary's mouth fell open. 'No!'

'Yes. The terrorists, the vile, blood-hungry terrorists got through our security system somehow,' Richard said distastefully. 'I didn't want to tell you until I was sure. But we've checked and . . .' he shook his head. 'I don't know how it happened, but it did.'

Hillary's mouth was still hanging open. 'How many?' she gasped. 'How many tablets did they contaminate?'

'We're trying to establish that. Enough to have gone out of this country. Enough to mean that there are going to be more . . . bodies.'

Hillary was staring at him uncertainly; he felt his shoulders rise slightly, felt his chin lift. He had the upper hand again. For now. For a little while.

'I should have told you before.' He looked at her intently. 'I'm sorry, Hillary.'

Hillary took a deep breath, then let it out. 'I see,' she said. 'I see.'

'The fact of the matter,' Richard continued, warming to his theme, 'is that we are in the grip of the worst terrorist attack of the past two hundred years. And people need to know that. You want the trust of the public? Get more police on the streets. Assign Pincent Pharma more guards. We need to root out the Underground once and for all and we need to work together. I need all Catchers and police working directly for me until the Underground is destroyed.'

Hillary blanched. 'We will work together Richard,' she said. 'But the Authorities are still in charge.'

'Of course they are,' Richard said impatiently, 'but if the Underground has its way there won't be anyone left to be in charge of. We have to destroy them, Hillary. We need to do it now.'

Hillary nodded uncomfortably. 'Very well. I'll let the Chief of Police and the Catchers know,' she said, her voice quieter. 'So what do we say? What do we tell the people? Foreign governments?'

Richard allowed the corners of his mouth to curl upwards. 'We tell the truth. A population gripped by fear is a good thing. It will help us. If we encourage people to suspect their neighbours then it will make them welcome police swooping in at the dead of night. We will take bodies at the first sign of illness instead of when it's taken hold. A slight fever and we'll swoop. If there are protests, we'll take the pro-testers. We'll take anyone who challenges us, Hillary, and the ones left will let us do it because they will be afraid.'

Hillary nodded silently. Then she looked up at

Richard tentatively. 'The batch that was contamin-ated,' she said. 'Is there any way of knowing . . . who might be . . . where the batch might have . . .'

Richard nodded seriously and did his best not to smile. It had almost been too easy. She was afraid, just as everyone else would be, and in fear she turned to him, the benefactor, the saviour. He reached into his desk drawer, took out a blister pack of tablets and handed them to her. 'Take these. You can be sure they're safe,' he lied. The contamination may have been fabricated, but if the drugs had been weakened by endless copying, who knew if this batch was any safer than another?

Hillary took them. 'Obviously it's because of my job,' she said quickly. 'And we'll need more safe batches for all key workers. Police, Catchers, and so on.'

'Yes,' Richard nodded smoothly. 'They'll be with you tomorrow.'

'And you'll find out how many? We need to be pre-pared. I need to talk to my counterparts around the world.'

'Of course you do,' Richard said. 'You'll be the first to know when we're sure of the scale of this disaster. I'm very grateful, Hillary. I know this isn't easy for you.'

'No, it isn't,' Hillary said, standing up. 'But at least you have finally told me the truth.'

'I'd have told you sooner if I could,' Richard said, looking at her earnestly, 'but a whiff of this could turn to mass panic.'

'It could,' Hillary said, nodding, frown line etched into her forehead.

'However, mass panic would enable more pressing measures to be taken,' Richard continued. 'We have to prevent another attack. We need to focus all our resources on crushing the Underground once and for all. All its supporters. Anyone who has ever shown any sympathy for their cause.'

'Road blocks, more police, limited movement, more surveillance – yes,' Hillary nodded.

'Protesters taken into custody, gatherings banned,' Richard suggested. 'Opt Outs and suspected Underground sympathisers rounded up.'

'Yes, yes, of course,' Hillary said, standing up. Richard pressed a button on his desk and immediately a guard appeared to escort her out of the building. 'Well, thank you, Richard,' she said as she left. 'We'll work together on this. From now on. You tell me everything.'

'Everything,' Richard assured her, waiting until the door had closed behind him before he picked up the phone. He had bought some time; now he had to use it wisely. 'Derek,' he said. 'Come up, please. We have some work to do.'

Chapter Eight

Julia Sharpe poured herself another gin and tonic and returned to the plump cushions of her sofa. It was 4 p.m. – an in-between time that Julia had, lately, begun to fill with a drink and programme downloads. In truth she'd have preferred wine, but that wasn't an option nowadays. Nothing that had travelled more than fifty miles was allowed, and the recent cold summers had put a stop to the south-east's wine production. But gin was OK. It did the job.

She'd already been to the gym, had her hair done, made sure that the house was in order, organised supper, popped round to a neighbour's for coffee and read a chapter of her book, but still the afternoon and evening stretched out in front of her like a long journey. Her husband would not be home for another four hours and even when he did return, he would bring little to alleviate the monotony. He would pick up the paper, sit on his chair, put on a CD, and wait to be called for dinner. Then they would eat, perhaps talk about their day, retire to the sitting room for more reading, watching, listening. Then bed. Then morning again. But at least he would be there. Few people were married these days – monogamy seemed almost laughable when lives stretched out indefinitely. But Julia didn't like to be alone and her husband had no time to find anyone else to fall in love with. And they were fond of each other. They offered each other comfort.

She took a large gulp of her drink and enjoyed the kick, followed by the warmth that seemed to fill her body – every bone, every vein. She felt her spine relax, felt her shoulders fall back. She switched on the computer. Immediately she heard tense and agitated voices on the news feed, but she quickly navigated away. Too depressing – full of stories of whole populations starving to death, of water restrictions being increased. Nothing, of course, on the subject that was on everyone's lips: the Missing. Stolen away in the middle of the night, Julia had heard. There were rumours of screaming, of disease, of plague. But that was ridiculous – why people insisted on suggesting such things when everyone knew that illness didn't exist any more was a mystery to Julia. Were they so bored that they had to invent catastrophes just to keep themselves going?

She leant back on the sofa and closed her eyes briefly, allowed herself to remember sun-drenched holidays, decorating her house, spending time with friends. Her life had always been comfortable. Enjoyable. And yet somehow, at some point – she couldn't remember when – something had happened.

Perhaps it was simply external factors – tighter and tighter rationing of energy didn't help – but Julia knew that wasn't it. It was inside. A growing dissatisfaction. A growing gnawing in her stomach, questioning . . . but questioning what? The point of it all? Of the endless days, the endless trips to the hairdresser's, the endless reading of newspapers that rarely had anything new to say? Did she use to find them interesting? She didn't know.

And it wasn't just her. She saw it all around her. The enthusiasm people had for high-risk sports. The way some, like Julia herself, obsessed over every new wrinkle as though it were a sign of a more fundamental decay, while others had given up, letting everything go, becoming heavy and grey and wrinkly because they just didn't care any more. Perhaps they couldn't care any more; perhaps the demands of eternity were simply too much.

And then there were those who had given up completely. The very few who took extreme sports to the true extreme – jumping out of buildings, jumping off bridges. There had been more of those recently, Julia couldn't help noticing. Perhaps that was what the missing people really were – people giving up hope, giving up their own existence because they didn't know what to do with themselves any more.

Julia shook herself. This was why she didn't like to be alone, she reminded herself – because she thought too much. It was something that had crept up on her. A few years ago, thinking about things usually entailed trying to decide which outfit to wear to an event, or which neighbours to invite to a party. These days it meant allowing dark, disturbing thoughts to wash over her; it meant questions that made her uncomfortable, conclusions that left her despondent and numb. Ever since the Surplus girl . . . Anna . . . Ever since she'd discovered her hiding in her garden room, such fear in her eyes, the boy with all his bruises . . .

No. Stop, Julia told herself firmly. What she needed was something cheerful to focus on, to keep her vaguely entertained without worrying her unduly. After all, her husband, a senior Authorities manager, had assured her that everything was under control, that she shouldn't listen to gossip. And what were the newsfeeds if not serious gossip?

No, a chat show was a far better idea. The presenters felt like friends; they were more familiar than anyone else she knew. She enjoyed their company.

She found the channel and sat back, smiling.

'It just shows, doesn't it, what a difference a bit of extra care can make.'

'It certainly does. In fact, it's inspired me to get myself fit again.'

'Again? You were fit once?'

The audience laughed – or perhaps it was canned, Julia wasn't sure. The presenters were like an old married couple – a couple who still held affection for one another. Like Julia and Anthony, only . . . better. They flirted, they bickered, they laughed. They made it look so easy. Perhaps she should try harder, Julia thought to herself. Perhaps she should be more coquettish.

'But now to a more serious subject.'

'Serious? You can do serious?'

'Of course I can do serious.' The man affected a hangdog expression and there was more laughter.

The woman shook her head, rolling her eyes and smiling. 'Come on, Michael. Now you may have heard rumours about people going missing – or perhaps you've read about the Missing in a newspaper. There are lots of theories doing the rounds regarding who these people are and why they've been taken away, aren't there, Michael?'

Michael nodded gravely but there was still a twinkle in his eye. 'There certainly are, Sophie. You know, I heard one rumour that people are being taken to trial a new civilisation on the moon!'

Julia squirmed slightly in her chair; she'd heard that particular rumour and had even asked her husband about it.

'Now that I would like to see.' Sophie smiled. 'But more seriously, we all want to know what's going on. Just yesterday, lawyers acting for the families of an alleged Missing person said that the failure of the Authorities to inform them of what was happening and the denial of any access visits was a breach of human rights, which have fallen down the agenda in recent years.'

'That's right,' Michael said, shaking his head – Julia

wasn't sure whether it was in incredulity or sympathy. 'So we thought we'd get Hillary Wright, the Secretary General of the Authorities, on the show, to tell us what's really going on. Didn't we, Sophie?'

'That's right, Michael. So, shall we get her on?'

Julia's eyes widened. Hillary Wright? On a chat show? She rarely appeared on television and when she did it was a carefully orchestrated Authorities press conference. Perhaps it was the only way to quell the rumours once and for all. Yes, that must be it.

'I think we'd better, don't you?'

Sophie smiled and the camera panned over to a door, through which Hillary Wright walked. Julia recognised her – hers was a familiar face anyway, but Julia had met her in the flesh once at one of the Authorities' Christmas parties. She had seemed a little cold, Julia thought, her handshake a little limp, but then she supposed a little coldness was probably required for such a high-octane job. Hillary was looking tired, a little ragged around the edges. It just showed, Julia tutted to herself – being busy might seem appealing, but it was probably utterly exhausting. Really, she was very lucky not to have many demands on her time. She could have a nap whenever she wanted.

'So, Hillary!' Sophie looked at the Secretary General, her face full of concern. 'Can you tell us what's happening? Are the Missing just the result of rumours, or is there something going on?'

Hillary smiled ruefully. 'I'm afraid to say that

what's going on here is that there are people out there, evil people, who wish to take away our basic freedoms – people who for various reasons want to see us suffer. These people, the terrorists who call themselves the Underground, will stop at nothing to achieve their goals, including attempted and real sabotage of the source of our freedom, Longevity drugs. At a time when we should be focusing our minds on the strategic plan that the Authorities are working on to improve the health, well-being and standard of living for everyone who lives in this great country, these people are hell-bent on creating mayhem and unrest even, I'm afraid to say, to the extent of taking away people's lives.' She looked into the camera and Julia's eyes widened in fear. Longevity drugs? Longevity drugs had been sabotaged? Her hand moved involuntarily to her throat.

'That sounds very serious,' Michael said, looking rather taken aback. 'Are you saying that Longevity drugs have been tampered with?'

Hillary nodded gravely. 'I am sorry to say so, yes,' she said. Julia took a sharp intake of breath. 'We have been investigating this for the past two weeks, which is why we have been unable to say anything until now. Obviously this is devastating news. But the Underground – the terrorist organisation that hates science and life – managed to break into Pincent Pharma and sabotage a batch of the drug.'

Michael and Sophie looked at each other blankly. 'But . . . but . . .' Sophie stammered. 'But what does that mean? Are we safe? How do we know which drugs?'

Hillary cleared her throat. 'We are safe, Sophie – let me make that absolutely clear,' she said. 'It was a one-off event, and security is now even tighter at Pincent Pharma. But the criminals who perpetrated this crime are at large and the Authorities will not rest until they are caught.'

'The Missing?' Sophie gasped. 'Are they . . . Did they . . .' She appeared unable to end the sentence. Death was not a word used lightly; it didn't happen, except to Opt Outs, soldiers fighting wars and people in faraway countries with bad sanitation. It was dirty. It was alien.

Hillary shot her a tight smile. 'An investigation at Pincent Pharma has revealed that Underground supporters did in fact break through its highest security during a power cut and managed to tamper with one batch of Longevity. The drugs have, of course, been withdrawn, although tragically some innocent people have been made very ill. But our investigation has revealed that the Underground could do this because they have their tentacles in every street of this land. Far from being a small group, the Underground has grown in numbers and is a real and present danger to our civilisation and, indeed, our lives. They hate our freedoms, hate our right to live indefinitely. They want only to cause havoc, to destroy innocent lives. And so we are upping surveillance, increasing our number of raids – because it is only by stopping the

Underground that we can protect our citizens.'

'Answer the question,' Julia heckled anxiously. 'Have people died?'

Sophie seemed to have the same thought. Regaining her composure slightly, she sat up a little straighter. 'So, to get this straight, what exactly are the Missing? Are they people with Underground links who've been taken away or are they people who've been affected by the sabotaged drugs?'

Hillary smiled tightly. 'As we understand it there have been just over two hundred people affected by the Underground's despicable actions,' she said, 'and these people are receiving state-of-the-art medical attention from the doctors at Pincent Pharma. Their families are being kept informed at all times. But in the main, what we are seeing with the so-called Missing is anyone with suspected links to terrorist organisations being questioned and held until we have a clear picture of the Underground's network. Naturally we have had to suspend our usual rules and laws governing the arrest and questioning of suspects. The day these terrorists attacked Longevity, the day they tried to end our way of life, was the day they lost any right to the criminal justice system that was established to protect our citizens. These are dangerous people and what we need is to get them off the streets, to question them, to find out what they know and to prevent this kind of catastrophe from happening again.'

Sophie and Michael glanced at each other. They looked pale and Julia felt a sudden kinship with them.

They were sharing this moment – this moment that had changed everything. 'So the rumours of men turning up in the dead of night, taking the ill away?' Michael asked.

'Are actually our security forces turning up to take away suspects,' Hillary said tightly.

Michael looked at her searchingly. 'And there really is evidence that all these people are associated with the Underground?' he asked. 'Because we've had calls from hundreds of people who say that the Missing are friends of theirs, innocent people who –'

'These are not innocent people,' Hillary interrupted angrily. 'They are terrorists. And as such, we are not interested in calls from people who think that they are their friends. Terrorists do not have friends – they have targets and people they use. But we will not allow them to achieve their aims. We will do whatever is necessary to protect the sanctity of human life.'

'Of course,' Sophie nodded, her eyes wide. 'So are there more, do you think?'

'Terrorists? Absolutely,' Hillary said. 'We have been living with blinkers on, I'm afraid, thinking that everyone in this country appreciates what it has to offer. Evidently there are people who seek only to destroy what we have built up, and our job now is to stop them. No stone will be left unturned in the search for these terrorists. We will hunt them down and we will punish them. And we will punish anyone who helps them. We urge anyone who knows of any Underground sympathisers to let the Authorities know. The time for tolerance has gone.'

'Absolutely right,' Michael said. The camera zoomed in and a trickle of sweat could be seen wending its way down his forehead. 'So in terms of those affected by the . . . in terms of the . . . do we know, are we safe? Are our drugs safe?' He looked terrified. Julia swallowed uncomfortably waiting for the reply; she imagined that everyone else watching was doing likewise.

Hillary's face seemed to shift slightly, as though her mask was slipping. Dread crept through Julia's heart. If Longevity wasn't safe, then . . . everyone was vulnerable.

'We are confident that it was only one batch that was affected by the attack,' Hillary said eventually. 'However, we know that people will be worried. Which is why we have a special helpline number to call if you have any concerns. In the meantime it is of paramount importance that everyone continues to take their Longevity drugs as normal. The risk of ingesting sabotaged drugs is very small, but as we all know, not taking the drugs is . . . is not an option. For anyone.'

Michael wiped his forehead. 'So we're safe?'

'Everyone is safe,' Hillary said, nodding to reinforce the point.

Sophie exhaled loudly. Julia felt her own shoulders relax slightly. 'And other countries?' the presenter asked. 'There have been reports of Missing around the world.'

Hillary nodded, and her expression was serious. 'Unfortunately, the contaminated batch included some drugs that went overseas,' she said, lowering her head sadly. 'But I can assure you that the numbers affected are small, and we are working with other governments to crack down on worldwide terrorist rings.'

'Thanks, Hillary,' Sophie said warmly.

'And Longevity Plus?' Michael asked, smoothing his hair back as he spoke, his forehead now sweat-free. 'We've all been waiting on tenterhooks for the launch, so is there any news? I'm sure our viewers would love to know.'

'Oh, I'm sure they would, and I'm very happy to say that we are at the final testing stage. Obviously we would never launch a drug until we were absolutely convinced that it was one hundred per cent safe,' Hillary said, her expression more relaxed now.

'Absolutely,' Michael said, his white teeth showing as he spoke. 'Do we know when it's going to be hitting the shelves, so to speak?'

'Very soon,' Hillary said brightly. 'Pincent Pharma are working night and day on it. But their hard work is absolutely worth it. Longevity Plus will, I believe, revolutionise the way we feel.'

'It's really that good?' Sophie asked, her eyes lighting up.

'It will do for the skin, the soul, the spirit, what Longevity does for the rest of our bodies,' Hillary said. 'Cell renewal will become energy renewal, skin renewal.'

'Well, I can't wait then,' Michael said. 'And thank you, Hillary, for sparing the time to talk with us today.'

'It's always a pleasure, Michael, Sophie,' Hillary said, looking from one to the other.

'Now, in association with Magic Mix, it's time for our cooks, Eleanor and Gary, to rustle up a feast in ten minutes . . .'

Julia took a deep breath. She felt as though she'd been on a roller coaster, taken to the brink of panic before being brought safely back to ground again. One batch. What if they had done more? What if there were more attacks? Her life, her world, had suddenly revealed vulnerabilities that she had never seen before, never even considered.

But she was safe. The Authorities would catch whoever was responsible. They wouldn't let it happen again.

Downing the rest of her drink Julia closed her eyes briefly, then opened them again and started to watch the cookery slot.

Chapter Nine

Roberta Weitzman leant against the wall briefly to catch her breath. She'd been feeling out of sorts for days now and had finally made an appointment to see the doctor to get her Longevity levels checked. It was an irritation – she was busy, always busy, but her fatigue was getting in the way of work; only that persuaded her to make an appointment. That and the reddish spots that had appeared on her stomach. A reaction to something, she had no doubt. Nothing serious. Not . . . She shook herself. She wasn't ill. She hadn't been one of the unlucky ones. And she wasn't the sort to get hysterical either. She just felt a bit tired, that's all.

The doctor's surgery was on the fifth floor of an office block in Maida Vale. She'd lived in the area for over thirty years and, like most people, had visited the surgery only a few times – for Longevity level checks, for a contraceptive implant, and when she was younger, for a broken bone which had required a plaster cast. Even now the visit felt like a waste of time. Some people talked about eternal life in such strange terms, as though they had trouble filling the hours, the days that stretched ahead, but Roberta couldn't understand them at all. She had so many things to do – books to write, paintings to do, sonatas to learn on her new piano. Her mother had been an Opt Out – a concept that terrified Roberta. No one else's mother had died; no one else had been forced to watch their beloved parent disintegrate gradually, losing both mind and body until there was nothing left. When her mother had died, all her ideas had died with her – all that potential, all the thoughts that hadn't yet been written down, argued for, worked through. And however much she'd protested to the contrary, she'd feared her death – Roberta had seen it in her eyes. 'I'm a burden on you,' she'd say sadly, and Roberta wouldn't know what to say because it was true – she was a burden of her own making. No one wanted to look after a rotting old lady, not even her own daughter.

Roberta was relieved to find the lift working and pressed the button, heaving herself in when the doors opened and pressing '5'. She waited as it trundled slowly upwards before stopping with a jolt and wheezing as the doors opened again, as though it were all just too much effort. She knew how the lift felt and found herself writing a story in her head about a building where the lift, the stairs, the rooms themselves had feelings, that they grew tired of ferrying and containing the humans who used them, decided to rebel and do things their way. Smiling to herself, she gave her name to the receptionist and sat down to wait. In front of her was a television screen with serious-looking people discussing something that they obviously considered of the utmost importance. Idly Roberta glanced at it. Along the bottom the headlines scrolled past: 'Missing confirmed as part of terrorist attack to sabotage Longevity. Crackdown to arrest Underground agents . . .'

She frowned. Roberta rarely listened to the news, but even she found herself wanting to know more. She had heard about the Missing, had dismissed it as rumour-mongering. But had there really been a terrorist attack? The doctor poked his head out of his door and called her name and she got up reluctantly. The fatigue hit her by surprise, forcing her down again before she could gather herself and, shaking her head in embarrassment, walk into the doctor's office.

'Ms Weitzman. And how are you today?'

Roberta smiled flirtatiously; it was instinct to do so. 'Oh, I'm OK. Just need my levels checked, I think.'

The doctor nodded, turned to his screen.

'Let's just have a look at your identicard reader, shall we?' He looked at her file and keyed in her code. Then he frowned.

'You've been tired?'

Roberta nodded. 'A little. But then I have been burning the candle at both ends, so to speak.' Another flirtatious smile. He was actually quite attractive, this doctor, she found herself thinking. She might suggest a drink. Later. When they had both finshed work.

'Any other symptoms?' He smiled reassuringly. 'While you're here.'

Roberta uncrossed and crossed her legs, then stifled a yawn. Maybe she'd forget that drink after all; even conversation was flooring her. 'No,' she said, a note of resignation in her voice. 'Oh, apart from a slight rash. But I think that's more likely to be my soap powder.'

'I see.' The doctor was still looking at his screen; eventually, he turned and bestowed another smile on her. 'Well, I think you need a booster jab and then we'll up your levels, shall we?'

'Oh, marvellous,' Roberta smiled, relieved. A booster jab. She'd be herself in no time.

She rolled up her sleeve and held out her arm and as the doctor pulled out a syringe, she returned to her story. It would be the lift that started it, she decided – began the revolution. It would tire of going up and down all day, carrying people. First it would reject them, push them out. Then it would decide it wanted to travel sideways, diagonally – to go wherever it pleased. It would urge the stairs to follow suit. The stairs would be apprehensive, nervous of what might happen, but eventually would . . . She looked over at the doctor. Everything had suddenly become blurry. Her eyes wanted to close. She felt like the air was heavy around her, forcing her backwards.

'I think something might be wrong,' she said uncertainly. 'I feel more sleepy than before. Are you sure you gave me the right medication?'

'Don't worry,' the doctor said soothingly. 'Don't worry about a thing.'

He picked up the phone and dialled a number. Roberta could feel herself slipping in and out of consciousness and did everything she could to focus on staying awake. Something was wrong and she wanted to know what it was.

'It's Doctor Brandon from Surgery 561,' she heard him say, his voice low, irritable almost. He sounded like he was a long way away even though she knew he was only two metres from where she sat. 'I've got another one.'

Her eyes closed – she couldn't fight much longer. She was drifting away. It was too strong for her – sleep beckoned.

'Be quick,' he said as she lost consciousness. 'I've got patients waiting.'

Chapter Ten

Jude picked up the phone. 'Hotel Sweeney. How's the weather with you today?'

'Cloudy in the north, but getting warmer all the time,' came the reply. It was a woman and she sounded tense, but that was nothing new. Since Hillary Wright's appearance on television a few days before, the phone had been ringing non-stop and all the callers sounded tense. Pip had manned the phone for the first day and night and Jude had listened to him tirelessly trying to explain to people that Hillary had been wrong, that the Underground hadn't set out to murder huge numbers of people, that they still needed support and help. By morning he had looked exhausted, pale, wiped out. Then came the news that people were beginning to hand children over to the Authorities in fear for their lives. Two small children had been left at the door of the Underground; Pip had managed to find someone to take them in, but a fear hung in the air – a fear that they were losing, that something terrible was going to happen.

Jude had taken over the phone the next day – it

was the least he could do, particularly as Pip had left with the abandoned children to take them to their new home. But two days on, with barely a break, he was beginning to feel like he was fighting a losing battle.

'State your business,' Jude said, as always.

'I'm number 6492. I've just had a brick through my window,' the voice said breathlessly. 'A group of people ran past shouting, calling me a murderer. I'm afraid. I'm hiding a . . .' She lowered her voice even more. 'I have a child here. I don't know what to do.'

She sounded terrified. 'Are you known to be a sympathiser?' Jude asked.

There was a pause. 'I'm an Opt Out. Of course I'm known to be a sympathiser. People treat me with contempt or pity most of the time. But not this, not violence. What shall I do? Can you send protection?'

Jude looked at the database. South-east London. Numbers of potential guards had already dwindled to barely a hundred across the country, and there was no one near her. All the available guards in London were already deployed; the capital city had the highest density of Opt Outs and Underground supporters, all of whom were now clamouring for help. 'Are you on your own?'

'Yes,' the woman said bitterly. 'No one wants to be associated with an Opt Out these days.'

'OK. Can you lock your doors? Sit tight until they lose interest?'

'You think they're going to lose interest? Listen.'
The woman held the phone up; Jude could hear distant chanting: 'Surplus out! Surplus out! Kill the traitors!' Suddenly a separate voice could be heard, a man with a hoarse voice. 'Hand him over, lady. We know he's in there. Dirty Surplus, stealing our water, contaminating our drugs! Hand him over and you won't be hurt.'

Immediately the chant changed to, 'Hand him over! Hand him over!'

'You see?' the woman said in a strangled voice. 'Do you think they're going to go away?'

Jude closed his eyes. He was exhausted – the kind of exhaustion that leaves you shaky, that makes your head feel as though it will explode if you don't shut your eyes.

'No, they're not going anywhere,' he said. 'OK, sit tight. I'm sending someone over.'

'How quickly can they get here? And won't they get lynched by the mob?' the woman asked anxiously.

'Don't worry,' Jude said, swallowing uncomfortably. 'Just stay where you are. Keep your son safe.'

The phone went dead and Jude stood up. Immediately the ringing started again. 'Sheila,' he called out urgently. 'Sheila, I need you to take over the phone. I have to go out.'

Sheila appeared immediately and looked at him searchingly. 'The phone? Why? Where are you going?'

'To get someone. A child,' Jude said. 'The mother's under attack. There's no one else.'

Sheila's eyes widened in alarm. 'But you can't go. You'll be caught. Send someone else.'

'There is no one else,' Jude said grimly. 'I'll be fine. I know how to take care of myself.'

'But . . .' Sheila stared at him helplessly. 'But we need you here. I need you. I . . .' She bit her lip. 'Please don't go.'

'I have to go,' Jude said, grabbing his coat. Then he stopped. 'You need me?' he asked. 'Really?'

'Really,' Sheila whispered. She was looking right at him, her face defiant, scared, beautiful all at once. Without warning Jude grabbed her, pulled her towards him and kissed her, before letting her go and running towards the door.

'I need you too,' he whispered, too late for her to hear him. 'You have no idea how much.'

The freezing air outside stung his skin and he pulled his coat tightly around him as he made his way through the streets. He'd memorised the address, knew he could get there using one of Pip's tried and tested routes. London was really two places: the place where most people lived, and the place the Underground inhabited – disused Underground tunnels, little-known alleyways that Legals would never walk down, particularly after dark, the cracked, unkempt main roads that years ago had been clogged with cars and which now lay empty but for the odd vehicle driven by someone very rich or very well connected.

Jude knew that what he was doing was rash, ill-considered; he knew that Pip would never have let him go. But he also knew he had no choice. He'd heard the crowd baying for blood; he couldn't leave the woman and her child – he couldn't. So instead he ran, ignoring the pounding in his head, ignoring his muscle spasms as he forced himself onwards. He took out his handheld device and searched for the woman's address. Soon he had a live CCTV image on his screen which revealed that while the front of her house was surrounded, the back was clear. On he ran. She was only twenty minutes away, but twenty minutes was a long time when you were under siege. He ducked through an alleyway and under a disused flyover, then pulled back against a derelict building. A sign above it revealed its history: St Thomas' Hospital. Through a gap in the boarded-up doors behind him Jude could see a blue sign, only just legible, pointing to A&E, to a Maternity Ward, to ENT. He'd never seen an old hospital before – they had all been converted long ago into apartment blocks, like the schools and universities. But this area was down on its luck – the high-speed surface rail hadn't yet reached it and until it did, buildings like this would be left to rot.

Pulling his eyes away, Jude listened for footsteps then carefully edged away from the hospital and ran, ducking into doorways, behind buildings, on to the main road that led to the woman's house. Her road was on the left; a few metres before the turning he jumped over a fence into one of her neighbours' gardens, then into hers. Here he ran to the back and, as the crowd shouted, kicked an opening in the fence ready for their escape before turning and making his way stealthily towards the house. He took out his handheld device and called her number.

'Hello?' The woman's voice was shaking.

'It's the concierge from Hotel Sweeney,' he said in a low voice. I need you to come to your back door. Slowly. Carefully. Don't let anyone see you.'

'Yes. Yes,' she said. He could see her through the back window, her outline moving into the hall. She was large, moving slowly; Jude silently willed her to speed up.

'She's coming!' someone shouted at the front of the house.

'Kick down the door!' someone else shouted.

'Legal killer!'

'Terrorist!'

The woman froze; Jude looked around desperately. He had minutes to get her out. Seconds, even. He ran to the door just as the woman got there. In her arms was a young child, his eyes wide with fear.

She opened the door and stared at Jude. 'But you're just a child yourself! I thought there would be more of you,' she gasped. 'We'll never get out alive.'

'We're going this way. Through the fence,' Jude said, holding his arms out for the child. 'You've got to come now.'

The woman looked at him, then at her child, then she shook her head. 'I can't run,' she said. 'I'm not strong enough.'

'Yes you are,' Jude said through gritted teeth. 'Come on.'

'I'm an Opt Out,' the woman said, her eyes shining with tears. 'My body doesn't renew itself and my heart . . .' She shook her head again, then looked at Jude desperately. 'Take him,' she begged. 'Take him, please. Leave me here.'

'I can't leave you here. They'll kill you,' Jude said vehemently. 'Come. Now. We can get away.'

'No.' The woman shook her head. 'I'll slow you down. They'll catch us.'

A large crash made them jump and the woman grabbed Jude by the shoulders. 'They're breaking the door down,' she said. 'Go. Go now. Look after my boy. Make sure he knows I loved him. That I wanted him. His papers are in his pockets. Look after him, please?'

Jude shook his head but the woman was already closing the back door. Reluctantly he pulled the child to him and started to run. As he squeezed through the hole in the fence he heard the crowd rushing into the house; then he ran, ran as fast as he could away from the screams as the woman surrendered to her tormentors, holding the child tightly to his chest to silence his whimpers, to stop from crying out himself. All he could think about was Sheila when she was little, being taken away from the parents who loved her on a night like this. All the children who'd been wrenched from loving homes to be imprisoned, murdered, enslaved.

'It's OK,' he whispered. 'It's going to be OK.'

As he rushed back to the Underground, stumbling with tiredness, his arms barely capable of carrying the weight of the child, he realised he had to make his promise good – he had to make sure everything would be OK. His body was crying out for sleep, for food, for water. But as he dashed madly through the door of the Underground, completing the security checks, explaining the child's presence to the Underground guard at the door, he was met with Sheila's eyes, wide with fear as she put down the phone. 'I don't want to answer the phone any more,' she said, her bottom lip quivering. 'I don't want to, Jude. I don't like it here. I hate it.'

'I know,' Jude said, handing the child to the guard. 'I know. But we've got to be strong. We've got to keep fighting.'

'I don't think I can,' she said quietly, standing up as the phone started to ring again.

Her eyes were swimming with tears; as they started to cascade down her cheeks, she fell against him. Jude held her tightly, his forehead creased, his eyes dark with worry. 'Leave the phone for a while. I'll answer it,' he said softly. 'You go and get some rest. OK?'

Sheila nodded, her body juddering slightly. 'I don't need rest,' she said stoically. 'Let me do something else. I can man your computer, answer messages.'

'My computer? But I turned it off when I went out,' Jude said hesitantly. His own security protocol meant that computers were always shut down when unattended for more than ten minutes. He was religious about it; he of all people knew how vulnerable networks could be.

'So I can turn it on again,' Sheila said quietly. 'Can't I?'

Jude looked at her uncertainly.

'Don't you trust me?' Sheila asked, her lips forming a little pout. 'Why did you teach me to use it if you never let me on it? I can help, Jude. Let me help.'

Jude didn't say anything for a moment. Then, eventually, he nodded. He didn't have a choice – Sheila was right. She was offering to help and he needed all the help he could get. 'OK,' he said, his voice rather strangled. 'But don't – don't do anything stupid.'

Sheila took his hand and gave it a squeeze. 'I won't,' she promised. 'I . . .' She looked at him searchingly as though about to say something then apparently changed her mind. 'I won't,' she repeated instead, then ran lightly from the room.

'Jude,' Pip said, suddenly appearing at the door. He looked even more exhausted than Jude felt; his eyes had dark circles round them. 'Jude,' he said, his voice low. 'Where have you been?'

Jude glanced up. 'I just had to pick someone up,' he said, rubbing his bloodshot eyes. 'We've got another child. He's with the guard.'

Pip looked at him carefully. 'You went out? That was very risky, Jude.'

'Yes, well, I'm not just a techie,' Jude said, irritation

suddenly getting the better of him. 'I can actually help people as well.'

Pip didn't say anything for a moment, then he nodded. 'Of course you can,' he said quietly. He sighed heavily. 'Jude, I . . .' He trailed off for a few seconds, then took a deep breath. 'I want to tell you something. Something important. I . . .' He looked at Jude intently, then took a deep breath. 'I . . .'

'What?' Jude asked impatiently. 'Is it really important, or is it about books again? Because people are under attack and the phone is ringing because they need our help, and someone's got to answer it.'

Pip smiled gently. 'Of course they do. You're right, Jude, as always. You are . . .' He put his hand on Jude's shoulder. 'I'm very proud of you, that's all.'

Jude felt a jolt of electricity shoot through him at Pip's words – no one had ever said they were proud of him before. No one. But there was no time to bask in the praise, no time to thank Pip or to wonder why the words meant so much to him. Instead he met Pip's gaze for a second, nodded, then raced to the phone.

'Hotel Sweeney,' he said. 'How's the weather with you today?'

Chapter Eleven

Richard Pincent was scared. It was not an emotion he knew well, not one that sat comfortably with him. Over and over again he paced the floor of his sumptuous office; over and over again he stared out at the London skyline, the dark, cold sky punctuated by tower blocks, by monuments to man's success, man's power – his power. He had bestowed the vista of eternity on mankind and now its very existence was threatened.

Even as he watched out of his window, he knew that people were on the streets marching. They were calling for the Underground to be found and bombed; suspected sympathisers were being locked in their houses and torched. A few months ago he would have sat back and enjoyed the spectacle, but now it simply made him more fearful, because eventually the mob would turn on him. Eventually they would discover his lies, realise that he was the enemy and not the Underground, and when they discovered the truth they would come to his doorstep.

He lifted his head miserably and looked out of the

window, the darkness and howling wind an apt reflection of his own thoughts. Was this how the Pharaohs felt as the Egyptian empire crumbled into dust? Would Pincent Pharma be a relic like the pyramids, explored by ignorant tourists snapping photographs, understanding nothing? Would Richard die here, in this large white tomb, to be discovered centuries later? He shook his head. Who would find him? Who would be left to find him?

Sighing, he turned to his computer and pressed a button, bringing it out of hibernation. Work had to go on. Memos must be answered, the veneer of normality maintained.

As if on autopilot, he started to decline appointments, agree budgets, delete anything that didn't interest him. Perhaps if he continued as normal things would be normal, he found himself thinking. But he knew this was a fallacy. Others might believe his lies, but he could no longer deny the gravity of the situation, could no longer avoid the terrible truth. He was the captain of the *Titanic*; he alone knew about the iceberg, knew that the ship was sinking, that no one would survive.

He felt sick. Felt like crying out. But as he wondered to himself if ever a man had felt more wretched than he, his attention was drawn by an icon at the bottom right-hand corner of his screen telling him that he had a network message. Messages were rare – all were filtered by his secretary and her team, ensuring that only the essential got through. But this message was even more curious because it had bypassed the usual route – it had come direct to him instead of through the Pincent server. Only Derek Samuels had a direct line to Richard's mailbox; only his messages arrived in this way. And yet this message was not from Derek. He looked at the time badge – the message had arrived just seconds before. Apprehensively, Richard opened it. And then his heart lurched.

'If you want the circle of life, I can give it to you.'

Richard stared at the message, blinked several times to make sure he wasn't imagining it, then looked around the room fearfully. Was this a joke? Had someone been watching him? No, impossible. There were cameras in his room now – introduced after the Underground broke into the building when Peter had worked here – but only he had the code to watch the images captured. So how did this person know? Who was it?

He sat, unable to move for several minutes. Then tentatively he leant forward.

'Who is this?' he typed back, his heart thudding in his chest.

'That doesn't matter. If you want the circle of life you can have it. But there's something I want too.'

Richard's eyes widened, then he pulled his chair towards his desk. It was a trick. It had to be a trap. But what kind of trap? And what if it wasn't? What if this person really had what he so desperately needed? If they had a lifeboat, if they had the ability to mend the ship, then he had to accept their offer. Didn't he?

'I want it,' he typed slowly, tentatively. 'What do you want?'

'I'll come to that. You know you gave it away once. If you want it back, you're going to have to do as I say.'

Richard's mind was racing. He'd given it away? Was it a riddle?

'I gave it away? I don't understand.'

'No. I imagine you don't. You had a ring, didn't you? Peter's ring?'

Richard's stomach lurched. Peter's ring. His grandson – the grandson Richard thought was dead until he was discovered by the Catchers. The ring had been with him, had been taken into custody, had found its way to Richard because of its initials – AF. Albert Fern. It had been Albert's ring. Given to Margaret, then to Peter. And Richard had never even thought to look at it properly. It was an ugly thing – he remembered Albert wearing it. Was it really the circle of life? Why would Albert have wanted to protect it? Why was it so important?

He closed his eyes and tried to picture it, turning it over in his mind. On the inside, Albert's initials. On the top, an engraving – a poor one, as if Albert had done it himself. Of a flower. Some kind of flower.

Richard opened a drawer and pulled out Albert's notes and scribblings. Frantically, he turned over pages until he found it. A sketch only, but it was unmistakable – the flower. But what did it mean? He picked up his phone. 'Derek,' he said urgently.

'Derek, I need you in here now.'

A minute later, Derek was by his side, his eyes widening as he saw the messages. 'How?' he asked, his face paling as he realised it was his own security system that had been breached.

'That doesn't matter now,' Richard said quickly. 'What matters is the ring. What was it Albert said when you took him away? That the circle of life had to be protected? Could he have meant the ring? Do you think this is a hoax or could the ring really be important.'

Derek didn't say anything for a few seconds. Then he shook his head slightly.

'Derek?' Richard asked, frowning. 'Derek, what is it?'

Derek looked up, his eyes narrowed, deep in thought. 'He knew,' he said simply.

'Knew what?' Richard asked impatiently. 'What are you talking about?'

'Albert,' Derek said. 'He knew. Before I took him. The way he reacted. He was expecting it.'

'Expecting to be killed?'

'He said that you'd never find the formula. He said you could search everywhere but you'd never find it. The way he said it, I think he knew you would try to find it. I think he was prepared.'

Richard nodded, frowning as he frantically tried to cast his mind back, tried to remember. He remembered the ring, remembered seeing it in Maggie's jewellery box one day. He'd assumed it had been there for a long time, that Albert had given it to her long before. He hadn't asked, hadn't wanted to draw attention to it because of the inevitable questions – about Grandpa, about what had happened to him. It was the ring she'd given to Peter, the ring Richard had held in his hands.

'The ring was Maggie's though. How did he get it to her?' he asked, trying to make sense of what he'd been told. 'Maggie never saw him before he died.'

'Who knows?' Derek said. 'She went to school, didn't she? There were opportunities. He must have had it engraved with the formula, then given it to her.'

'Yes,' Richard breathed. 'Of course. The eternal circle of life. He put the formula on the ring.'

'And you had it all that time,' Derek said.

Richard looked at him, his teeth gritted. 'And I'll get it back. You'll get it back for me.'

Derek didn't reply, but Richard barely noticed. All he knew was that his prayers had been answered. The ring. He would have the ring and he would have his salvation. Everything would be restored.

He turned back to his computer. 'You have the ring?' he typed. 'Then you also know the whereabouts of my grandson?'

Catchers had been looking in vain for Peter and Anna for a year, ever since Peter had humiliated him in front of his employees, in front of the media. Richard's heart quickened at the thought of finally finding him, of wreaking his revenge.

'You need the circle of life, not Peter,' the message came back.

Richard's eyes narrowed. Then he shook himself. First the ring; everything else would follow. 'Very well,' he typed. 'The ring. Name your terms.'

He read the message that came back and smiled, then laughed. He felt so happy, so relieved, he could have danced. He was being asked for so little for so much. His heart lifting, he turned to Derek. 'I want every Catcher to be given Peter's picture and told to search only for him. Do you understand?'

'Perfectly, sir,' Derek said, his eyes glinting.

'Good,' Richard said, leaning back in his chair as relief was replaced by delighted malevolence. 'I think we need to up the stakes. I want the Underground destroyed beyond any chance of repair. And in the meantime, I've got a visit I want to make. Call the prison, will you? Let them know I'm on my way.'

There was a bang at the door and Peter, who'd been dragging potatoes into the store, looked up in surprise. Anna, who'd been changing Molly's nappy – a makeshift affair of tea towels, loo roll and cotton wool – turned round and caught his eye. He could see a flicker of something cross her face – anxiety, he presumed. He shot her a reassuring look, then went to the door, opening it cautiously.

But it was only the wind. Of course it was, Peter thought ruefully. They never had visitors. They were miles from anyone.

'There's no one there?' Anna asked. She sounded worried as always.

Peter rolled his eyes. Ever since he'd received a message from the Underground that morning he'd been restless, agitated. He'd assumed the message was from Jude; it had come from his address. But there had been no sign-off, no banter, just a request. It made him feel insignificant – increased his feeling of isolation, of being cut off from everything.

'Believe me,' he said, more sarcastically than was warranted, 'if we were in any kind of danger we'd know about it. Pip would tell us right away.'

Anna looked at him piercingly. 'You make it sound like that's a bad thing.'

Peter blanched slightly – he hadn't meant to. Not really. Then he shrugged. 'It's just that Pip said we were going to be up here for a few months,' he said. 'We've been here a year now.'

'I know. It's amazing, isn't it? I mean, it's lovely up here. The children can play outside and we're left alone . . .' She met his eyes; he could see that she wanted to say more but was loath to in case he reacted badly. They'd had this conversation so many times lately, Peter always venting his boredom, his frustration, and Anna getting more and more anxious. It was his fault, he knew it – he should be happy up here. But he couldn't be, not so far away from the action, not so far away from everything.

'Left alone. You said it,' he said gruffly, knowing as the words left his mouth that he should have kept them in. It wasn't Anna's fault he felt out of the loop, wasn't her fault that he'd been turning Jude's message over and over in his head all morning. What did it mean? Why hadn't he said more? Had Pip told Jude not to tell him? Were they gradually severing the link? Did they not think Peter was useful any more?

'We'll go back eventually, you know we will,' Anna said gently, standing up, moving towards him, putting her hand on his shoulder. He knew he was in the wrong and yet she was mollifying him, was being so understanding. He loved her more than he could ever put into words, and yet . . .

'I have to go. I got a message. I have to go to London.' He said it quietly, braced himself for Anna's response. The message had said to send his ring down to London via their watcher. Not to ask any questions, not to tell anyone else about the message. It hadn't said to bring it himself. It hadn't suggested that Peter should leave the safe house.

But that only made it more important to Peter that he go. It was time – time for him to be in the thick of things again. He was sick of being at arm's length from the Underground, sick of being out of the loop, treated like a child. He'd heard about the attacks; he'd heard about Underground sympathisers being stoned on the streets. But he hadn't heard it from the Underground itself, only from the newsfeed. He should be there to fight, not safe and sound in the middle of nowhere.

'What?' Anna's hand had left his shoulder; now,

instead of quietly supporting him, she was towering over him. 'Why?'

'Because they need me. Because I want to be part of the Underground again.' His voice was tentative, like a child asking for something it knows it isn't going to get.

'You *are* part of the Underground. It was the Underground's idea for us to be here, remember?' Anna moved away; he knew she wanted to end the conversation.

'We're not doing anything,' he heard himself say, unable to leave it, unable to accept his frustrations. 'Except grow food and eat it. People are disappearing. The Underground has sabotaged Longevity. Things are happening and we should be part of it.'

'No we shouldn't,' Anna said defiantly. 'It's too dangerous.'

'It's not dangerous. Come with me. We could all go. We could live in the Underground headquarters, like Jude and Sheila.'

'Peter, no,' Anna said. 'Can't you see what we've got up here? We're self-sufficient. We don't need anyone. We don't have to hide – not really. If people are getting ill, why would you want to risk one of us getting ill too? Risk the children getting ill? If the world is slowly drying up, why would you want to leave our well?'

She looked at him for a few seconds, her look the same one Peter remembered her giving him when they first met. Haughty, insecure, desperately trying to stay in control.

But they weren't in Grange Hall any more.

'It's not up to you,' he said quietly. 'There are things happening in London. Important things.'

'There are important things happening here too,' Anna said, her eyes flashing now. 'Like Molly learning to crawl. Like Ben learning his numbers. And we're up here for a reason, remember, because we're safe here, because your grandfather and the Authorities can't track us down to kill us all.' She was on a roll now, her expression darkening as she spoke. 'But I suppose those things aren't important to you,' she said, angry now. 'I suppose being in London where the "action" is is more important than ensuring the next generation survives.'

'I didn't mean that,' Peter started to say, but trailed off. He couldn't tell her the truth. If she knew the truth, she'd read the message – she'd know that Jude had not asked him to come. Would she realise that his not asking Peter to come was the very reason why he felt compelled to go?

'If you want to go to London, you go without us,' Anna said, her voice low. Then she picked up Molly, took Ben by the hand and walked out of the room, leaving Peter staring at the space they had filled just moments before.

Chapter Twelve

Margaret Pincent sat very still. She could feel the dryness of her clasped hands, could feel the overwhelming fatigue begin to take hold. It was all she deserved and she welcomed it – welcomed death with its release, its finality. Other convicted murderers were taken off Longevity quickly – a short, sharp shock – but not her. For her they'd strung it out bit by bit, little by little, supposedly because being Richard Pincent's daughter bought certain privileges. But Margaret suspected that this was yet another punishment. Her decline was so gradual that she was hardly aware of it and questioned every symptom, not sure whether it was in her head, whether she'd lost her mind, whether it was ever going to end.

But now, now she could feel it. She was an old woman. Twelve months ago she'd been the House Matron of Grange Hall – feared, respected, obeyed unquestioningly. Now she was slowly decaying. Rotting flesh, collapsing organs, inevitable death – these were the things that lay ahead. These were her future.

She'd do it again if she had the chance – she'd kill him again and again. Stephen, her former husband, had taken their child from her, made him a Surplus. He'd made her believe Peter was dead – her little boy, the older boy she'd tortured unknowingly, like all the others she'd punished for not being him, for not being her baby. For that, Stephen had deserved more than just death; she regretted that she hadn't made him suffer more.

But her own decay still revolted her. In a world where death had been averted, mortal, frail flesh was feared and despised. Margaret felt the same abhorrence for her condition that she saw on the faces of her guards, their eyes squinting, their lips curled as though they were facing a plate of rancid food. She was vile, disgusting. She smelt of decay – something that the grey walls surrounding her seemed only to enhance. Death was a revolting spectacle, a vile concept. Even her doctor found it hard to look at her, as though her symptoms might be catching, as though she might tarnish him with her weakness.

She deserved it all, she knew. It was this knowledge that stopped her from curling up in a ball and howling inconsolably. It was this knowledge that gave her the smallest sense of control, for she had brought it on herself. She was no victim.

In a notebook that Margaret kept by her bed, she kept a running list of all the changes she'd experienced since being imprisoned, since her Longevity dosage had gradually been reduced. First had been her skin – dry and rough to the touch, then sagging, as though it had given up any pretence at being fit for purpose. Cuts wouldn't heal, sores appeared out of nowhere, her eyelids hung heavy over her eyes.

Her hair was the next most obvious symptom. Undyed, her roots were growing through white as snow – such a contrast to the black she was accustomed to, the black strands which she pulled into a bun each morning. Black and white. Old and new. Now and then. The 'now', the whiteness, was growing longer each day. Margaret had read once that hair continued to grow after death; she wondered how long for, and why.

The cold was unbearable. Her muscles, previously a form of internal heating, their strength spreading warmth around her body, were wasting away and her limited fat stores were unable to protect her, helpless against the relentless cold of the prison. Margaret Pincent, who had always prided herself on her hardiness, who had continually rejected the requests of her staff at Grange Hall for one more radiator, for an increase in the thermostat, now found herself unable to prevent her limbs shaking, shivering against the icy air that surrounded her.

Some of the symptoms were more welcome than others. Myopia, Margaret's virtual blindness, was a comfort to her, for who would wish to see a prison clearly? Who would wish to look upon the face of her gaoler, the dull grey walls of her cell, the vile slush they told her was food? Grange Hall had been grey too but it had been *her* grey, *her* vile slush, *her* domain.

Others symptoms filled her with fear, with desperate loathing. Worst of all were the nightmares which accompanied her every time her eyes closed. Memories dredged up from years and years ago now haunted her: her mother, white and lifeless, staring at her from her bed; her grandfather, who'd promised to look after her and had killed himself instead; her baby son, snatched away from her before she could hear his first cry. Everyone had abandoned her. Everyone she had ever loved.

She picked up her notebook. It was easier during the day. During the day she could focus on facts – facts and truths and revelations. Only at night did her demons have free rein to plague her, to make her cry out in pain, to make her anguish so unbearable. Pushing the pages away from her so that she might see a little more clearly, she began to write. Today her breathing had started to deteriorate – her breaths had become rasping, her chest compressed. The day before her bowels had failed her, soiling her bed linen and humiliating her so much she would have taken her own life if she could have done.

Oh Peter! Oh my son!

She sighed and pushed the notebook from her; even writing his name was too much, made her wounds too fresh. She would never speak to him, would never see his face again.

The letter from the girl had arrived just days

before. Margaret had still not recovered from the feeling of hope that had seemed to physically lift her body up when the guard had given it to her. Her feet had left the floor, she'd been sure of it. But seconds later, the descent to earth had seemed to crush her organs, her bones, her mind, her soul. He was not coming. He would not acknowledge her.

Anna's letter had been kind, but that had made it worse. Margaret despised the girl – for taking her son away, for showing him the happiness that Margaret herself never could, for being with him when she could not. And she despised her because after all this time, after all that Margaret had done, Anna still could not turn from her completely. Unlike Peter, she could not ignore Margaret's letters, and this only revealed how weak she was. Margaret had always hated the weak; they reminded her of herself. Peter might hate her, but in a strange way she almost drew comfort from the fact. He knew his mind. He was strong. He was a survivor. Worth dying for, worth the suffering . . .

Leaning against the wall, she heard the familiar sound of heavy footsteps coming down the corridor, then her door opened fractionally.

'Grub's up,' a voice said. Margaret peered at the large figure in the doorway. She caught his eye and saw him shrink back.

'Put it down, please. Over there.'

Even in prison, Margaret did her best to keep command.

The prison guard shuffled over and put the food on her table, then leapt back behind the doorway again. It was a cheap, rickety table, so different from the large, authoritative desk she had sat behind at Grange Hall. The desk that Surpluses had clung to as she beat any hope, any self-worth out of them. The desk that had contained her gun for so many years – a gun she'd never expected to use. Until Stephen . . .

The man began to shut the heavy metal door that separated her cell from the corridor outside, then stopped momentarily.

'You always eat in here, alone,' he said, looking at her suspiciously.

Margaret let out a small sound of displeasure that this man felt able to address her directly, felt no fear at asking her such a personal question. At Grange Hall no one had asked her anything directly.

'I was just wondering why,' the man said after a few seconds of silence. 'I'd have thought you'd want to get out of here, is all. Canteen's just down there.'

'The canteen,' Margaret said icily, enunciating each word carefully, 'holds no attraction for me.'

She had been alone all her life and she saw no reason to change now.

The man nodded; he seemed in no hurry to leave.

'What is it?' Margaret asked sharply. 'If you have something to say, spit it out.'

Even now she had no patience for time wasters, for dawdlers, for anyone who did not live their life according to order and rules. It used to be her rules that governed everyone around her and she missed that.

'I just wondered . . .' The man frowned, looked uncomfortable.

'Wondered what?' Margaret stared at him insolently.

He took a deep breath. 'What it's like,' he said quietly. 'To die. To know you're going to die.'

The question shocked Margaret, silenced her for a minute or two. No one ever mentioned death, not even here in prison. The word was skated over, euphemisms used in its place as though the very word could contaminate.

'It makes me sick with fear,' she said eventually, shooting a glance at the guard. She was beyond lies, beyond any pretence. 'Is that what you want to hear? I hate myself, I hate what I have done. And yet I fear the end. I fear nothingness.'

The man nodded uncomfortably. 'They say,' he said, looking down, 'they say that people are dying. Getting ill.'

Margaret's eyes narrowed. 'And who are they? Fanatics? No one dies. You know that.'

She had heard the rumours, of course. As much as she tried to ignore the other prisoners she still brushed up against them on occasion, in the bathroom, on the corridor. But she believed none of it.

'Authorities say Longevity was contaminated by the Underground. Say they made people ill. But no one's come back yet. Not one of the ill. My next-door neighbour – she's never come back.'

Margaret looked at him carefully. The Underground. Terrorists. Evil men. But evil men who had kept her son alive and were now poisoning Legals. Right and wrong had ceased to have meaning, she realised. Everything had shifted. She took a deep breath. 'Your name,' she said. 'I don't know your name.'

'John,' the man said.

'Well, John,' Margaret said, 'my grandfather used to tell me that the only people who fear death are the ones who haven't lived.' She surprised herself with the statement; she'd forgotten it until now.

'And you have? Lived, I mean.' he asked.

Margaret laughed darkly. 'No,' she said. 'I haven't lived. And that is my torment. That is my pain.'

She sighed and turned to her food as the door shut with a loud clunk. It was the usual vile slop, enough to keep her going but no more, and she ate it unenthusiastically. She put the bowl on the floor then leant back on her bed, allowing her eyes to close momentarily.

The rap on the door surprised her – an hour couldn't have passed, could it? She looked at her food suspiciously, looked around the room as though she might find a clue somewhere. Perhaps she had fallen asleep. Perhaps . . .

'Yes?' she asked.

The door opened slowly. It was John again. 'You're here already?' she asked.

He looked down at the bowl, then back at her. 'You've got a visitor.'

Margaret looked up in shock. 'A visitor?' She had not had one visitor in all the time she'd been in prison.

'That's right.'

'Yes, yes, I . . . Just a moment. Just one moment, please.'

It's him. It's Peter. He's come.

No. Pull yourself together, woman. It's not him. It will never be him.

Desperately Margaret ran her hands over her white hair, looked down at her frail body, smoothing down her overall. Then she held out her shaking hands to be chained together and, trembling with anticipation, wobbling on frail legs, followed the guard down the corridor.

Anna watched in silence as Peter tried to fold a jumper. He made three attempts but each time the sleeves fell away as soon as he picked it up. She didn't step in to help and eventually he gave up, stuffing it untidily into his suitcase. He looked up and met her eyes.

'A few days,' he said again, as though it made a difference. 'One week max. You'll hardly notice I'm gone.'

Anna stayed mute; she knew her eyes spoke for her, knew that Peter could read her thoughts, that speaking them out loud wouldn't help.

'You were right about staying here,' he continued,

adding trousers, socks and T-shirts to the heap inside his suitcase. 'It's safer, I know that. So me going on my own makes sense. This way I can just find out what's going on and be back in no time.'

He looked down again as he spoke and Anna knew why. Guilt was seeping out of his pores. She sat down on the bed. She could stop him if she really wanted to – she knew that. But for how long? How long could she live around those pained eyes, the restlessness, the voice full of reproach? Yet she was angry with him for needing to go, for having any needs that didn't centre on her, on Ben, on Molly. They should be enough. This should be enough.

She sighed and self-consciously pulled a jumper from the suitcase, folding it neatly in what was almost a reflex action. Sleeves across the shoulder then fold at the chest. She had done it a thousand times at Grange Hall; taking in laundry had been one of the ways it had demonstrated its 'usefulness' to the local community. Then she picked up another. Peter looked at her gratefully.

'You're not angry?'

He seemed relieved, like he really thought everything was OK now. Anna's eyes narrowed; she threw the two jumpers back into the suitcase, ignoring the mess lying beneath them.

'Of course I'm angry.' His words had revealed his complete lack of understanding of the situation. Now she wasn't even going to pretend to be OK with what he was doing.

Peter looked stunned. 'I won't go for long,' he said, as though that made a difference.

'You won't go for long?' Anna looked at him in disbelief. 'An hour is long. A day is long. Peter, you're leaving us alone up here. Richard Pincent wants you dead, wants us all dead, and you're going to London? All because you want to be close to the action? What action, Peter? What could matter so much?'

Peter sighed, cleared his throat, took a breath. 'You know what matters so much.' He was looking at her, but she refused to meet his eyes.

'No,' she lied. 'I don't.'

'Yes you do,' Peter said tightly. 'We might be safe up here for now, but we won't be for ever. I know you want to stay here and pretend that the world doesn't exist, but it does. What about the Surpluses, about the children hidden in attics? And now there are dead bodies. Can't you see? We need to fight, Anna. I need to fight.'

Anna could feel her hands clenching into fists. He was right and she hated him for it. 'Why can't other people fight?' she said in a strangled voice. 'We've been fighting all our lives.'

'Other people *are* fighting. Every day. But I can't sit back and let them do it for me. You know I can't.'

'I know you *won't*.' Anna saw Peter's face tighten, could feel him drifting away – already she seemed to be losing her grip on him. 'Anyway, you can't go now. We've hardly got any food,' she said, resorting to practical obstacles, knowing already it was futile.

'I'll dig up some vegetables before I go.'

'And I won't be able to do all the planting while you're away. Not if I'm looking after the children all the time.' She sounded petulant and it irritated her, but she could see that it irritated Peter more. Impatience filled his eyes.

'Whatever,' he said, banging the lid of his case shut. 'I'm sure we'll manage.'

'There's still a "we"?' Anna asked, sticking out her chin.

Peter's eyes met hers and immediately she regretted the words.

'I didn't mean . . .' she said, but it was too late. He was heaving his case off the bed, dragging it out of the room, down the stairs.

'I'll get the vegetables now,' she heard him say.

'Don't bother,' she called back. It was his fault, after all, that she'd questioned their future. He'd driven her to it. 'Go to London. See if I care. See if any of us do.'

Margaret paused outside the door to catch her breath, collect her thoughts. It was open – the visitor was already in the room waiting for her. The visitor . . . But who?

'You going in?' The guard looked at her impatiently. She nodded.

Slowly, she walked into the room. There was a man sitting at a small table on the other side of the toughened glass that separated them. A man who was utterly familiar and yet a total stranger.

'I didn't expect you,' she said, her eyes narrowing. 'Why come now? Why come at all?'

The man stood up and smiled. 'Margaret,' he said. 'It's good to see you.'

She pursed her lips. 'I doubt it,' she said. 'I can't imagine you relish the sight of me. The decay. I'm part of you and yet here I am, fallible. A failure. That must be hard to accept.'

Her eyes were stony; she felt nothing but contempt for the man who was her father.

He nodded slowly, appearing to digest her words. 'You're right,' he said eventually. 'It is hard. And yet I have made my peace with the disappointment you have given me over the years.'

It still hurt, even though Margaret would die before letting him know. She steeled herself. 'What are you doing here?' she demanded.

Richard Pincent smiled. 'You received a letter,' he said. 'I'd like it, please.'

Margaret stared at him for a few seconds. 'You mean it wasn't read before I got it?' she asked flatly. 'Surely not.'

'It was checked for seditious content,' Richard said, a smile on his face but not in his eyes. He looked strained, Margaret realised. He never looked strained. 'But then it was given to you. Only then did anyone think to tell me about it.'

'And you want me to give it to you?'

'Yes,' Richard said.

Margaret nodded. 'What you mean is that my room is being searched, am I right?'

Richard shrugged. 'You are a prisoner, Margaret. Possessions are a luxury that you cannot expect to benefit from.'

A guard appeared at the door and nodded his head. Richard smiled and scraped back his chair, walking to the door and holding out his hand. Margaret watched tight-lipped as the guard whispered something in her father's ear and gave him Anna's letter. He quickly scanned it then walked back to her.

'Apparently the envelope was postmarked Scotland,' he said, leaning towards her so that she could see the fine red veins that covered his nose, the slightly enlarged pores around his eyes. Even as a child she hadn't trusted his face, but she had also been scared of him. She'd thought she had nothing left to fear, but she'd been wrong.

'He's protected by people cleverer than you,' she said, her voice low but the shake in it audible to them both. 'You will never find my son.'

Richard sat down again. 'Oh, but I will,' he said, leaning back, a relaxed expression on his face. 'Right now, though, I'm more interested in how you managed to write to him. To the girl. How does a prisoner of the Authorities track down two dissidents that have managed to evade the Catchers? You've had no visitors. So is it another prisoner? A guard?'

Margaret said nothing.

'Tell me,' Richard said, his eyes narrowing. 'Who

took your letters for you? Who sent them?'

Margaret looked him right in the eye and suddenly she realised that she wasn't afraid of him any more. 'There are people all around the world who hate you, just as I have always hated you,' she said quietly. 'There will always be people who will fight you, who will attack you, who will eventually destroy you. And I hope that Peter is one of them. I hope he wins. So I'll tell you nothing. Not one thing.'

Richard didn't say anything for a few moments, then he shrugged and stood up. 'Suit yourself,' he said. 'You were always a disappointment to me, Margaret, and it's no surprise that you should disappoint me today as well. We'll track down your accomplice – it won't be hard. In the meantime, I'll suggest to the guards that they withdraw your drugs completely. No use extending your life any more, is there? You can die knowing that I remain unbeaten. That you failed, just as you have always failed. I'll send Peter your best, shall I? Tell him that your weakness failed him yet again.'

'Tell him . . .' Margaret started to say, her eyes filling with tears in spite of her best efforts to stop them. 'Tell him . . .' But it was already too late – her father had stood up and was striding back towards the door.

Chapter Thirteen

'Unfortunately the Underground do not appreciate the sanctity of human life, nor do they respect it. What we are dealing with here is unadulterated evil. And we will crush it, be assured of that. The Authorities and Pincent Pharma will not stop until these terrorists are stopped and brought to justice . . .'

The brick came through the window at 9 a.m., three days after the Authorities had first pointed the finger of blame at the Underground. Jude heard it immediately; he'd been listening to the radio, manning the phone while Sheila caught up on some sleep. The crash sent him running to the room he called his office, fearing the worst. The noise had come from the room that housed his computer, the only possession he truly valued, but it wasn't the computer he was worried about this time – it was the children, six of them now, huddled on the floor. The boy he'd rescued, a girl brought here by one of the Underground guards, and four more who had been left by their desperate parents and guardians.

He arrived to find glass on the floor, the window shattered, the brick in the middle of the room wrapped in paper. Cautiously he unwrapped it and spread the paper out, looking up at the window every few seconds. This time it was just a brick; next time it would be worse. If one person knew they were here, soon more would. Even if it was just a lucky guess, even if it was just a random act of violence, Jude couldn't risk it – they had to move. They had to get out of here.

'What was that sound? What's that on the ground?' He turned to see Sheila who'd appeared next to him, her gaunt frame barely seeming strong enough to support her head. She was staring at the brick worriedly.

'This,' he whispered, 'is a warning that we're under siege.'

'We?' Sheila looked at him warily.

'The Underground,' Jude said quietly. She sat down next to him and crossed her legs.

'Did we really kill people? Did we really sabotage the Longevity drugs?' she asked softly. She sounded fragile. Jude wrapped his arm around her, then realised that actually he was feeling fragile too, that he needed comfort just as much as she did.

'No.' He shook his head. 'No, we didn't.'

'And where's Pip?'

Jude looked around helplessly. He hadn't seen Pip for days; he had convinced himself that he was out rescuing Surpluses, developing a plan, doing something important. But if any of those things were true, he would have been in touch. Jude had heard nothing. No one had.

'What was that noise?'

The door guard, a man called Sam, appeared. 'The noise?' he asked again.

'A brick,' Jude said grimly, holding it up.

'A brick? Through a window?' Sam's face changed suddenly. 'We have to move. People know where we are. We can't hang around here.'

'I know,' Jude said. 'But Pip's not here.'

'Pip'll find us. Regulations are, any form of attack and we move immediately. We need to be out of here within the hour.'

'But where would we even go?' Sheila demanded. 'Where would we move *to*?'

'There are places,' Sam said.

Jude nodded. 'They're in here,' he said seriously, walking into Pip's office and pulling open a drawer. 'Here. Locations,' he said, showing Sheila. 'These are all possible alternative headquarters. Pip showed me two weeks ago. We pick two, tell everyone we're going to one and then change it on the day, just in case anyone . . . Well, you know, just in case.'

He looked back at the smashed window and shivered at the cold wind whistling through it.

'Let's get packing then,' Sam said matter-of-factly. 'Can't wait here, not if people on the Outside know where we are. Turn off the computers and shut everything down.'

'I'll shut them down,' Sheila said quickly.

Jude nodded, but he wasn't really listening. He was looking at something on the newsfeed. A rolling headline. 'Head of the Underground hands himself in for terrorist atrocity.'

'Turn that up,' he ordered Sheila, who was about to turn it off. 'Now.'

Silently Sheila turned the volume control. And then she gasped.

'Yes, Sandra, that's right,' a woman was saying into the camera. And next to her was a man – a man with long grey hair and a long grey beard.

'No!' Jude shouted to no one in particular, but it was no use. It was Pip, right there on the screen. In handcuffs.

'I can confirm that the man who calls himself Pip, the elusive leader of the Underground movement, is here with me now,' the woman continued. 'He approached the Newsfeed Service to announce that he is handing himself in, that he takes full responsibility for the sabotage to Longevity drugs. He told me earlier that he broke into Pincent Pharma on his own initiative, and that the Underground has ostracised him for the deed.'

'Tell me, Vanessa, does that mean that Pip is no longer the leader of the Underground?'

'It certainly does, Sandra. Now, the Authorities have requested that Pip is not allowed to answer questions directly, but earlier he told me that he is no longer part of the organisation, that many within the organisation were unhappy with what he was doing. Shall we run the clip?'

The image faded away and was replaced by one of Pip staring into the camera. Jude's mouth fell open and his skin felt prickly all of a sudden.

'And why have you decided to hand yourself in?'

'I'm tired of running, tired of fighting,' Pip said gently. 'I realised that I'd taken a wrong path and caused a great deal of suffering and that I'm ready to take responsibility for my actions and make amends. I acted alone in contaminating the Longevity supply; I betrayed and let down my own Underground supporters, who never condoned such an attack. The Underground deserved better leaders, leaders who stayed true to the cause. It now has such leaders. Man was not supposed to live forever, but I had no right to curtail the lives of Legal people, I realise that now.'

The image faded and was replaced with the news reporter, Pip at her side.

'And what's happening now? What's going to happen to Pip?' a voice asked.

'What indeed, Sandra,' the reporter said. 'Well, the police and Hillary Wright are both on their way here, along with Richard Pincent. What Pip's fate will be, only they will know. But one thing we can be certain of is that justice will be done. Pip is a terrorist, and he must pay the price for that.'

'Thank you. That was Vanessa Hedgecoe reporting from the Newsfeed central office in London, where just hours ago the leader of the Underground, a man who refers to himself as Pip, handed himself in to officials and asked to make a statement . . .'

Jude turned the volume off then turned round to Sam and Sheila, who were both looking at him in shock. 'Let's pack,' he said, his throat constricting as he spoke. 'Let's get out of here.'

It hurt to walk. Hurt so badly Margaret winced with the pain. But she had to keep going, had to keep shuffling down the corridor towards the canteen. She had been there perhaps once in her time in prison and she despised the place, felt only contempt for those who ate there. Some desperate, some aggressive, some defeated – all were reminders of what she'd become, who she was now.

But contempt was no longer an excuse; revulsion did not matter and nor did her pride. She had to find the woman who had taken the letters. It had been chance that brought them together. Her toilet – a 'luxury' offered to those whose sentences were terminal, whose Longevity drugs were being withheld or reduced – had become blocked and Margaret, suffering from an upset stomach, underwent the humiliation of having to use the communal facility along the corridor while it was cleared. It had been in that horrible place, after throwing up bile, that she had been approached by Gail. And the approach had not been friendly – Gail had accosted her, pinned her against the wall, told her that she was evil incarnate for manning a Surplus Hall, for taking in stolen children and subjecting them to years of abuse. Margaret hadn't had the energy to fight back and that had given Gail confidence. The words poured out. She was a proud Underground supporter. She was a fighter, and there were more like her. Margaret's father would be revealed eventually as the terrible blight on humanity that he truly was. 'Your son,' she had said, eyes flashing, 'your son will bring Richard Pincent to his knees.'

And so when Margaret had written her first letter to Peter, it had been Gail that she had sought out, Gail that she had persuaded to give the letter to someone who could forward it. It had taken some time, some tears, some threats and some promises of money, but eventually Gail had agreed.

Now Margaret needed something else from her. She needed Gail to warn that man. Pip. The man who had looked after her son. She needed to warn him that her father was on his way to Scotland. She had to make sure that Pip knew, that he could protect him, that he could do what Margaret herself couldn't – what she had never been able to do – look after Peter.

Pausing briefly to regain what remained of her breath, Margaret took the last few steps into the canteen. It was a sea of people, of colour, of noise; she felt dizzy and put her hand to the wall to steady herself. People were looking at her but she didn't care. Slowly, deliberately, she began to move forward again, scanning the room. Was she here? Please let her be here. Then suddenly she saw her with a cluster of women, queuing. She rushed forward, nearly falling.

'Gail.' Her voice was hoarse, a whisper. 'Gail, I . . .' But Gail wasn't listening, didn't even notice her. She was staring at the screen on the wall. 'Shhhh,' someone shouted. 'Shut up!' someone else called out. People stopped talking. Silence descended like a wave.

And then she heard it. The newsfeed. Pip, the hope of the Underground, Peter's protector, had given himself up to the Authorities. As she listened, Margaret went white and felt her heart crashing in her chest. Because he had been her hope too, and now she had none. Now all that lay before her was the emptiness of oblivion.

Julia held up her identicard and waited for the green light. It took a few seconds – longer than usual – but eventually the small printout appeared, the barriers opened, and she was ready to shop. She enjoyed her trips to the Maxi-Market, enjoyed the rare feeling of plenty. For although her purchases were restricted by her identicard reading, she could still look, touch and smell the wonderful display of foods on offer. Even if they weren't real. Even if her journey here had been stressful, difficult and unnecessarily so in her opinion.

The checkpoints were everywhere now and police patrolled the street. A simple journey involved a million questions, body searches, horrible intrusion into one's personal life. Where are you going? Why are you going there? When will you be back? But she didn't mind. The world was different now and they needed such checks for their own protection. Not just from the Underground terrorists but from the crowds of deranged, angry people. Fear made people forget themselves, Julia found herself thinking. Fear was a terribly destructive force.

She looked up at the building and felt her spirits lift a little. She remembered being young and going to the supermarket. People had been free to choose to shop where they liked in those days and no one thought anything of buying fruits from halfway across the world – and while the Maxi-Market wasn't the same, not really, it still gave her the thrill she got back then – of potential, of wonder, of desires being met.

Unfortunately her printout didn't allow for many of her desires, particularly the overwhelming desire she felt for chocolate. But it did give the green light for pasta and even pesto which, if it wasn't good for her hips, was certainly good for her general mood. Humming to herself, she walked towards the vegetable section – it was all root vegetables at this time of year, large and heavy and begging to be stewed with beef or sausages. But beef was off the menu. Beef hadn't been on the menu for a long time – not for Julia, not for anyone. She felt sorry for the cows really, but they required too much space to graze, caused too much havoc to the environment; they were not efficient, and efficiency was what it was all about, wasn't it? Still, she would buy a small portion of lamb instead, which was still available, if expensive. She pressed her identicard to the reader next to the imitation vegetables and waited.

Sweet potato, five hundred grammes, added to trolley, the voice said. *Marrow, three hundred grammes, added to trolley. Two vegetable credits left. Thank you.*

She walked on to the bread section, her favourite. The food on display might not be real but the smells were, and she inhaled deeply as the scent of freshly baked loaves wafted towards her.

Granary loaf, five hundred grammes, added to trolley. Try the latest butter substitute on aisle fifteen. Thank you.

'You're only buying one?'

The woman's voice startled Julia and she turned round to see a neighbour she'd occasionally come across at drinks parties. Belinda. No, Brenda – that was it. Julia frowned. 'I only need one,' she said, thinking to herself what an odd question it was to ask someone. 'Why?'

Brenda looked at her contemptuously. 'You're not hiding any more Surpluses in your house? Any terrorists trying to kill us all?'

Julia's heart seemed to miss a beat and she fought to control herself. 'I really don't know what you mean,' she said, moving away. 'Now if you don't mind . . .'

Brenda moved closer. 'I do mind. It's people like you who have created this mess. People are dying and all because of liberals like you. Everyone knows it was you who helped those Surpluses, Legals now. And what did they do to thank us? They poisoned our Longevity. Surpluses aren't people, Julia. They're not human. They're evil. They should be put down at birth like in other countries.'

Julia could feel her skin getting hot and prickly. It seemed so long ago, that fateful day when Surplus Anna had turned up in her garden room with the boy, hiding from the Catchers. She hadn't intended to help them escape but they'd been so fragile, so helpless, and they were only children. Of course she understood now that it was she who'd been vulnerable, she who'd been weak, exploited by their manipulative minds. Her therapist had explained it all to her. Her husband had too. He'd blamed himself for being absent so much of the time, had promised that they would spend more time together.

But no one knew. They'd been promised secrecy. Hadn't they?

She swallowed uncomfortably. 'I haven't created anything, Brenda. You must have seen the news. It was Pip, the Underground's leader, who infiltrated Pincent Pharma, not the Surpluses. Now, please excuse me. I have to get on.'

'It's liberals like you who have allowed this murder, you know. Surpluses shouldn't be kept alive. Those halls are breeding grounds for terrorists. They should all be shut down in my opinion. Full of evil.'

An image of Anna flashed into Julia's mind – sweet little Anna listening to Julia's stories with an expression of wonderment on her face, the same face months later telling Julia about the cruelty at Grange Hall, fear etched into frown lines on her forehead, the determination that they wouldn't go back, couldn't.

But that was before the Underground had wreaked such devastation. Could such a person as Anna really be a terrorist?

'They are children,' Julia said tightly. 'The Underground terrorists are to blame, not Surpluses. But really, I do have to get on.'

'Suit yourself.' Brenda moved away, letting Julia pass. But moments later she was beside her again. 'I'd stock up if I were you though,' she said icily.

Julia didn't say anything; she looked ahead stonily.

'Word is that it wasn't Longevity they sabotaged,' Brenda continued regardless. 'It was the air we breathe. They're poisoning us with disease. If it was just one batch, why are people still Disappearing? They're not all terrorists. My aunt's gone. She hated the Underground. Hated them.'

'Maybe that was a front,' Julia said hesitantly, her stomach clenching with anger. 'Maybe she only pretended to hate them.'

Brenda's eyes widened with outrage. 'How dare you!' she said. 'My aunt wasn't a terrorist. She wasn't! Not like you. We all know about you, Julia.' She looked so angry, so desperate. Julia quickly turned and started to walk. She wouldn't listen to another word. The air wasn't poisoned. It couldn't be, could it? No. The Authorities would have told everyone to stay inside if it was. No, Brenda's aunt was obviously involved in the Underground after all.

Although, Julia thought with a thud, she herself had been involved in the Underground. She'd hidden

Surplus Anna. Would the Authorities be coming for her too?

Rushing now, Julia completed her shopping and left the Maxi-Market still feeling shaky. She was convinced everyone was looking at her. Who else knew about the Surpluses? Who had Brenda told? Did she actually even know anything or had she just been guessing? But as the shop steward filled her car with the produce she'd bought, Julia began to relax. Brenda was just agitated. She would apologise soon enough. Pip had been captured, no one else would disappear, and soon everything would return to normal. Julia took a deep breath in, then exhaled, feeling her shoulders relax slightly, her forehead smooth.

Then, thanking the steward, she started her car and made her way home.

Chapter Fourteen

Derek Samuels gripped the briefcase that rested on his knee – the briefcase he took everywhere with him. It contained the tools of his trade – the implements he used to encourage people to talk to him, to tell him their secrets before he ended their lives. He could tell as soon as he met someone what they would respond to, how to take them to the edge of desperation before offering a glimpse of hope, of salvation, if they were to do his will, if they were to tell him what he wanted to know.

'You must give him to me,' he said quietly, looking straight ahead as the Pincent Pharma car sped towards the Newsfeed offices. 'I can get what you need from him.'

The news had been a shock – Pip handing himself in, confessing to a crime that Richard and Derek both knew he had not committed. But they knew why he had done it, and now Derek had to amend his plans accordingly.

Richard nodded, then turned back to Hillary. 'He's right,' he said. 'Derek can break this man. Let him take him. Let him see what he can learn.'

Hillary shook her head. 'He surrendered to the Authorities,' she said firmly. 'There is due process to be followed, Richard. Everyone will want to know what is happening to him. He is the most wanted man in the whole world, the most dangerous terrorist. We can't just let Derek take him to a darkened room somewhere. We must be seen to punish him. To hang him if necessary.'

'Hang him and he will become a martyr,' Derek seethed, not allowing his voice to rise. 'That is what he wants. He has surrendered to save the Underground, to stem the attacks, calm the anarchy that his actions created. Hang him and people will feel safe again, they will become complacent. Hang him and another will take his place. Give him to me and I will root out every supporter, every sympathiser. Give him to me and the Underground will no longer exist.'

'Hillary, you know it makes sense,' Richard said evenly. 'I understand that this is an Authorities matter, but this man Pip will have information that Pincent Pharma will find very useful. How they breached our security, what else they had planned –'

'What matters is that he won't breach your security again,' Hillary said tersely. 'The priority is to restore public confidence.'

'But not to restore it too much,' Derek interjected silkily.

Hillary pursed her lips. 'A state of national emergency was declared last week,' she said tightly. 'Half the world is threatening to declare war on us unless we put to death the man who murdered their people.'

'Then he dies,' Richard said with a shrug. 'But later. He should suffer first. Derek can ensure that. Derek knows all about making people suffer and about getting information from them. Let him have Pip first. We need him.'

'You need to concentrate on containing the contamination,' Hillary said, her voice low and angry. 'You said that it was one batch. And yet there are more and more bodies. I have just been on the phone to my counterparts in Sweden, Korea and the US, where the death tolls are rising. You assured me everything was under control. And it isn't, Richard. It isn't at all.'

Derek looked at Richard meaningfully, then he leant forward and lowered his voice so that Hillary had to strain to hear it. 'If I may,' he said. 'The only way to ensure that the death toll does not rise is to ensure that all Pip's allies are caught before they can attempt more contamination.'

Richard smiled gratefully at him. 'Hillary,' he said, 'Derek's right. The contaminated batch was bigger than we'd hoped, but everything is under control.'

'Really?' Hillary asked, leaning towards him as she lowered her voice. 'There are rumours of large pits being dug within the walls of Pincent Pharma, Richard. Smoke has been spiralling above your land for weeks. What have you been burning? And where are those affected being treated? You won't let me see them. You won't let anyone see them.'

'Of course I won't,' Richard replied, his eyes narrowing. 'No one can see the victims of contamination because they are in sterile units. The contamination has opened their systems to bacteria, to infection which must be contained. Everything we use in those units has been burnt or buried to protect the healthy. And in the meantime, with your help, we have been rounding up all the sick, all the liberals, all the Opt Outs, all those hidden children that people keep like little pets. You know that calls to the Surplus hotline have gone through the roof? People are falling over themselves to point the finger, to voice their suspicions, to snitch on their neighbours. We are winning. But we can't rest on our laurels. We need Pip to tell us everything he knows. Only then will the world be safe again.'

'So there will be no more Missing?' Hillary asked tersely.

Richard shot a conspiratorial look at Derek, who moved his head just enough to encourage his master. There had been another message that morning. The ring was on its way. Things were in motion.

Richard nodded. 'Yes, Hillary. They will stop.'

Hillary blinked slowly; her hands were gripping her bag so tightly that her knuckles were white.

'One week,' she said. 'One week is all you have.'

'That's all I need,' Derek said, sitting back. 'That's enough.'

An hour later, Jude looked for the last time around the room he'd spent the past two months in. It always amazed him how easy it was to pack up what represented the Underground headquarters, how quickly the spaces that had contained it returned to their former existence – dank, squalid buildings good only for being knocked down. Packed up, the Underground could be condensed into three piles and his computer. He knew that the operation's sophistication wasn't focused in one place, that its armies were not stationed in the building nor its information held in physical form alone. But still, standing there, he couldn't help feeling that far from the wide-reaching terrorist organisation Hillary Wright insisted on talking about, the Underground was really a fragile thing, a butterfly hoping that by flapping its wings huge changes would come about.

Two supporters had been called in to help him pack and the work had been done in silence. Whether because of Pip's surrender, the crazed attacks on Underground sympathisers or the whimpers and cries from the children, Jude didn't know, but no one said a word as they methodically shifted the piles of papers and equipment into rucksacks for easy transport.

Sam appeared again. His shift – the guards worked one week on, three weeks off – had come to an end, but his replacement had not turned up yet. Jude had a feeling the replacement wouldn't be turning up ever; he suspected Sam thought the same, but neither of them admitted it. They continued to talk as though things hadn't changed irrevocably, as though any minute now another guard might appear.

'You going to take over running things? Till Pip escapes?' Sam asked.

Jude didn't say anything for a few seconds. 'He'll be out before you know it,' he said. Then, knowing that it was an empty promise, 'He'll escape. He's got a plan.'

'Course he will. I know that,' Sam said.

Jude nodded gratefully. Until a few hours ago, Sam had been an anonymous guard stationed at the top of the stairs. Jude had barely registered his face, and Sam hadn't spoken except to check the credentials of visitors and to tell them where to go. But now – well, now things were different. Since they'd watched the newsfeed together, it felt like the two of them were carrying everything on their shoulders. They would be too, quite literally, Jude thought wryly, looking at the rucksacks.

Sam looked at him awkwardly. 'There was another one twenty minutes ago,' he said.

'Another . . . ?' Jude asked, but he didn't have to finish the sentence; he knew what Sam meant. He meant another supporter had called to say they no longer wanted anything to do with the Underground. If Pip had hoped that handing himself in would draw a line in the sand, stop the attacks, stop supporters from deserting them, he'd been wrong. If anything, his admission of guilt had just made things worse.

'Said she didn't want us contacting her again. Said she was resigning her support.'

'Right. Thanks,' Jude said tightly. 'Well, it doesn't matter. We've still got supporters. We'll be fine.'

'Right.' Sam breathed out heavily. 'Thing is,' he said, 'people don't want to get ill and die, do they?'

Jude stopped packing the box next to him and looked up.

'The Underground didn't sabotage the drugs,' he said quietly. 'You know that, right?'

'I know.' Sam nodded. 'But it does – death, I mean – it does focus the mind, doesn't it? Like, people want new life, they do. But then when the reality hits, they realise that if there's new life, then there's got to be death. Which is OK in theory, but when it's in practice, when you hear about people dying . . .'

'Yeah,' Jude said, closing his eyes and seeing the blistered bodies in the Pincent Pharma lorry, the woman clawing at him in pain as she died. He met Sam's eyes and saw real fear in them. But before he could say something, reach out, explain that he understood, there was a loud bang on the door. He looked at Sam in alarm as the door guard jumped up.

'Who's there?' he asked. 'What's the weather like out there?'

He looked back at Jude, his eyes wide with fear. Then a voice called out, 'It's windy in Scotland, but here it's quite mild.'

Jude stiffened as he recognised the voice. 'Peter?' he called out as Sam opened the door tentatively. 'Peter! What the hell are you doing here?'

Peter scanned the room as Sam hurriedly shut the

door behind him. His face was blue and black, his clothes covered in dirt. 'You're moving?'

Jude nodded. 'Yeah. We're – it's safer.'

Peter appeared to digest this, to take in the sound of crying, the emptiness, the bags under Jude's eyes. 'You were waiting for me?' he frowned.

Jude shook his head in bewilderment. 'I didn't know you were coming. What are you doing here? Where's Anna? And the children?'

But Peter didn't answer and Jude watched wide-eyed as he fell to the floor. It was only when he looked down that Jude saw the footprints on his clothes, realised that he had been literally trampled, the black marks on his face the bruises and dirt from having his face pressed into the ground. Where? How? He wanted to know, but he couldn't ask. Instead he turned to Sam, who immediately leant down and picked Peter up. 'I can carry him,' he said in answer to Jude's silent question. 'Come on. We have to go.'

'Yeah,' Jude said on autopilot, then, rounding up the children, he assigned rucksacks to Sheila and the supporters, picked up his computer, silently pointed the way and followed them out.

Chapter Fifteen

In the Cut was busy that morning, bustling with men and women having their hair coloured and dyed, wigs fitted, eyelids injected with botox and skin rubbed with almond oil. As the world outside descended into chaos, In the Cut was a sanctuary of civilisation, of peace, of denial. No mob rule here, no checkpoints, no fear to grip them – just dim lights which cast flattering shadows on clients as they sat back on comfortable chairs, in this temple to the god of beauty, of self-preservation.

Julia Sharpe flicked over the pages of her e-magazine, but her eyes weren't focusing on the articles or pictures that it contained. Instead she was staring ahead at her reflection in the mirror, fearful, afraid. No rash. There was no rash. She was safe. But for how long? Would she be next? Two of her neighbours had been taken in the night – were they terrorists or had they taken the contaminated drugs? She went to the same pharmacist as one of them. Would she be next? How would she know?

Forcing her eyes away, she found herself looking

surreptitiously at the woman reflected in the mirror next to hers. Her name was Sylvia and she was wearing a mask – a protective mask that had been explicitly prohibited by the Authorities because there was no need for them, because those selling them were profiteers, because the rumour of a virus was sedition. There was no illness. It was impossible. It was the work of Underground propaganda.

Julia looked away; it unnerved her.

'So, the same colours?' her hairdresser Jim was asking her. Julia looked at him vaguely.

'I'm sorry? Oh, colours. Yes. Same as usual. Thank you.'

She forced her eyes back to her own reflection, to the wrinkles under her eyes, the drooping jowls she so despised. Was it her imagination or did her eyes look tired – not just the skin around them but the irises themselves? Then she shook herself. She was imagining it. Everyone was going mad, caught up in fear. It was what the Underground wanted. She would not fall for it.

She scratched her arm then, realising what she was doing, stopped herself. The itch was imagined. Next she would start to believe the prophecies that were being spouted on street corners about the end of the world, about the eternal winter coming finally to an end.

Eternal winter? There was a reason for the cold weather – something to do with the sea. Everything had a rational explanation. She would not allow herself to fall so easily into the insanity that appeared to be gripping the nation.

She was having her hair done. What could be more normal than that?

Clearing her throat, Julia tried to think of something to say – one of her usual topics of conversation: her bridge evenings; the cost of petrol; the new, ugly developments being erected for immigrant labourers which were a blot on the landscape and a constant reminder, as her husband regularly remarked, sighing, that the small island of Great Britain was simply getting too full. She usually enjoyed her conversations with Jim – enjoyed the opportunity to regale him with her opinions as he listened and nodded, never butting in to disagree with her as her friends and acquaintances so often did; never shaking his head and telling her that she didn't understand as her husband *always* did.

But today her mind was full of everything and nothing, hope and despair, neither of which she'd countenance. It made small talk a little difficult.

'So how are you today?'

'Me?' She forced a smile. 'Oh, I'm . . . I'm fine, thank you. Very well.'

Her eyes strayed involuntarily back to Sylvia's reflection. Jim saw and grinned. 'We've got some of those if you're interested,' he said conversationally. Julia's eyes narrowed.

'You . . . have?'

'Sure. They're infused with tea tree oil. Protect you

from, you know, pollution, dust, whatever really. They're getting very popular.'

'Pollution?' Julia nodded, felt relief flood though her. People weren't afraid of getting ill, not rational people. She wasn't ill. There was nothing to worry about.

'Oh, thank God. I thought they were . . . I mean, you hear about people panicking about these supposed Missing, and I thought . . .' She met Jim's eyes and her voice trailed off. Thought what? That people were worried about dying? That the Authorities couldn't be trusted? That the vans that came in the night, glimpsed through windows, filled with grim-faced policemen wearing masks, were not prison vans rounding up Underground supporters? No, these were not things she thought. She refused to think them, refused to let herself even recognise awareness of them.

Jim was twisting foil round strands of her hair with studied concentration; Sylvia, meanwhile, had glanced up sharply before looking back at her magazine. Julia reddened; she felt stupid suddenly, awkward.

'They're really popular?' she asked, her voice more cautious now, softer.

Jim shrugged. 'People like to be careful,' he said evenly.

'And they're not . . . the disallowed ones?'

Jim met her eyes briefly in the mirror and Julia felt a thud of fear.

'They're legal, so far as I know,' Jim said. 'So, shall I turn the volume up?'

Julia frowned, uncertain what he was talking about, then she realised he was looking at the small computer screen embedded in the wall. It wasn't usually on; Julia knew it was Jim's way of stopping dead their conversation. He didn't trust her. She didn't trust herself.

'Today saw the demise of Margaret Pincent, daughter of Richard Pincent of Pincent Pharma, granddaughter of Albert Fern, the inventor of Longevity, and former House Matron of Grange Hall, who shot her former husband last year. The murderer died after a gradual, humane reduction in Longevity. Her former Surplus son, Peter Pincent, an Opt Out, is a known Underground supporter and on the most wanted list. And in other news, the United States has announced a state of emergency as the death toll from contaminated Longevity drugs reaches 2,565. In the UK, the Authorities have confirmed only two hundred affected people, and say that anyone caught protesting or attempting any seditious activity will be imprisoned immediately . . .'

'Bet a lot of women have thought about killing their ex-husbands, don't you reckon?' Jim was smiling again; Julia managed a slightly strangled laugh.

'I imagine they'll think twice now,' she said. Her arm was itching unbearably; not scratching it was taking all her concentration, rendering her hot and uncomfortable.

'Bit warm today, isn't it?' Jim said. 'Bit unseasonal, don't you think?'

Julia looked at him uncertainly. 'I'm not hot,' she lied. She was sweating; she wondered if Jim had noticed.

'No? Must just be me.' Jim shrugged. He looked as though he was going to say more, but he was distracted immediately by a gust of wind as the door opened. Julia turned her head to see who it was, but she didn't recognise the woman who rushed in. Her hair was short and severe, the skin on her face lined and coarse. She met Julia's eyes and came running towards her and Julia found herself shrinking back into her chair.

'Water!' the woman gasped, grabbing at a glass that had been left on a shelf and bringing the whole unit tumbling to the floor. 'Water!'

Everyone stared at her in horror, Julia recoiled violently and Jim immediately dropped the foils. 'This is a hairdressers, not a cafe,' he said, attempting a smile as though it might defuse the woman's anger. 'Maybe you should go somewhere else.'

Julia was staring at the woman in fright. She was on the floor now, clutching at her throat. 'Water!' she screeched. 'Give me water!'

'Give her some water!' Julia heard herself shout, then she clapped her hand over her mouth as two policeman enter the salon. Quickly they bundled the woman out of the hairdressers and into a van that was parked outside. Two salon assistants, meanwhile, lifted the shelving unit back up and started to rearrange the objects on it. For a few minutes everyone sat in silence. Then slowly, gradually, conversation started again and the salon resumed its low hum of activity.

'Well!' Jim said, turning Julia round on her swivel chair, asking her to face up towards him so that he could do her hairline. 'That was a bit out of the ordinary, wasn't it!'

Julia nodded. Her hands were shaking and she quickly moved them under her gown. There was another policeman in the doorway; she could see him out of the corner of her eye. Jim saw him too.

'You just missed the nutter,' he called out. 'She's been taken away.'

The policeman looked at him for a moment, then entered the salon. He headed straight for Julia. She started to sweat. They were coming for her. She'd known they would. She'd known it. She was shaking; she was terrified.

'Jim Harrison?'

Jim turned and smiled. 'That's right. What can I do for you?'

The policeman didn't return the smile. 'I'm afraid you'll have to come with me,' he said.

'Come with you?' Julia nodded and started to stand up.

'If you don't mind.' The policeman took Jim by the arm and frogmarched him outside. Julia stared after them uncertainly. Jim? They'd come for Jim? He was an Underground agent? It was impossible. No, not impossible, but unlikely. So unlikely.

'My foils!' she called after them foolishly. She ran

to the door, out on to the pavement. There was a van right outside and the policeman opened the back. The road was empty; checkpoints and blockades had been set up around the salon. She followed the policeman and Jim. 'Can't he finish my foils first? I'm sure there's been a mistake. My husband works for the Authorities. I can call –'

'Back inside, please,' the policeman said to her curtly, but it was too late – she'd already run a few metres down the road, had seen inside the van. The bodies, some alive, some dead, were piled on top of each other like animal carcasses, the stench overwhelming. Not Underground supporters. Not terrorists. They were ill. Like the woman who'd wanted water. They were all ill, Julia realised with a thud.

Jim had seen too. His face was white. 'Wait! What are you doing?' he shouted desperately as the policeman threw him inside with the rotting bodies. 'There's been a mistake. I'm not –' But his words were lost as he was thrown in the back, the door closed behind him.

The policeman got into the van and stared at Julia who was rooted to the spot, unable to move. 'You get back inside,' he said. 'Else you're going in the van too, understand?'

Julia nodded. She edged back towards the salon, walked in and closed the door. Then she stood there, stock still, unable to move for several minutes. Because she did understand. Finally, she understood completely.

Chapter Sixteen

The rain was lashing down and Molly's battered pram kept getting stuck in the mud as Anna attempted to push it with one hand and pull Ben along with the other down the winding lane that led to her house. Their house. Peter was only gone for a week, she knew that, but she also knew that it was empty without him.

She tried not to think about it, tried to remember the steel wall that she'd built up at Grange Hall – a wall that protected her from disappointment, that kept everyone out. But the wall was no use now, she knew that.

Anna hadn't needed anybody back then, had seen it as a matter of pride that no one could ever disappoint her because she didn't hope for anything. She'd thought she was strong, but now . . . now she could see that she'd been weak, fragile, so easy to break. These days she allowed herself to feel – allowed anger to flood her veins, joy to fill her heart and pain to fill her eyes with tears. She knew that each emotion came and went, knew that she could cope with whatever life threw at her. Even Peter going to London.

She reached for her keys; her hands were soaking wet

and it took an age to work one into her pocket. Eventually, though, the door swung open and she pulled the pram in. She'd turned the heating off the day before when the icy weather broke and clouds appeared, offering some natural protection from the cold, but still the house felt warm. Warm and safe. Anna couldn't understand desires that stretched outside of those two words. Or three, perhaps. Warm and safe and free. Warm and safe and free and loved . . . She shook herself and lit the candle on the kitchen table, took off Ben's coat and gave him a drink of milk. Peter never used candles – he laughed at her attempts to save on energy, told her that a few hours on the computer and a few lights on weren't going to make any difference to anyone, particularly as their energy came directly from a secret generator provided by the Underground. They were off the grid and no Authorities rationing could be imposed on them. But Peter didn't suffer from the guilt that Anna did; she still felt the pressure to tread lightly on the world, to use as few of its resources as necessary. And anyway, she liked candles. They were cosy and reassuring.

She picked up Molly and took off the layers of blankets enveloping her. Molly had been sleeping and opened her eyes, smiling in delight as she always did when she woke up. Anna found it amazing that a baby could be so entirely happy when it knew so little of the world; it terrified her that she was responsible for that happiness, for making it continue, for ensuring that Molly's smile never faded.

'There's a good girl,' she cooed, as she lay the baby

down on a sheepskin rug on the floor. 'I'm just going to scrape the vegetables. Good girl. Now, Ben, would you like to help me?'

'Vegebles,' Ben agreed. 'Scape vegebles.'

He started to rummage half-heartedly through the shopping on the pram, then wandered off to play with a wooden dog on a lead that Peter had made for him a few days earlier. It was too dangerous to take the children shopping. Underground supporters left dried goods and other supplies for them once every couple of months and they had to grow most of their food, but every so often, an excursion to the nearest convenience store was unavoidable and Peter would usually go alone with the fake identicard that Pip had given him. Today though, with no Peter, Anna had been forced to go herself, tying Ben to Molly's pram and hiding it out of sight half a mile from the shop. People had looked at her – they always did – but no one said anything, no one challenged her. The village was sympathetic, Pip had told them; twenty years before Catchers had descended looking for Surpluses and a skirmish had ensued. Four Legal children had been killed, one just a baby, and that wasn't the sort of thing anyone forgot easily.

'Doggie!' Ben yelped excitedly as he pushed it along the floor towards Molly. 'Doggie roll!'

'Careful of the baby,' Anna sighed, then started to unload the shopping herself: a few poor cuts of meat, some milk, yogurt, bread. When she'd worked for Mrs Sharpe, she'd imagined that everyone on the Outside ate chocolate every day, that their homes would be brimming with wonderful food. But she'd soon realised that even on the outside food was scarce.

That was fine with her. She loved growing her own food, loved watching vegetables and fruit ripening, nature at its proudest. She loved the feeling of control over her destiny, loved spending most of her life outdoors and the rest of it inside, cooking, cleaning, making a home for her family.

She sat down and looked over at the children. Ben's wooden dog was scampering all over Molly, who was giggling in delight. Anna found herself smiling too. She was so lucky, she realised. So incredibly fortunate. Perhaps she would start her diary again. She'd been meaning to for ages, but never seemed to find the time. Now, with Peter gone, she could write in the evening when the children were asleep. She could read, too, curled up in bed . . .

Her thoughts were disturbed by a gust of wind that swept past her face and blew out the candle. Immediately Anna felt a jolt of fear – an irrational one, she knew. It would be a broken window, a gap in one of the dilapidated walls that they'd yet to fill. She had always been scared of the dark, a fear borne out of spells in Solitary at Grange Hall, a dark, dank, miserable place that aimed to break the spirit of its inhabitants and succeeded in doing so. All except for Peter, that is. Peter didn't allow Solitary to break him; instead it was he who did the breaking – tunnelling out, taking Anna with him, giving her a taste of freedom and excitement that she'd never thought possible.

Using this memory to steel herself, Anna got up and felt around for the matchbox then, using her hands to protect it from the wind, she struck a match and relit the candle. Immediately its warm glow turned the kitchen back into a safe, warm place. Ben, who had momentarily stopped playing to look around in confusion, resumed trotting his dog up and down Molly's body as she gurgled and kicked in enjoyment. Anna stood up and walked around the room to find the source of the gust of wind that had plunged it into darkness. The door was firmly closed; there was a small draught from underneath, but not enough to extinguish a candle. The window to its left was also shut; Anna lifted her hand but couldn't feel any wind coming through it. Frowning, she walked towards the bigger window on the other side of the kitchen. And then, suddenly, she stopped and screamed. Because in the reflection of the window, she saw a pair of eyes looking at her from inside the room. Immediately, Ben began to yell and, like an echo, Molly followed suit. Terrified, Anna turned to them, but an arm looped around her, preventing her from moving.

'Cooperate and everyone will be just fine,' a voice said – a deep, threatening voice. Anna did her best to breathe. She had to be strong for Molly, for Ben.

'Cooperate. Yes. Yes, I . . .' Anna managed to say. Molly's cries were searing through her like physical pain. 'The children,' she said. 'Please let me go to them.'

'Don't worry, they're coming too,' the man said.

He grabbed her hands and pulled them behind her back. Anna felt her stomach clench. 'Please,' she said.

'Please. We're not Surplus. I've got papers. I've got our documents . . .'

But the Catcher was already taking out his phone to call his haul in. 'I've got the girl,' he said. 'The children too.'

Then, pulling Anna, he dragged her out of the house.

Derek answered his phone immediately. 'It's definitely her?' he asked.

'Definitely,' his guard replied. 'The Covey girl and two small ones. Shall I tell Mr Pincent, like he said?'

'No,' Derek said, smiling to himself. 'Tell no one. Bring her to me.'

'But –'

'But nothing,' Derek cut in angrily. 'You report to me, *I* report to Richard. And the orders have changed. You bring them to me, do you understand?'

'Yes, sir,' the guard said quickly. 'Yes, I understand.'

'Good.' Derek put down the phone and breathed out slowly. Everything was coming together. Anna Covey and her children were his and soon there would be more. Many more.

Twenty vans were parked outside, waiting for his word. He would go with them, he decided. Make sure the job was done properly.

He stood up and moved silently along the corridor, then down the back steps of Pincent Pharma to where the vans were waiting. Quickly he inspected them, then nodded to the drivers.

'It's time,' he said, a little smile playing on his lips. 'It's time to collect.'

Chapter Seventeen

Ella Blunden sighed and turned off the news broad-cast, searching for some music instead. There was enough grey at Grange Hall without having more descend from the outside world. She'd thought of Grange Hall as a prison when she'd first arrived but now, with fear on the streets, it felt like a refuge. Missings, police checkpoints, the Underground poi-soning the Longevity supply, people ranting on the radio about death, about God, about conspiracy theories . . . Grange Hall itself had received numerous phone calls from people offering to torch the place, telling her to kill the Surpluses before they had an opportunity to grow up and become terrorists them-selves. Chance would be a fine thing, Ella thought to herself with a sigh. Although it would put her out of a job.

She found a music station playing swingsong and turned up the volume. The Surpluses were all asleep; they wouldn't hear, anyway. The House Matron's rooms were soundproofed – Ella had seen to that. She hadn't exactly jumped when they offered her the job, not after what had happened to the last House Matron. But money was money, and they'd held out all sorts of incentives, including the refurbishment of her apartment and a new office. One that no one, to her knowledge, had committed murder in. She had standards, after all.

She sat back in her upholstered chair and poured herself a glass of wine, taking a sip, then a larger gulp. Perhaps if she drank the bottle she'd fall asleep again, snatch a couple of hours before the new day began.

It wasn't a nice place to be. It was safe, perhaps, but cold – a sinister house that sucked any life out of you, took away any humanity. She'd been here nearly a year now, a year that felt like for ever. And yet the Authorities had made it clear she was to stay for at least ten years, that this was part of the deal.

They didn't know what it was like, she thought to herself as the music played: they'd cleaned the streets of the vile young things and had forgotten what it was to be around them all day long. Perhaps that was why she couldn't sleep these days, she mused. Perhaps she was waking up at 4 a.m. so that there was a buffer between her dreams and her reality – a time to adapt, to accept.

She took another gulp of wine and let the music soothe her active mind. It was the girls she found the hardest, she mused, as she felt the alcohol slowly warm her blood. The boys were easy to discipline because they understood about dominance. They tried to fight back, failed, were beaten and then fell into line. Girls, on the other hand . . . She took another gulp of her wine, then another, then reached out for the bottle to refill her glass. Girls were tricky. You never knew what they were thinking, what they were planning. They unnerved her. She was pleased that the liberals were being hunted down, pleased that everyone was seeing the Underground for what it really was. If those sympathisers had only come to work here they'd have realised the truth. If they spent one week in this place, they'd repeal any legislation protecting the little brats.

A buzzer sounded in her room and Ella's eyes shot to it angrily, warily. It could only mean one thing – trouble. No one would dare call her at this hour unless it was important, unless it was very bad news. She shrank back into the protective comfort of her chair, wishing she was somewhere else, anywhere else. But she wasn't. She was there. She had to move. Steeling herself, putting down her drink, she reluctantly stood up, walked over to her desk and picked up the receiver.

'Yes?'

'Mrs Blunden, there's someone here to see you.'

'At this time of night?' Ella asked impatiently. 'And you let them in? I've made it clear that I don't expect to be disturbed unless there's a real emergency. A breakout. A death. Unless that's what's happened, there is no reason to call me at this hour.'

'If you could just come down –'

Ella put the receiver down, breathed into her hand to check her breath and, satisfied that the wine was undetectable, slipped her shoes on and made her way out into the corridor. As she did so she shivered – already she missed the sanctity of her rooms with their warm colours, plumped-up cushions, radiators that worked.

At the bottom of the stairs her Deputy Matron was waiting for her.

'Well? What is it?'

Sarah nodded her head towards the door to the visitors' reception. Ella looked up and as she did, a face appeared – a face she recognised. She'd never seen him in the flesh, but she knew who he was immediately. Everyone did. They called him the Dark Knight.

'Mr Samuels!' she gasped. 'You should have told me you were coming. I'd have made preparations. I'd have –'

'No need,' Derek Samuels said smoothly, walking towards her. 'This is a Code Red. I will be taking the Surpluses with me.'

'The Surpluses?' Ella said uncertainly. 'I'm not sure I understand. You're taking –'

'All of them,' Derek said confidently. He clapped his hands and more men appeared through the doorway, their Catchers uniforms putting a chill through Ella even though she knew she had nothing to fear from them.

'But shouldn't there be . . .' her mouth twisted uncomfortably, 'paperwork, notification, something?

For my records, I mean,' she said, smiling nervously. 'You know what the Authorities are like.'

'There is no need and no time for paperwork,' Derek said.

Ella bit her lip. 'So shall I wake them? We could ring the bell.'

'Please don't trouble yourself,' Derek said briskly. 'My men will not need any assistance. I'd be grateful if you would return to your quarters.'

Ella nodded mutely. Many times she'd hoped that the Surplus Halls would be closed down and the Surpluses got rid of. The rich would have to forgo their slave labour, but they could pay people properly if they wanted help, she'd reasoned. People like Ella herself. Give her a decent wage and she'd clean their houses and cook their meals. It would beat staying here, that was for sure.

But now that the Surpluses were being taken, she felt unsettled. 'Perhaps I should phone the Surplus Department. Just to be sure,' she said. But the look Derek Samuels gave her made her wish she hadn't spoken. 'Or I'll just retire to my apartment,' she said quickly, tugging at Sarah's arm. 'Both of us.'

'That would be wise,' Derek said. He clapped his hands again and watched as his men silently dispersed around the building.

Chapter Eighteen

Jude moved his arm, swatting away what he supposed must be a fly, but he missed and the fly turned into a stick being prodded into him by his father. He was taunting him, saying, 'You're not Peter. You're the inferior brother. You'll never be Peter. I wish you were Surplus.' He lunged at his dad, eyes blazing, heard him yelp and woke up. It wasn't a stick, he realised; it was Sam's finger. 'What the – What time is it?' he asked groggily.

'Five thirty.'

He glanced at his watch. That meant he'd had, what, three hours' sleep? He pushed off the grimy blanket and pulled himself up. It was only then that he realised how white Sam was. His heart fell.

'What's happened? Have we been found?'

Sam shook his head. 'It's the Surpluses,' he said, his voice hoarse.

'The children?' Jude looked at him in alarm. 'Are they back?' The night before, he'd persuaded the supporters who'd helped them move to take the children with them – they'd agreed eventually, but uneasily. It was a great deal at any time to ask someone to hide a child and right now it was almost suicide.

'Not those ones,' Sam said bitterly. 'The Surpluses in the halls. They've all been taken away. A woman called. The Northern Watcher. She said the Steadley Hall Surpluses were taken away by Catchers in the middle of the night. And the Southern Watcher said that Grange Hall was emptied at 10 p.m.'

Jude stared at him wide-eyed. 'You're sure it was the Watchers? Sure it wasn't a fake?'

'They knew all the codes. The Northern Watcher was crying. She said she hadn't been able to do anything. She said the Catchers came. They sneaked in and bundled everyone out.' He looked down. 'What next?' he whispered. 'What next?'

'We track them down, that's what,' Jude said, jumping up, but he didn't believe his own words.

'You can't fight the Catchers,' Sam murmured. 'No one can.'

Jude walked over to the phone, read the transcript of the Northern Watcher's description of the Catchers pulling up outside, the Surpluses being led out into the cold night then bundled into the back of the vans. He shivered. 'OK,' he said grimly. 'Here's what we do. You're going to get some sleep and I'm going to think.'

'No,' Sam said, his expression one of defeat. 'Pip's gone. The Surpluses are gone. No one is on the Underground's side any more. It's over. Can't you see that?'

'It's not over,' Jude said tersely. 'We've got something that Richard Pincent wants, and if he wants it badly enough we can get Pip back and maybe even the Surpluses. And if he doesn't want it badly enough then we'll think of something else. But we're not giving up. No way.'

His eyes travelled to his brother, who was lying on the floor; he'd been unconscious since he'd arrived the night before. He walked over and woke him up.

'Peter,' he whispered. 'Peter, wake up.'

Peter sat up with a start. 'What? What?' he said fearfully, then registered Jude's face. 'What is it?' he asked.

'Why are you here?' Jude looked at him intently.

'Why am I here?' Peter's face crumpled with confusion. 'I brought the ring,' he said. 'Like you asked.'

'Like I asked?' Jude said uncertainly. 'I don't know what you're talking about.'

'I'm talking about the message you sent me. To send the ring down. I messaged back, remember? Said I was coming with it.'

Jude looked at him blankly. Then he swallowed uncomfortably as a terrible thought struck him. He walked over to his computer and quickly navigated past the security codes into the messaging centre. He hoped he wouldn't find anything; hoped there had been a mistake, that his unthinkable suspicion was completely wrong. But there in front of him, hidden in the 'Deleted' folder, he saw it: the message that had been sent to Peter. He saw other messages too, messages to

Richard Pincent, messages back again. He breathed in sharply.

'The good news is that Richard Pincent wants the ring,' he said uncomfortably.

'And the bad news?' Peter asked. Jude didn't answer. 'Where are we anyway?' Peter asked, looking around.

'New headquarters,' Jude said flatly. Then he turned to Peter. 'Do you have the ring?'

'Of course,' Peter said, reaching into his pocket. Then he frowned. 'I had it . . .' he said, going white.

He stood up and searched every pocket. 'I had it when I got here. I know I did,' he said frantically. 'Is it important? Why do you need it anyway?'

Jude didn't say anything for a few seconds.

Then he looked around. 'Where's Sheila?' he asked quietly.

Sam, who'd been staring at Peter as though he were a ghost, appeared to shake himself. 'In there,' he said, pointing to a door. Jude ran towards it and pulled open the door. 'She's not there,' he said, turning back to Sam. 'Is she with the children?'

Sam rushed around, pulling open cupboard doors, but within seconds they knew she had gone; the new Underground headquarters were half the size of the last place and there were few places to hide.

'I don't know how . . . I was on the door all the time. Except for unpacking. Except for –'

'Sheila took the ring?' Peter asked incredulously. 'Is that what you think? Why would she do that? What's going on, Jude? Tell me what's happening.'

Jude turned back to his computer and opened recent files; as he scanned them he filled Peter in on what had been happening.

His brother didn't take the news of Pip well. 'He's been captured? He turned himself in? It's impossible . . .' he was saying.

But Jude wasn't listening. He was staring at a file he thought he'd deleted, a list of the Palmers that he'd tracked down. Uncertainly he scanned the names.

'What?' Peter demanded again. 'Do you know where she is?'

Jude looked at him uncertainly. 'I don't know,' he said, a feeling of dread rising up within him. What had his princess done? Why had she been driven to this?

He bit his lip, trying to think. She had the ring, but she was still looking for the Palmers. Where would she be? There were nearly fifteen names and addresses on the screen and they didn't have time to go to every one. Had she contacted them? Surely she knew where she was going before she left?

He stared at the desk in front of him, then noticed a notebook. The top page had been ripped out; beneath it the imprint of writing could be seen. Immediately he grabbed it.

Peter ran his hand through his hair. 'Jude, forget about Sheila,' he said. 'If she's gone, so be it. We need to get Pip. That's what matters.'

'Sheila is what matters,' Jude said grimly, his mind

racing. Already a plan was forming in his mind. But the plan required preparation. He needed to get back to his computer; needed to get back into the Pincent Pharma security system. But most of all he needed to find Sheila. 'It looks like Sheila has your ring. Your grandfather wants your ring. Without it, we've got nothing to bargain with. We need Sheila, otherwise we've got nothing.'

'So where do we start looking?' Peter asked.

Jude looked back at the scrap of paper, his mind clouding with worry, with anger, with uncertainty. 'She's in Muswell Hill,' he said. 'At least I think she is. You wait here and I'll go and see.'

Peter looked down at his clothes, which still bore footprints on them. 'I'm not waiting anywhere,' he said gruffly. 'If you go, I go. Understand?'

Jude thought for a moment, then nodded. 'In that case, give me five minutes and we'll go.'

Chapter Nineteen

Julia heard the front door open but didn't move. She was sitting on the sofa in the bay window at the front of the house, the sun streaming down on her through the double-glazed windows. She felt warm, she felt comfortable, she felt happy.

She heard her husband's footsteps on the wooden hallway floor, the same footsteps she'd heard for decades, as he took off his coat, put down his keys, straightened his tie in the hallway mirror. She lifted her head slightly; any second now he would appear in the doorway, his expression serious as ever, offering her a sherry, enquiring what time supper would be ready even though they always ate at exactly the same time. Always had.

And there he was. She smiled. 'Hello, darling.'

He frowned; it had been a long time since she'd used that word. A long time since she'd said a lot of things. A long and successful marriage, people called it, raising their eyebrows, looking at her in wonderment. So few relationships had lasted so long. Longevity had given some the impetus to start afresh (many, many times), had instilled in others the fear of commitment – for a lifetime of commitment was now so long, so terribly long. Without children there was no need for stability; with no family, there was no family unit, just individuals with their own agendas, their own pleasure-seeking journey.

But not Julia. Not Anthony. They were old-fashioned, she would say to those people with raised eyebrows. They had got used to each other. And if the romance had died long ago, the companionship hadn't. The kindness hadn't either, not entirely.

They were fond of each other.

They'd come a long way.

'Sherry?'

Julia smiled. 'I'd love one.'

Anthony walked over to the drinks cabinet and took out two glasses and a bottle, filling them to the same spot he always filled them. So many little routines, Julia found herself thinking. Long life, short life – did it matter when each day was the same, when humans were incapable of living for the moment because of their fundamental need for order, for the comfort of everyday routine?

He handed her a glass and she took a sip.

'What time's supper?' he asked, already walking towards the door.

She smiled. 'Does it matter?'

There was a silence; Anthony took a few seconds to register her answer. Slowly he stopped, turned round. He looked tired. Everyone looked tired these days.

'Whatever do you mean?'

'I mean, does it matter?' Julia said. She stood up, walked towards her husband, put her glass down on the mantelpiece and wrapped her arms around his neck. 'We've had a good life, haven't we, Anthony?' she asked. 'We've had our adventures, our holidays. We've lived well, haven't we?'

Anthony nodded. 'We live very well,' he said. 'And we will continue to do so. So, what time is supper?'

'For how long?' Julia whispered.

He frowned. 'Julia, what's wrong with you? What are you trying to say?'

'How long will we continue to do so?' Julia said. 'It isn't going to last, is it, Anthony? We're going to die. I know we are.'

'We are not going to die.' Anthony stepped back, his eyes flashing with anger. 'I won't have you say such things in this house. The Authorities are clear on the matter. Longevity supply was sabotaged. The perpetrator is being held and questioned. There is no reason to –'

'I saw the van,' Julia said quietly. 'They took my hairdresser. He wasn't an Underground agent. The van was full of dead people, diseased people.' There was a flicker of something in her husband's eyes. Fear? Recognition?

'I saw inside,' Julia continued. 'The Authorities are lying.'

'Lying?' Again the anger, the defensiveness. 'The Authorities do not lie. It is sedition to utter those words.'

Julia shook her head defiantly. She could feel tears pricking at her eyes. 'I won't be taken away like that,' she said hoarsely. 'I won't. I'd rather stop taking Longevity. I'd rather die here with you, comfortably, on our own terms.'

Anthony's eyes widened. 'You're talking like a mad-woman,' he said uncertainly, downing his sherry in one. He stood up, walked back to the drinks cabinet and poured himself another. 'What has got into you?'

'Nothing has got into me,' Julia said, blinking away a stray tear. 'Just . . .' She walked over to her husband. 'We've had a good run. We've been happy. Haven't we?'

'Of course we have,' he said irritably. 'Julia, please stop this rambling. Are you drunk?'

She leant against his chest, remembered how small she used to feel when he wrapped his arms around her in the early days. He was a tall man and she'd loved that about him – loved the feeling that he would always look after her. Now she wanted to look after him.

'I've already stopped taking my Longevity,' she said in a quiet voice. 'I didn't take any today. Not after what I saw . . . I want you to stop too. I want us to stay here. I don't want to go back outside.'

'You've what?' He stared at her incredulously. 'What are you thinking?'

'I'm thinking,' she said carefully, 'that I have always been in a position to make choices. We've been lucky in that way. And now I am making this choice. They won't take me away in a van. They won't take you. I want us to grow old together. Even if we're only old for a few weeks, days even.'

'Die? Get old?' Anthony shook his head. 'Julia, will you please listen to me? I told you, the Authorities have made it clear that –'

He was trembling. 'You're wrong, Julia. The Authorities are clear that everything is under control.'

'And you believe them? You believe what you have been told?' Julia demanded, her eyes gripping his, her voice quivering with emotion. 'Really?'

He swallowed, looked away. 'The Authorities' line is that –'

'There are bodies piling up, Anthony,' Julia cut in. 'I saw them with my own eyes. When I left the hairdressers, I walked and walked. They can't collect all the bodies, can they? Tell me the truth, Anthony.'

'It's not my job to know the truth,' her husband said hesitantly. 'My job is to follow the rules, to manage efficiently, to ensure that protocol is adhered to . . .'

'And what if it doesn't matter any more?' Julia said. 'What then?'

'I . . . I . . .' He looked at her helplessly. 'I don't know,' he said. She led him to a chair, where he sat down, let his head hang forward. Then he sat up again, his eyes wide. He looked at Julia mournfully; suddenly he seemed very tired. 'They're digging up land,' he said, his voice barely audible. 'The file states that it is for vegetable farming. But they are digging trenches two metres deep. Four in some places. Vegetables aren't planted four metres underground.'

'No, they're not,' Julia said, stroking his head.

'And so many people collected for seditious activity,' he continued desperately. 'Hundreds of thousands of names. But there aren't that many prison places. I asked where they had all been taken but no one could answer me. They've just . . . disappeared.'

Anthony sat up, pulled her towards him so that she was sitting on his knee. She hadn't been there for decades. 'I love you, Julia,' he said, burying his face in her neck. 'I have always loved you.'

'And I love you.' Julia smiled, tears in her eyes. 'I love you very much, Anthony.'

They sat in silence for a few minutes.

'How many days?' he asked eventually.

'They say it can be weeks,' Julia said, smiling through her tears.

'Take some today, then,' her husband said, looking at her fervently. 'We'll stop together. Wait for me. We'll stop together, we'll go at the same time. We'll shut the door, we'll hole in. We'll do this our way.'

'Yes.' Julia nodded happily, tears now cascading down her cheeks. 'We'll do it our way. Together. It's time to start saying goodbye.'

Chapter Twenty

Derek Samuels sat on the edge of his chair waiting. Soon. Soon it would be time. Everything was in place. The children locked away downstairs. Pip. Jude would arrive before long, bringing Peter and the girl, Sheila, with him.

Finally, Derek would wreak his revenge. He had waited a long time. Too long.

But soon it would be over.

Soon it would all be over.

A few minutes later Jude and Peter emerged on to a grubby London street, their collars up, their hats pulled down low. Jude's hands, thrust in his trouser pockets, belied the urgency in his walk. Since he had joined the Underground he had known that the streets all carried danger, but now it was different. Now it wasn't just Catchers or Authorities police he was fearful of, it was everyone. Everything. Death and the fear of death had changed everything, had changed everyone. Now it was each man for himself and anger erupted easily, devastatingly.

The street itself was largely empty; Jude soon realised why. In several doorways lay bodies – some alive, some dead – that had not been picked up yet, their diseased and rotting flesh attracting flies, creating a stench that forced passers-by on to the other side of the road. Jude tried to pull Peter away, but he didn't do it in time. He watched uncomfortably as his half-brother registered the bodies, then he turned to look away and pretended he didn't notice Peter retching into the gutter.

'That was pretty grim,' Peter said a few seconds later as they turned into another side street.

Jude nodded. 'Yeah,' he agreed. 'So, look, let me fill you in on what's been going on.'

As they walked, Jude told him everything – about his grandfather, about the ring, about the Missing, about the attacks; about his suspicion that Sheila sent the message to him asking for the ring. And Peter told him about his journey, about the crowd he'd thought was chasing him but which trampled over him as they ran towards their real target, a doctor's surgery. A dealer in sabotaged drugs, they'd shouted. A murderer.

Then they stopped for a moment.

'You shouldn't have come,' Jude said, 'but I'm glad you did. It's lonely. Down here, I mean. Boring too.'

Peter looked at him in surprise. 'Boring?' he asked. 'Really?' He managed a rueful smile. 'I thought you were having all the fun.'

'Fun?' Jude raised an eyebrow. 'Sure. I suppose you

could call this fun.' He caught Peter's expression and shrugged. 'I thought you'd got the good deal, that's all. Pip's favourite. Hero of the Underground.'

'Farmer, you mean,' Peter said wryly. 'And I left it to get trampled on by a hysterical crowd torching houses. Great plan, right?'

Jude grinned sheepishly. 'You are an idiot,' he said. 'But you're here now, so . . . This way.' They ducked down and inched towards a busier road. People were scurrying along it faster than usual, their faces slightly pinched, their eyes averted, some of them wearing masks. Jude pulled Peter round the corner, then they darted past a health-food shop with posters in the window promoting vitamins that boosted the immune system and into a narrow passageway. On a tram stop poster, someone had scrawled 'Kill the Murderers. Destroy the Underground.'

Suddenly a woman appeared in front of them. 'My husband!' she screamed. 'They've taken my husband. They've taken him –' Jude pulled Peter away. She didn't seem to have noticed that they were young, but she would soon enough.

'Look!' the woman called after them. 'My blisters. He had them too. They took him away. Will they come for me now?'

Jude saw Peter turn round, saw his eyes widen as he caught sight of the woman's pustules. The same pustules that had covered the dead bodies in the doorways, the same pustules that Jude had seen on the bodies in the Pincent lorry. 'Don't look,' he said, dragging Peter towards a grate in the pavement, heaving it open and jumping down. As Peter followed him they heard a van pull up and police leaping out, followed by the woman's screams as she was dragged away.

'Down here,' Jude said, pulling Peter along a cramped tunnel. 'It used to be a sewer,' he added as they heaved open a trapdoor. 'We can go north from here.'

Peter gulped. 'A sewer?'

Jude looked at him archly. 'What do you prefer? The sewer or the police? Come on, it doesn't even smell. Not really, anyway.'

'Fine, the sewer,' Peter said grimly, jumping down after him.

It was 10 a.m. by the time they got to the address Sheila had written down, slipping into the front garden and hiding between the wall and a hedge. It was an ordinary terraced house on a residential street, the little garden well cared for with plots for vegetables and fruit.

'You sure this is the right place?' Peter asked nervously.

Jude nodded. 'Look,' he said. Through the reflective double glazing, a girl could be seen, her long red hair framing her face. It was unmistakably Sheila.

Jude stood up. 'I'm going in,' he said. 'You go back to the sewer and wait.'

'I'll wait here,' Peter replied.

'No.' Jude shook his head. 'It's too dangerous. If I don't get out, you have to go to Pincent Pharma.'

Peter met his eyes, then nodded and ran off. Jude walked up to the front door and rang the bell, then slunk back and hid. A man came to the door and opened it a little. He looked old – very old, Jude realised with a start. His hair was grey, nearly white, his eyes watery and pale. He had a slight stoop. 'Hello?'

The man looked from left to right then quickly closed the door. Immediately Jude slid out and rang the bell again. This time the man called out from behind the half-open door, 'Who's there?'

Jude looked around then ran out. Grabbing the man, he pulled his hands behind his back and pushed him back into the house before shutting the door again.

'I've come for Sheila.'

The man didn't say anything, but Jude wasn't waiting for a reply. He pushed the man down the corridor towards the stairs. 'I know she's here,' he said, taking the stairs two at a time and pulling the man up with him.

'Wait!' A woman appeared at the bottom of the stairs, pale but for the all-too-obvious pustules which she'd done her best to disguise with make-up. Her eyes were wide with fear. There was no sign of any of Richard Pincent's men, no sign of any Catchers or guards. 'Who are you?' she called after him. 'What are you doing?'

'Sheila?' Jude ignored the woman. He let go of the man and continued up the stairs.

'Jude?' Sheila emerged from behind a door, her skin as translucent as always. She looked at him for a moment, her eyes lighting up, then, feigning insouciance, she raised her eyebrows. 'What on earth are you doing here?'

The woman was following him up the stairs; he could hear her rasping breath behind him. 'Go back to bed, darling,' she said to Sheila, grasping at Jude's jacket. 'You have to go now,' she told him. 'Sheila's our daughter. She's come to look after us.'

Jude looked at Sheila, who was gazing at him triumphantly, like she'd won a game or something.

'These are my parents. My actual parents.' She beamed at the woman who was trying to loosen Jude's grip on her. 'I found them on your computer. They didn't want to give me up, Jude. They've been looking for me for years. And they were so happy to see me.' She was smiling, her eyes full of tears, and she reached out to take Jude's hand. 'You don't have to worry about me any more,' she said.

'But I want to worry about you,' Jude said miserably. 'I thought you needed me.'

'I do,' Sheila whispered. 'I mean, I did. But you've got other things, Jude. And you don't need me. My parents do. I'm home now. I've come home.'

'This isn't your home,' Jude said bitterly. 'The Underground is your home. I'm your home.'

At the mention of the Underground, he saw the

woman's eyes darken. 'Underground? That group of murdering terrorists?'

'You should go, Jude,' Sheila said quickly. 'My parents don't approve of the Underground.'

'They are not your parents,' Jude said angrily.

'We are,' the woman said desperately. 'I'm Mrs Palmer. I'm Sheila's mummy. We've waited so long for her. Haven't we, Billy?'

'So long,' the man called up. 'For our little Sheila.'

'You did?' Jude asked, his eyes narrowing. 'So your husband Opted Out?' he added. 'I mean, that's why he's . . . old?'

Mrs Palmer nodded. 'That's right.'

'But you didn't. I mean, you're on Longevity.'

Mrs Palmer nodded again. 'A life for a life. Just one life.'

'Yeah,' Jude said. 'A life for a life.' He felt as if he was choking; his chest was constricting and he was finding it hard to breathe. He couldn't lose her. He wouldn't lose her. Desperately he looked around for something, anything, that would make her see the truth . . . and then he saw it. A photograph.

'That your husband?' he asked. Mrs Palmer's eyes followed his; the photograph showed Mr Palmer playing tennis, a big grin on his face.

'A long time ago, yes,' she said. 'Now, please let me go. You're hurting me.'

'Funny that neither of you have red hair,' Jude said.

Mrs Palmer cleared her throat. 'Red hair?'

'Like Sheila. I mean, you're both dark. Bit unusual

214

to have a red-haired child, isn't it?'

He pulled Mrs Palmer round so that she was looking at him. Her eyes flickered slightly.

'How old is Sheila?' Jude demanded suddenly. 'When was she born?'

'Jude, you know when I was born,' Sheila interrupted. 'It was –'

'I want your mother to tell me,' he said, putting his hand up to stop her.

Sheila sighed in mock irritation, then looked at Mrs Palmer expectantly. 'Go on, tell him,' she said.

'Well, you're . . . fourteen,' the woman said.

'Fourteen? She's not fourteen.'

'Fifteen, I mean. Yes, she's fifteen. She was born, now let me see, in 2123 – 24. Yes, she was born in 2124.'

'And where was she when she was taken by the Catchers?'

'Where? Well, here, of course. Oh, it was a terrible night. Terrible.' She was twisting her head to look at her husband.

'Here?' Sheila asked. 'I was here?'

'That's right,' the woman said. 'We tried to stop them. We begged them –'

'So not at her grandparents' then? Only that's what's in her file.' Jude was staring at them angrily now.

'Grandparents? Yes, of course. You remember, dear,' Mr Palmer said, coming up the stairs. 'The details – they become a blur. When you're so upset. When you lose –'

'A daughter?' Jude said angrily. 'You never lost a daughter, did you?'

Mrs Palmer put a protective arm round Sheila. 'Of course we did. We did, didn't we, Sheila? But we've got you back now. Safe and sound.'

'Yes, you have,' Sheila said, squinting as though she were having trouble focusing. 'Go away, Jude. I don't need you any more. I've got my parents now. And I'm tired. I'm very tired.'

'What have you done? Drugged her?' Jude stared at Mrs Palmer angrily. Then he turned to Sheila. 'They're not your parents.'

'Yes they are,' Sheila said, folding her arms defiantly. 'You just don't want me to be happy.'

'Happy?' Jude let go of Mrs Palmer and pulled Sheila to him. 'Sheila, all I want is for you to be happy.'

'No,' Sheila protested. 'You wouldn't help me find my parents.'

'Because they're dead.' Jude closed his eyes, pulled Sheila closer. 'They're dead, Sheila,' he whispered. 'I looked for them and found them. They died, Sheila. I'm so sorry.'

'No,' Sheila said, her body starting to judder. 'No.'

'Yes,' Jude cried. 'They lived in Kent. Your grandparents' house was three streets away – you were staying there one weekend so your parents could go away for the night. A neighbour called the Catchers and your grandparents didn't have the paperwork showing you were Legal, and . . .'

He drew back slightly so he could look at Sheila. 'I'm so sorry,' he said, gripping her tightly. 'I wanted to tell you but Pip thought it would upset you. But these people – they're not your parents. We have to leave here now.'

Sheila didn't say anything for a few seconds. Then her eyes narrowed and she turned to Mrs Palmer. 'You said you were my mother,' she said. 'Why?'

'I . . . We . . .' Mrs Palmer floundered. 'We got your message and we talked and –'

'We always wanted a child,' Mr Palmer said stoutly, appearing from behind his wife. 'She wanted parents to look after. Is it so wrong?'

Jude's eyes flickered over to Sheila, who was staring at her supposed mother.

'You wanted a child?'

'Always,' Mrs Palmer nodded, opening her arms out. 'Just like you, Sheila. We've been waiting for you all our lives. When you called us up we were so happy. Come to your mother, Sheila. Come here.'

Sheila looked at her tentatively.

'No, Sheila,' Jude said, but she wasn't listening. She moved towards Mrs Palmer, whose outstretched arms enveloped her. Jude noticed the woman's eyes flicker over to her husband's. Something wasn't right, but Jude didn't know what it was.

'Sheila,' he said. 'We have to go. We have to go now.'

'No, Jude,' she said. 'I'm going to stay here. It's warm here. They need me here. I'm going to stay . . .'

'You hear that? She's staying. You're the one who's going,' Mr Palmer said, advancing on Jude. His eyes were watery; Jude could see his reflection in them. And then he saw something else. His eyes widened; Mr Palmer noticed and froze.

'You hold on to her,' he ordered his wife. 'I'll get this one. Two of them will buy us much more.'

Mrs Palmer nodded and her grip tightened around Sheila, who looked over at Jude uncertainly.

Jude looked through the window at the men getting out of the unmistakable Authorities van. Then he lunged at Mr Palmer and pushed him down the steps. Grabbing Sheila, he pulled her down the stairs and into the kitchen as the front door flew open and two men entered wearing protective uniforms with masks, gloves and hoods. They froze, breathless, but the men walked straight past the kitchen door and up the stairs, where they seized hold of Mr and Mrs Palmer.

'No!' the woman screamed as she was dragged down the stairs. It was a scream of abject terror, of fear so deep it made Jude tremble. 'No, leave us be! We have Surpluses. We called the hotline. Take them, not us. They're in the kitchen. They're –'

The man didn't appear to listen; he carried on dragging Mrs Palmer out through the front door. Immediately Jude pulled Sheila out of the back door and through the garden to an alleyway, and they sprinted back to the sewer where Peter was waiting, ashen-faced.

'I thought they'd got you,' he breathed.

'I did too,' Jude said grimly.

'So has she got the ring?' Peter asked as Jude crouched down to get his breath back. Sheila was still glassy-eyed, but her face was flushed from running.

Jude took Sheila's hand. 'Did you take Peter's ring, Sheila?'

Sheila nodded and reached into her pocket, pulling it out.

Peter snatched it, staring at it and turning it over in his hands.

'OK. Pincent Pharma?' he asked.

Jude nodded uncertainly. 'Sheila's been drugged,' he said. 'She can barely walk.'

'Then leave her here,' Peter said. 'We'll get her later. We need to get Pip out safely. He's our priority.'

'Pip,' Sheila whispered. 'Yes, save Pip.'

Jude looked at her translucent skin, her unfocused eyes, and felt a knot in his stomach. He'd saved Sheila once before and he'd do it again, as many times as it took. If she was broken, he'd mend her. If she was sad, he'd do everything in his power to make her happy. 'Pip is a priority,' he said quietly, 'but so is Sheila. Sheila is my priority,' he went on, his voice low. 'She isn't safe here.'

'Perhaps she should have thought about that before she stole my ring,' Peter said bitterly. 'Perhaps you should have thought of that before you let her send messages to me and my grandfather.'

'Don't you criticise me,' Jude said angrily. 'You've been up in Scotland playing happy families while I've been down here living in basements, tracking lorries full of dead people, watching everything collapse.'

'And I'd still be there with Anna and the children if Sheila hadn't tricked me into coming to London,' Peter said equally angrily. They stared at each other for a few seconds, each daring the other to respond. Instead, Sheila opened her eyes.

'Richard Pincent?' she asked anxiously. 'Is he here? Has he come for me?'

'No, Sheila. No one's taking you,' Jude said quickly.

'All right,' Peter relented. 'We'll bring her. She might be better by the time we get there. OK?'

Jude nodded. 'OK.' Then he held out his hand. 'And I'm sorry,' he said quietly. 'I didn't mean –'

'I know you didn't.' Peter looked down. 'I didn't either.' He took Jude's hand; they clasped each other in a wordless communication, then let go.

'So listen, what's the plan when we get to Pincent Pharma?' Peter asked lightly. 'Do we just stroll in and demand that Pip is released?'

'Something like that,' Jude said with a shrug and a half-smile. Then he slapped Peter on the back. 'Don't worry. I've got a plan. I'll fill you in on the way.'

'A plan?' Peter said quizzically. 'One that involves more tunnels, I presume?'

Jude grinned. 'You know me so well.' Then he looked at Peter carefully. 'Oh, and I think you should give me the ring.'

'You? Why?'

Jude raised an eyebrow. 'It's Peter Pincent's ring. I think most people would expect it to be with Peter Pincent, right?'

'I suppose so,' Peter said uncertainly.

'So it's safer with me,' Jude said seriously. 'You can trust me, you know.'

'I know.' Peter hesitated briefly, then took off the ring and handed it to his half-brother. 'So, off we go then,' he said, leaning down to pick Sheila up.

'It's OK, I've got her,' Jude said quickly, lifting her into his arms.

'Thank you,' Sheila whispered as he walked slowly behind Peter. 'Am I really your priority?'

'My only priority,' Jude whispered back, his eyes pricking with tears. 'I need you, Sheila. I need you just as much as you need me. I love you.'

'I love you too,' Sheila said happily, tightening her grip around his neck. 'And I'm sorry I took the ring,'

'I know,' Jude said, watching as her eyes closed.

'I just didn't want you to take it, Jude.'

Jude glanced over at Peter. He was only a couple of metres away.

'Me?' he whispered back uncertainly. 'I wasn't planning to take it.'

'Yes, you were. I saw the message you sent to Peter. I saw the ones you sent to Richard Pincent too,' she said sleepily. 'You shouldn't talk to that man, Jude. He's not very nice. He's not very nice at all.'

'What was that?' Peter asked, turning round. 'What did Sheila just say about my grandfather?'

Jude looked down at Sheila, but she was already fast asleep. 'Nothing,' he said carefully. 'She didn't say anything. Come on, let's get a move on. We haven't got much time.'

Chapter Twenty-one

The trees were bare of leaves, the ground hard and unyielding beneath Jude's feet, the barren landscape one of death, not life. Flies buzzed everywhere, gloating at the newly abundant landscape.

Behind Pincent Pharma, he could hear diggers. But they were not part of some construction programme – they were digging large pits, unofficial graves for the unmourned, the unacknowledged. He looked down at Sheila who had curled up like a cat in the brambles where they were hiding and was now fast asleep, her gentle breathing and soft skin incongruous against the harshness of their surroundings.

His heart thudding in his chest, Jude watched silently as Peter walked towards the perimeter gate of Pincent Pharma. He was stopped by the guard, who looked at him curiously then made a call. Two minutes later the guard ushered Peter through and another rushed from the reception area to escort him in. Jude stared at the doors as they closed behind his half-brother. Jude's plan was actually happening now. It was too late to change his mind now. Too late for any regrets, for second thoughts.

His eyes travelled back to Sheila, his flawed, difficult, beautiful sleeping princess. Then, with a sigh, he shook her. 'Sheila? Sheila, wake up.'

'Mmmmm. Jude?' She shook her head, disturbing her red curls so that they tumbled across her face. 'I don't want to. I'm asleep.'

'You have to wake up. We're going into Pincent Pharma.'

Suddenly Sheila was wide awake. 'Pincent Pharma? I don't want to go in there, Jude. I don't want to.' She started to shake, and Jude knew it wasn't from the cold.

'We have to,' he said. 'We'll be OK. I'm going to look after you. I promise.'

Sheila's eyes widened. 'Are you going to give Richard Pincent the ring?' she asked. 'Is that why you got Peter to give it to you?'

Jude didn't say anything for a moment. Then he took her hand. 'I'm sorry I didn't tell you about your parents,' he said quietly. 'I did look for them. I wanted to tell you . . .'

'That they were dead?' Sheila looked down, blinked slowly. Jude knew her eyes would be filling with tears. He pulled her towards him.

'They died a few years after you were taken to Grange Hall,' he said. 'Your mother joined the Underground. She trained as a nurse; she took out contraceptive implants so that supporters could have children. She was killed by an Authorities spy who pretended she wanted her implant removed. She was a hero, Sheila.'

Sheila nodded, a funny snorty noise coming from her throat. 'And my father?'

'He was the Opt Out,' Jude said. 'He died not long after. A heart attack. I think his heart was broken.'

Sheila sniffed loudly. 'They loved me then?' she asked tentatively. 'I do remember them loving me, but . . . but . . . at Grange Hall they said I'd made it up. They said I was Surplus, that my parents never wanted me.'

'They wanted you,' Jude whispered. 'Just like I do now.'

Sheila looked up at him earnestly. 'OK,' she said.

'OK?' Jude asked.

'OK I'll come in with you. I trust you, Jude. You tell me what to do and I'll do it.'

Jude looked down at her tenderly. He could hear Pip's voice in his head: *When you're ready to lead, Jude, you will know because people want to follow you.* Was he ready? Was he really ready for what lay ahead? He steeled himself. If he had doubts, he couldn't let Sheila see them.

'Good,' he whispered. 'Let's go then. Just do exactly what I say and we'll be fine.'

'Exactly what you say,' Sheila agreed.

Her eyes met Jude's; slowly, tenderly, he drew her towards him. As their lips met he felt an electrical charge shoot through him and for a moment, the plan didn't matter – nothing mattered except being here, holding Sheila. But he knew he couldn't stay there. Reluctantly, he pulled away and squeezed her hand. Then, moving tentatively to prevent himself from snapping twigs underfoot and alerting the Pincent guards to his presence, he crept towards the perimeter gate, motioning for Sheila to follow him, towards the door he had disabled earlier that morning. When got there he pulled Sheila towards him, flat against the wall. He tried the door, hoping against hope that no one had noticed the red light above it was no longer lit, then smiled with relief as it opened. Taking a deep breath, he jumped inside with Sheila and closed it behind them.

Peter felt a sense of foreboding as he was finally taken to a lift linking the reception area to the rest of the building. It was a terrifying plan, walking into Pincent Pharma and asking to see his grandfather, but he wasn't sure what the alternative was. And Jude was right: if his grandfather really needed the ring, then Peter would be safe. If his grandfather really needed the ring, they could name their terms.

He remembered the first time he'd been here, remembered trying his best not to be blown away by the whiteness, the newness, the sheer scale of the place. Now it felt different, it felt like a terrifying prison, the last bastion of an emperor who was losing his empire. Gone was the busy flurry of white coats; now fewer people could be seen, all walking with their heads down. Guards were everywhere, their grey uniforms reminding Peter of the corridors of Grange Hall; it was a colour that sucked out all joy, all life.

The guard who had been sent to meet him in reception had taken him into a small room and searched him comprehensively, stripping him of his clothes, of his dignity. Now, finally, he was being taken to his grandfather, the man he despised, to the man he wished more than anything he wasn't related to.

The lift felt slow – too slow, but eventually they reached the fifth floor and stepped out on to the luxurious carpet that covered Richard Pincent's suite.

His office door, a few metres away, opened and he appeared, the thin smile on his face not disguising the bags under his eyes, the strain, the exhaustion.

'Peter,' he said, walking towards his grandson.

'I've come for Pip,' Peter said levelly. 'I know he's here. I want you to let him go. Now. With me.'

Richard said nothing for a few seconds, then he laughed. 'And the ring? I understand you don't have it.'

'You'll have the ring when Pip is free. And the Surpluses,' Peter said, his voice wavering slightly with emotion.

'I'll have the ring now or Anna will die, do you hear me?' his grandfather said suddenly, his face going red. 'She will die and the Surpluses will die. Slowly. Painfully. And you will watch them suffer. They will die knowing that you didn't save them.'

'You don't know where Anna is,' Peter said levelly. 'Don't throw empty threats at me.'

'I don't know where they are?' Richard smiled

coldly. 'No, Peter. It seems that you are the one who doesn't know where they are. They are here. Derek brought them here. I only discovered them this morning – can you imagine what a delight that was?'

He laughed as the blood drained from Peter's face.

'You're lying,' Peter seethed. 'You're lying.'

'You are a fool,' Richard said, shaking his head. He moved forward, grabbed Peter by the shoulders. 'Get me the ring, Peter,' he shouted. 'Get me the ring now.'

Peter stared resolutely ahead. 'You don't have them,' he repeated. 'I know you don't.'

His grandfather let go of him. Then he walked back to his desk and picked up his phone. 'Bring the girl up. The Surplus girl and her Surplus progeny,' he said, his lip curling with distaste as he spoke. He turned back to Peter. 'We'll see whether you'll have nothing to say when the baby is killed,' he said darkly. 'We'll start with the smallest, shall we, and work our way up?'

Peter swallowed uncomfortably. In his pocket was the bleeper Jude had given him for emergency; silently he pressed the button. Jude would hear it; Jude would come.

Please, Jude, he thought silently. *Please don't let me down.*

Jude didn't notice the flashing light on his handheld device; he was too busy orienting himself, working out which way to turn. They were in a vast, bleak corridor, too visible, too vulnerable; they had to get to their destination quickly.

It was the smell that had made him freeze moment-arily. A smell of scrubbed floors, of disinfectant. Sheila smelt it too and he felt her stiffen with fear. He hadn't feared coming back until now, hadn't really understood what it would mean to be back inside Pincent Pharma, inside the centre of Richard Pincent's power base, the prison where Sheila had been kept. But the smell brought memories back more vividly than anything else, reminding him how dangerous this place was, how sinister. He took her hand and squeezed it; she gripped it hard.

'You ready?' he asked.

Sheila nodded.

'OK. This way,' he said, pointing down the corridor. They were on the west wing of the building, the opposite side from where he'd been kept a year before, but it looked the same: white soulless corri-dors, heavy doors with numbers on them hiding what lay behind. Silence surrounded them; the rooms could be filled with people but not a sound would escape. Jude moved quickly, tugging Sheila behind him, until they got to the door he was looking for: the door to room W576. He opened it and he and Sheila hurried in.

She glanced around the room apprehensively. Jude, however, wasn't interested in the room; he was already looking up at the ceiling, at the vent. He'd chosen this room specifically, had searched the whole of the ground floor for the easiest access to the hub, to the control centre.

'I'm going up,' he said to Sheila. 'I need you to help me.'

'Up there?' Sheila's brow wrinkled.

'The vent. I can get to the camera system that way. I can find out where Pip is, where Peter is.'

'Is that where . . .' Sheila looked at him searchingly.

'Where I found you? Yes,' Jude said quietly. He moved towards her, pulled her into him. Then he lifted up her chin so she was looking right at him. 'Can you do this? I'm going to go up and see what's going on. You have to wait here. Silently. Then I'll come back.'

'How soon?' Sheila whispered worriedly.

'Soon,' Jude promised. 'Very soon.'

'OK.' Sheila laced her fingers together, looking at Jude sternly when he appeared uncertain. 'I can take your weight,' she said tersely. 'I trust you. You have to trust me.'

'I trust you,' Jude replied, placing his foot in her hands and jumping up. He grabbed hold of the vent and punched it hard – there was no time to undo screws. As he punched he lost his balance and almost fell, but on the second attempt it gave way and he hooked his hands round the opening, pulling at the vent until it lay in pieces on the floor. Then he hauled himself up into the void above the ceiling.

'See you soon, princess,' he whispered, and started to wriggle through the cramped, hot ceiling cavities of Pincent Pharma. Keeping his head down to stop dust getting in his eyes, he pushed himself forward with his elbows and knees, wincing every so often when something sharp dug into him or dust and other material fell into his hair, on to his back. From what he could remember, if he travelled north he should get to a security hub in a few minutes.

And once he was there . . . Once he was there, he'd be in control again. Jude knew the Pincent Pharma security system better than any other. It might have been upgraded since his last encounter with it a year or so ago, but that didn't worry him. There was no system he couldn't take over and now this one – his old foe, old ally – was going to help him once more.

Jude took a deep breath and forced himself forward. The passage was narrowing and dust particles were getting into his mouth, into his chest, but he struggled on. He didn't have much time. Too much was depending on him.

Finally he felt the passage widen and saw a low light ahead. He sighed with relief and, upping his pace, squirmed towards it. Quickly he took out his trusted handheld video link device, connected it to the system hub and started to search the cameras. He flicked from image to image – the reception area, the corridors, the laboratories. It seemed spookily empty, apart from the guards who patrolled every corridor and stood outside every door. There seemed to be more guards than staff these days. A few white-coated men and women could still be seen, their faces serious as they tested, analysed and checked the white tablets in front of them. Jude noticed that a woman in one of the labs looked strange, her body bowed over the table in front of her. He zoomed in and saw that she was sweating profusely. Her hand moved to her throat. She picked up a glass of water and started to drink but then she dropped it and it smashed on the floor. Worried faces looked up; moments later, guards rushed in, their faces masked, and took her from the room. No one said a word. No one looked at anyone else. Jude felt a shiver go down his spine.

Shaking himself, he continued his search. He looked at room after room, many empty, then suddenly felt his heart quicken. Anna. Anna was here! He stared in disbelief – she was meant to be in Scotland. Peter had left her in Scotland, safe. This wasn't right. This wasn't right at all. Trembling, he zoomed in. She was sitting silently on the floor, a baby and a small child in her arms. The baby was crying and Anna's face was tear-stained. The child was silent, his eyes wide, afraid. Jude moved the camera to see if anyone else was in the room and as it moved Anna glanced up at it, a look of disgust on her face. Then she buried her head in her children's hair, pulling them more tightly towards her. The door opened and a guard walked in, grabbing her roughly.

Jude watched in horror, his mind racing. How many other secrets lay buried within these walls? How many more prisoners? He continued to flick through the screens. He found Sheila and had to force himself not to linger, staring at her freckles, her red hair, her frightened yet still determined eyes. He had to focus. He didn't have much time.

He gasped. The screen showed a room full of children, then another and another, more and more. Jude moved between the images, his eyes widening. He'd never seen so many children together. There were hundreds of them – ten, twenty to a room – holding each other for comfort, makeshift sanitation in one corner of each room and a bucket of what appeared to be food in the other. Like a farm, Jude thought with a thud. But farms had a purpose. What use would these children be? What sinister plan did Richard Pincent have for them? Jude narrowed his eyes. Whatever the plan, it would be abandoned. He would see to that. His hand moved towards his pocket and he felt for the ring, the ring Richard Pincent so desperately wanted. He took it out and looked at it for a moment, then put it in his mouth.

The madness would end, Jude resolved.

Everything would change.

Mama! Mamanana! Want go home. Want go home, Mamanana.'

Anna squeezed Ben's hand and pulled him towards her. 'Soon,' she whispered. 'Soon, my darling.'

At least Molly was asleep, she thought heavily. At least her daughter wasn't staring at the grey walls like her and Ben. Back in Pincent Pharma – she'd know this place if she were blindfolded. Everything she'd feared, everything she'd been so desperate to escape was here. It had happened; her nightmare had come true. And yet somehow she felt strangely calm.

The door opened suddenly and her grip tightened around Ben, who looked up hopefully. 'Home?' he asked. 'Go home?'

'Home!' The man laughed, then appeared to shake himself. 'You're coming with me,' he said, grabbing Anna and ignoring the children as though he couldn't bear to look at them. Anna managed to hoist Molly in one arm and take Ben's hand with her free one. 'I can walk more easily if you don't hold me like that,' she said tightly. 'It's not like we're going to be able to run anywhere, is it? Have you seen how long my brother's legs are?'

The guard glanced down at Ben with distaste, then shrugged. 'Suit yourself,' he said. 'But you try anything and you'll regret it, understand?'

'Where are we going?' Anna asked.

'None of your business,' the guard replied. 'Just follow me.'

'Teter?' Ben asked as they walked. 'Teter here?'

Anna shook her head. 'No, Ben. Peter isn't here. He's with the people who are going to burn this place to the ground. He's going to rescue us, Ben. Just you wait.' She spoke loudly; she wanted the guard to know she wasn't scared. Wanted Ben to know.

'Peter? He's the other one, isn't he?' the guard asked, turning round. 'The one upstairs?' He laughed again. 'Little brat's right. He is here.'

Anna felt her heart flip. 'Here?' she gasped. 'No, you're wrong. He's not here. He's –'

'Captured like the rest of them,' the guard said triumphantly. He stopped and leant down so that his face was only centimetres from Ben's. 'Your Peter is an idiot,' he said, a little smile on his face. 'He isn't brave, he's just stupid. Like your mum here. You should be scared, little fellow, because nothing good's going to happen to you. Nothing good at all.'

Ben's eyes widened and Anna pulled him away. 'I'm not his mother, I'm his sister,' she said angrily. 'And Peter is brave. He's braver than anyone else I've ever met. And if he's here, that's a good thing. You're the one who should be scared, not me, not Ben and not my daughter.'

She had wanted to protect Ben, reassure him, but as she spoke she realised that she meant every word. She wasn't scared. Not for herself or for her children. Because she'd faced her nightmares, faced her worst fears, and she was still standing – they all were. 'If you're going to take us to see Richard Pincent, can we move a bit more quickly?' she said sharply to the guard. 'There are a few things I'd like to say to him.'

The guard opened his mouth to respond, then appeared to change his mind. Instead he upped his pace and Anna lifted Ben up and, carrying him and Molly in her arms, strode after him.

Peter willed Jude to hurry. Without the ring, he had nothing to offer for Anna's freedom, her life. He could play for time, but it would run out eventually.

His grandfather was pacing up and down, sweat

dripping from his forehead.

'Why do you need the ring anyway?' Peter asked. 'What do you want with it?'

'What do I want with it?' His grandfather rounded on him angrily. 'I want what should have been mine years ago.' He stumbled slightly, grabbed hold of his desk. Then he snatched up a glass of water and drank it in one, looking at Peter insolently as he did so. He picked up his phone. 'Where is the girl? She should be here by now. And get me some more water.'

He turned back to Peter, as though almost surprised to see him there. His eyes were glassy; they appeared confused. 'Water,' he gasped. 'Water. Give me water.'

Peter watched him wide-eyed, then darted forward and wrestled him to the floor. This was his chance, he realised. Grabbing a computer lead, he managed to wrap it round his grandfather's hands. It wasn't much but it was enough. He would get out of this room, he would find Anna, they would escape. He didn't care about anything else.

His grandfather's eyes were bulging in anger as he wrestled with the lead, still calling for water.

Peter wasn't listening. He jumped up and ran to the door. He would surprise the guard bringing Anna and the children. He would overpower him, he would . . .

But as he got to the door it opened, knocking him sideways, and into the room walked a woman dressed in pale blue, her face covered in heavy make-up, her eyes dead, a large jug of water in her hands. Hillary Wright looked from Richard to Peter, then turned back to the corridor and called a guard to restrain Peter before putting the jug down on the desk. 'Your secretary gave me this,' she said to Richard as he struggled up off the floor. 'Perhaps you can explain to me what's going on here.'

Jude looked back at the images. There was one more person he needed to find, one more cross to mark in his mental matrix of the building. Frantically he sped through the images for the first floor, the second, the third. He couldn't see into Richard Pincent's office using this hub and could only guess that Peter was there waiting for him, wondering . . . He would have no idea that Anna was close by, Jude realised. But no matter. He had to stay focused.

At last he found what he was looking for – a simple room containing a single bed with no mattress. A frail-looking man was sitting on it, his face calm, his limbs still. Only his eyes were animated, their intense blue making Jude forget himself for a second. Pip looked old. Had they taken his Longevity away? Of course they had. His hair was white now, his skin thin and pale, but his jaw was still determined. This was not a man who had given up. Was it?

Something moved in the corner of the screen and Jude jumped as the door opened and his old adversary walked in. Derek Samuels. The man who would have had him killed given the chance. Jude felt the hairs on the back of his neck stand up. Would he beat Pip? Would Jude be forced to watch the leader of the

Underground being subjected to torture? To interrogation? Would he be able to save Pip before . . .

But as he watched, he felt his head clouding with confusion. Because as Derek approached Pip, his hands moved towards him not in a threatening way but in what Jude knew was a gesture of friendship. It was small – a hand on the arm – but unmistakable. Pip stood up, spoke, his face animated then serious. He nodded and Derek smiled.

Jude shuddered. The smile. He remembered it too well. The smile of an evil man. The smile of the devil.

He closed his eyes. He needed to think and the images in front of him were blurring his thoughts. This must be part of the plan, but how? Jude thought quickly.

Pip had brought him here. Pip, with his messages sent to Richard Pincent, to Peter, made to look like Sheila's, like an amateur's. Pip had known that Jude would suspect Sheila, had known that he would protect her. But when Sheila had told him she'd been protecting Jude, he'd realised that the real culprit could only have been one person. And he'd known instinctively that it was now up to Jude to take over, finish what he'd started, even if the path ahead was not entirely clear to Jude, even if he didn't yet understand the rules of the game he was playing.

The lion chasing his tail, the mouse running free . . . Jude had assumed that the lion was Richard Pincent, that he and Pip were the mouse, that Pip knew what he was doing, that everything was a diversion, a smokescreen. But it couldn't be. He'd missed something, had heard wrong. Hadn't he?

Jude closed his eyes. He knew he hadn't misheard, knew he hadn't missed anything. But that meant that Pip was . . . that suggested that Pip had lied, that he was on the side of darkness.

Even as the thought occurred to him he knew it couldn't be true. But he also knew that he needed to hear what they were saying. Frantically he pulled out his handheld device and connected it, sweat dripping off his forehead and making his fingers slip as they twisted wires together. As he connected it, he saw the light flashing, knew immediately that Peter needed him. But Peter would have to wait.

'They're downstairs,' Derek was saying.

'All of them?' Pip asked.

Derek nodded. 'They can't stay here for long. It's disgusting down there. The smell . . .'

Pip looked serious for a minute. 'And Anna?'

'He found her. She's going upstairs. To Peter.'

Pip nodded. 'Peter has the ring?'

'No,' Derek said. 'He was scanned at the door. But the other boy has it. Jude. He and the other girl are hiding in the west wing.'

Pip's eyes lit up. 'Yes, I knew I could rely on him to do my bidding and bring everyone here. It's all come together nicely, Derek. For a while there I was a bit worried.'

'Me too.' Derek smiled.

'So then it is time, is it not?'

'It is time,' Derek agreed.

He helped Pip up. Jude stared open-mouthed, struggling to breathe. His airways were constricting, his head clouding. Had this been Pip's game all along? Was the Underground the lion? Was Jude the lion? Had he been chasing his own tail while Pip, the mouse, had been working with Derek Samuels to deliver them all up to Richard Pincent? They were all here – Peter, Sheila, Anna, the Surpluses. There was no way out.

Except there was, Jude realised. He still had the ring. He had to leave, had to escape. Then he would issue his demands and Richard would acquiesce. He would have to. Desperately, Jude disconnected his handheld device and wriggled back through the ceiling cavity towards Sheila. He'd brought her here; he was responsible for her. He'd promised to protect her and he wouldn't break that promise. He wouldn't.

He could see the broken vent in front of him and moved frantically towards it. When he got there he could see Sheila's face looking up anxiously. He looked down, met her gaze. 'Sheila,' he whispered hoarsely, 'we have to get out of here. We have to get as far away as possible. Now.'

But Sheila didn't reply; her face disappeared from view and was replaced by the face of a guard. Before Jude could react, he was pulled down to the floor below.

'I'm sorry,' Sheila cried. 'He just came in. He saw the vent. I'm sorry, Jude. He threatened to . . . He said he'd –'

'It's OK,' Jude said as the guard grabbed him. 'It doesn't matter now anyway,' he added, his head slumping. 'It's all over, Sheila. It's all over.'

Chapter Twenty-two

Jude felt sick as he was pushed roughly down the corridor. Sick, dizzy and empty. Everyone had come here because of him. Because he thought he knew – thought he was ready to lead.

He was ready for nothing. He hung his head, unable to look over at Sheila, unable to offer her any hope, any reassurance.

He stumbled and the guard behind him kicked him angrily, told him to be careful, told him not to make any trouble. He took out his walkie-talkie. 'Mr Samuels, sir. I've got them. The boy and the girl. We're on corridor W3.' He listened to instructions. 'Yes, sir,' he said, and put the device away. Sheila was whimpering; all Jude wanted to do was to reach out, to protect her. But he knew he couldn't. He had failed. There was no use pretending.

Another guard appeared in front of them and looked quizzically at the first.

'I'm taking them to Room W467,' the first explained. 'Mr Samuels' orders.'

The second guard shook his head. 'Hillary Wright

is here. She has ordered that all guards report directly to her,' he said. 'I'll need to call up.'

'Directly to her?' the first guard asked sarcastically. 'Since when do we follow the Secretary General's orders at Pincent Pharma?'

'Since now,' the second guard said.

'Well, I'm calling Mr Samuels,' the first insisted. Jude watched him put his gun back in its holster. 'See what he has to say about this.'

'You don't understand,' the second guard said. No gun, Jude noticed. Maybe strapped to his ankle. Still, it would take time to pull it out. He looked at Sheila. They had to try, didn't they? Even if they died in the attempt. Maybe that would be better. 'It doesn't matter what he says,' the second guard continued. 'She's the boss now. She's in Mr Pincent's office. She –'

Jude took his chance, grabbing Sheila and running down the corridor. They tore round the corner, heading for the West exit. He could hear the guards charging after them, yelling at them to stop. Shouting that they would shoot. Still Jude ran, his heart pounding in his chest. He only needed a few minutes. He could lock down the system, close the doors, shut off the cameras. He could do something. He could get Sheila out. Get the others out, too. It couldn't end like this. He couldn't be a failure, an also-ran, the person who led Peter, Sheila, Anna, the children to their deaths. Not without a fight. Not without . . .

'Stop! Or we fire!'

He stopped, fell to the floor. Sheila screamed. The

noise, louder than anything he'd ever heard. A shot. A bullet. Then another one. Crack! He felt his chest. He wasn't hurt. Sheila? Had they shot Sheila? He opened his mouth and a strange sound came out, barely human. He grabbed her, pulled her towards him. 'No. Sheila, no.'

'She isn't hurt, Jude.'

A voice. A familiar voice. A voice he once trusted. He looked up. Pip and Derek Samuels were walking towards them. He edged backwards, turned. On the floor behind him the guards lay slumped in pools of blood. His chest constricted. He looked back at Pip. 'You,' he said hoarsely. 'It was you. You told Peter to come. You told Richard about the ring.'

'Yes,' Pip said, his blue eyes looking intently at Jude. 'And you came, Jude. I knew you would. Give me the ring, please.'

Derek was pointing his gun at Jude. He looked around desperately but there was nowhere to run, nowhere to hide. Hating himself, he handed the ring over.

'You knew I'd bring Peter and Sheila,' Jude said miserably. 'Like lambs to the slaughter. To him.' He looked at Derek Samuels with angry hostility. 'To this monster. Your friend.'

Pip looked at the ring, his eyes shining, and put it on. Then he glanced over at Derek. 'A monster,' he said thoughtfully. 'Yes, I suppose he is. But then again . . .' He looked back at Jude, holding out his hand to help him up. Jude ignored him, turning instead to Sheila, who was staring at Pip in horror. 'It's time,' Pip said. 'It's time for the truth to come out, Jude. Will you come with us?'

'Never,' Jude said bitterly. 'I trusted you. Everyone trusted you.'

Pip smiled sadly. 'Yes, Jude, I know.' Then he turned to Derek. 'Will you bring them, please?' he asked.

Derek looked at him for a moment, then quickly moved over to Jude and Sheila, taking their arms, pulling them up, then pushing them down the corridor towards the lift.

Chapter Twenty-three

The silence was electrifying as the lift containing Pip, Derek, Jude and Sheila shot up to the fifth floor, to Richard Pincent's suite. Jude felt as though he'd been kicked, punched, picked up and punched again. Pip had been like a surrogate father to Peter. All Jude had wanted to do was to earn his respect, to prove himself to Pip – and for what? Had the Underground been a sham all along? Was that why it had never come close to winning? Had Pip been Derek's agent, forming a resistance movement to ensure that all rebels, all those who disagreed with the system, could be carefully managed, contained, kept at bay?

He couldn't believe it, didn't want to believe it. Even now as Pip walked in front of them, even now as Derek pushed them roughly down the corridor towards Richard's office, Jude was waiting for the look, waiting for a twitch, something – anything – that told him Pip was playing a game, a complicated game that he didn't understand, a game that explained everything, that made it all OK.

Pip didn't even turn round; he just walked slowly,

shuffling along the corridor like an old man. Jude hated him. He hated him more than he'd ever hated anyone – even Richard Pincent. Because Richard Pincent had never pretended to be someone he wasn't. Because Richard Pincent had never earned Jude's love and then smashed it into little pieces.

As Jude approached the office, Pip stepped aside and Derek moved forward to knock. Slowly he opened the door to reveal Richard leaning on his desk looking terrible, his skin a strange green colour, his eyes bulging. At the sight of Derek he stood up and smiled. 'Derek,' he said. 'You have the Surpluses?'

He saw Jude and Sheila and frowned uncertainly, then his eyes lit up. 'You have these ones as well? See, Peter? There's no one left now.'

Peter's face was white as Jude and Sheila were pushed into the office. Sheila stumbled and fell to the ground. Peter immediately held out his hand to help her up but she shook her head, wrapping her arms round her knees and hiding her head in them. Peter looked at Jude searchingly, but Jude could barely meet his eyes – he had nothing but despair to communicate.

There was another knock at the door, another guard, another delivery – this time Anna and the children. Jude flinched as she walked in, her pained eyes seeming to bore into him. She saw Peter and walked slowly towards him, faltering on her feet, the children in her arms. Ben immediately reached for Peter's neck and Anna released her hold as Peter's arms wrapped around him, around her, around Molly, like branches –

a silent communication, a bond that inspired both awe and jealousy in Jude.

'I'm so sorry,' Peter said.

'No,' Anna said. 'Don't be. He should be the sorry one.'

She turned towards Richard, who staggered forward. 'The ring,' he said to Derek. 'You have the ring?'

Derek nodded, taking it from Pip and handing it to Richard. 'Here it is,' he said.

Richard took the ring and exhaled loudly, then closed his eyes for a second. 'Yes,' he breathed. 'Yes.' He stared at it, turning it over and over in his hands. 'But where is the formula?' He frowned, then shrugged and pressed a buzzer on his desk; two seconds later a scientist appeared at his door. 'Here,' Richard said, giving the ring to him. 'The formula is on here. Find it. Use it. Reboot the system. Do it now.'

The scientist nodded urgently, took the ring and left. Richard looked around grimly. 'You've done well, Derek,' he said. 'Very well.'

Derek smiled silkily.

'How has he done well?' Hillary asked suddenly. 'Richard, will you please tell me what's going on? What is this ring? Why are these people here, in your office?'

'The ring?' Richard laughed. 'The ring is our answer, Hillary. We will be reborn.'

'Reborn? What are you talking about?' She looked piercingly at Richard, but he wasn't listening – he had poured a large glass of water and drank it down in one before refilling it.

There was another knock at the door and everyone swung round. It was the scientist. 'Mr Pincent, sir,' he said tentatively. 'We've looked at the ring. Several of us. It doesn't appear to have the formula on it, sir. Just the initials A.F. and a rudimentary engraving of a flower.'

Richard looked at him angrily. 'Look again,' he barked. 'The ring has the formula on it. I know it has.'

'You know?' Pip asked quietly. No one seemed to have heard him apart from Jude, who froze. There was something about his voice. Something different.

'We have looked. We have scrutinised it,' the scientist continued, his voice shaking slightly. 'But there is nothing on it, Mr Pincent. Nothing that suggests a formula of any sort.'

'Formula?' Hillary asked. 'What formula?'

'Look again!' Richard screamed, ignoring Hillary. 'Look again and again and again! It's there. I know it is.'

'You know nothing, Richard.' Again, Pip's voice. Again, quiet, different. This time Richard heard. He looked at Pip curiously.

'You,' he said with distaste. 'Pip. What sort of a name is Pip?'

He turned to Derek. 'Have you not been torturing this man? Why is he still able to speak? Why is he still able to stand?' He lurched forward and steadied himself, grabbing hold of the corner of his desk.

'Pip is not my real name,' Pip said. 'But of course

you knew that.'

'I don't care what your real name is,' Richard said through gritted teeth. 'I care only that you suffer. That you are tormented.'

Jude looked down at his arms, which were covered in goosebumps. Peter was still wrapped around his family and Sheila was rocking gently backwards and forwards on the floor. But Jude felt like an electrical current had suddenly entered the room, a current only he could feel. He and Pip. He didn't understand it. He just knew a storm was coming. He just knew that lightning was about to strike.

'I have suffered,' Pip said quietly. 'I have suffered for many years. Too many.'

'You have suffered?' Hillary asked, her voice shrill. She walked over to Pip, surveyed him as though he were an animal being taken to market. 'You murdered people. You are a terrorist of the worst kind. You are despicable. Richard is right – you deserve only to suffer, to feel pain.'

Pip nodded slowly. 'You are right,' he said, his voice soft, hypnotic, 'but not for the reason you think.' He lifted his head and looked back at Richard. 'The ring,' he said. 'It isn't what you think it is. It isn't the eternal circle of life. You have been chasing a chimera, chasing your tail. There is no formula to be found on it.'

Richard's eyes bulged with anger. 'How dare you!' he shouted. 'How dare you talk to me! You know nothing. You are a criminal who knows nothing.' He glared back at the scientists. 'I thought I told you to

250

keep looking!' he shouted. 'I thought I told you to –'

'The eternal circle of life is the circle of life and death, Richard. That is what needs protecting. That is what I have been trying to protect all this time. The circle of life and death. I knew that Longevity would not work for ever. Nature can be interrupted by man – we can build dams, we can create drugs, we can erect houses, bridges. But it cannot be stopped forever. Nature finds a way through. Even through concrete, Richard, a weed will grow. The virus, the epidemic sweeping the world – it is not a result of Longevity being copied. It is a result of Nature finally finding a way in. Longevity has stayed the same while Nature's army has morphed, mutated. It has won, Richard, as I always knew it would.'

'Copied?' Hillary asked, beady-eyed. 'What do you mean?'

'Longevity was not contaminated,' Pip said gently. 'It simply ran out of steam.'

Richard stared at him. 'How dare you!' he seethed. 'Who are you to tell me –'

'You know who I am, Richard,' Pip said, walking towards him. He glanced over at Jude, his blue mesmerising eyes communicating something important that Jude only seemed to understand subconsciously, filling him with a warmth, with the knowledge that he had not been betrayed. 'You recognise my voice,' Pip continued gently. 'You are trying to come up with an explanation, trying to tell yourself that your memory is playing tricks on you. But you know it is me.'

'I don't know what you're talking about. You're a madman. You're –' Richard said, but Pip didn't take any notice.

'The ring never had the formula on it. It was a wild goose chase, Richard – something for you to focus on, something to absorb you as your world crumbled,' he continued, still moving towards Richard, his voice soft, gentle. 'And even if it had, the formula is not what you need. Longevity cannot fight the virus. Your reign is over.'

Richard shook his head desperately. He was looking at Pip as though he'd never seen him before, as though it was a surprise to find him in the same room.

'Scrutinise the ring again,' Richard pleaded. 'There must be something . . .'

'It's over, Richard,' Pip said. 'You know it's over. You can't lie any more. There's nothing to lie for.'

'What's over?' Hillary demanded, looking at Richard fearfully. 'What is he talking about?'

Richard didn't appear to hear her. Instead he walked towards Pip uncertainly, real fear on his face. 'The eyes,' he said, his voice barely audible. 'Your eyes.'

'Surgeons can't do much with eyes, I'm afraid,' Pip said, smiling now. 'Jawlines, noses, chins, the shape of cheeks, but not eyes. Not really. Still, I rather like my eyes.'

'No!' Richard said, shaking violently. 'No, it's impossible. You're dead.' He looked at Derek. 'He's dead. You killed him.'

'No.' Derek shook his head. 'No, Richard, I didn't.'

'Who's dead?' Hillary enquired anxiously. 'Who are you talking about?'

Richard opened his mouth then closed it again. He stared at Pip as though encountering a ghost. Then he started to shake.

'Albert Fern,' he whispered.

'Hello again, Richard,' Pip said, the smile leaving his face. 'It's been a long time, hasn't it?'

Chapter Twenty-four

For a minute or so, it felt as if the world stood still. No one said anything, no one moved. Then suddenly Richard ran at Peter, wrenching Molly from his grasp and holding her up in the air. 'Give me the formula, you bastard!' he shouted at Pip. 'Give it to me now or she dies! They all die!'

Molly's screams filled the room as Richard shook her. Anna stared wide-eyed, then leapt at him, kicking and biting him like a wild animal. 'Give me my child!' she screamed. 'Give her to me!'

Peter snatched Molly from his arms as Richard fell to the ground, and Anna continued her frenzied attack until Peter gently pulled her away.

'Derek,' Richard gasped. 'Derek, kill them! Kill them all!'

Derek turned slowly to look at him, then shook his head.

'Derek,' Richard said, his voice strangled, staring at his head of security uncertainly. 'Derek, don't do this. Not now. We've got Albert. He'll give us the formula. We can rule the world again, Derek. You and me. We can do it – you know we can.'

'No, Richard,' Derek said. He walked over to the desk and leant against it. He took a deep breath and let it out, then held his head in his hands.

'He's ill,' Hillary said cautiously. 'Guard's, he's –'

But before she could finish her command, Derek straightened up. 'So long,' he breathed. 'Too long. It's been too long.'

'What's been too long?' Richard seethed. 'What are you talking about?'

'I've been doing this so long I hardly know who I am,' Derek said. He looked around the room wildly. 'Who am I? What am I?'

'You know who you are,' Pip said gently. 'You know, Derek.'

'I don't know,' Jude said, his voice level, 'but I want to know. I want to know everything. You . . . You're Albert Fern?' he asked Pip incredulously.

Pip nodded.

'You invented Longevity?'

'No!' Richard yelped. 'No, Derek killed him. Albert Fern is dead.'

'Not dead,' Derek said. 'He's not dead, Richard. I didn't do it.'

There was a shocked silence. 'You couldn't do it,' Pip said gently. Then he took a deep breath and walked over to the window, before turning back to Jude. 'Derek understood,' he said simply. 'Richard paid him to kill me, but he wasn't a killer. He was a security guard. He was a man. A man with insight,

255

with intelligence. A brave man. A man who could see, like me, that it was already too late to stop Richard, that the wheels were already in motion, but that whatever happened, the circle of life had to be protected. That however Richard's new world played out, new life must be created, so that when this day came, all would not be lost. Humans are destructive animals, Jude, but they are also wise ones. They couldn't be allowed to die out simply because of the aspirations of one man.'

Jude was trembling and tears filled his eyes. 'I knew you were messaging Richard,' he said, his voice catching. 'I thought at first it was Sheila. But then she ran away to find her parents. She'd thought it was me. I realised . . .' He looked over at her beseechingly. Slowly, she uncurled herself and stood up, then reached over and took his hand.

'You realised that you'd thought what I'd encouraged you to think,' Pip said gently. 'I'm sorry, Jude. I couldn't tell you what was happening. It was a long game. A very long game. And the end was in sight. I had to keep Richard preoccupied while Derek and I implemented our endgame.'

'You sent me that message?' Peter looked at Pip uncertainly. 'You let them take Anna?'

Pip nodded. 'I didn't expect you to come to London. When we discovered . . . We knew Anna wouldn't be safe. Knew we had to get there before anyone else did. Richard was closing in. We had to act fast.'

'But she was taken by his men,' Peter continued, shaking his head in disbelief, in anger.

'Derek's men. There's a difference,' Pip said gravely. 'I understand why you're angry, Peter, but we had to do what we did. We had to keep you safe. We hadn't planned on . . . Events took over – the attacks on the Underground, Richard closing in on your safe house. I couldn't risk it, couldn't risk everything unravelling. Pincent Pharma is the most protected building in the world. It may not be comfortable, but it is safe.'

Jude's mind was racing. 'The Surpluses,' he gasped. 'You took the Surpluses too?'

'Yes,' Pip nodded slowly. 'Left in Surplus Halls, they would have been attacked, torched like everyone else under suspicion. We hadn't banked on the Authorities blaming the Underground. That changed things.'

'But Derek,' Jude said, looking at the man he'd feared for so long. 'He wanted to kill me. He would have killed us all.'

'No,' Pip said.

Derek looked up miserably. 'I'm sorry,' he said, falling to his knees. 'I'm sorry. I had to. We agreed. All that mattered was the endgame. The eternal circle of life.'

'That mattered more than us?' Jude asked Pip stonily.

Pip shook his head. 'You *are* the eternal circle of life,' he said. 'You, and Jude, and Anna, and Sheila and the children. Especially the children. You are true renewal. Longevity threatened to break that circle; we had to keep the link.'

'Longevity keeps the human race alive forever,' Richard gasped angrily from the floor where he still lay. He was shaking, clawing at his throat.

'No.' Pip shook his head. 'Not forever. Life is a changeable thing, Richard. Evolution taught us that adaptation is the key to survival. No drug could ever defy that fundamental tenet.'

'Derek. My friend,' Richard managed to say, his voice hoarse and pained. 'Derek, I forgive you for what you've done. We all have our weak moments. Derek, help me. Get me water. Torture this man. Get the formula. Everything will be OK again. Everything . . .'

Everyone turned to look at Derek, whose eyes darted over to Pip and back again. Then he laughed, a terrifying laugh full of pain, desperation and anger. 'Your friend?' He shook his head. 'I have never been your friend, Richard. Never.'

'Of course you have. You're delirious, that's all,' Richard groaned. 'You've been brainwashed. Albert's got to you – I can see that now. But you can't let him win. You can't, Derek.'

'Over a hundred years I've worked for you,' Derek said, his voice low and angry. 'Over a hundred years I've pretended. I've killed and maimed and done unspeakable things. And all for Albert.'

'No!' Richard shouted. 'No, it's not true!'

'For Pip,' Derek continued desperately. "That day

you told me to take him away, I did,' Derek said. 'I threatened to kill him. I beat him up. I did all sorts. And he just kept telling me that I didn't know what I was doing, that he forgave me, that his life didn't matter but that life itself did.'

'You've been . . . You've been on our side all this time?' Peter asked suddenly, staring at Derek uncertainly.

'No!' Sheila shouted out suddenly. 'No, he's lying. He's evil. He's not on our side. He's not. He can't be . . .'

'Hush,' Pip said softly. 'Sheila, Derek is telling the truth.'

'Then why didn't he help us?' Anna asked accusingly. 'Why did he lock me up? Why did he let Sheila . . . let the Surpluses . . . How could he?'

'Yes,' Jude said suspiciously. 'How could he?'

Pip moved towards him and put his hand on his shoulder. 'Jude, you must understand. Derek had to be closer to Richard Pincent than anyone. He had to be beyond suspicion. We couldn't risk him being discovered, even if it meant suffering. Even if it meant that we lost people.'

'Derek told you about Unit X,' Peter said suddenly. 'He's the reason I went in. He helped us save Sheila.'

Pip nodded. 'He alerted me to many things, but we had to ensure the intelligence appeared to come from other sources,' he said.

'All this time?' Richard gasped. 'All this time you've been working for him?'

'Albert told me what would happen. He predicted everything,' Derek said quietly. 'Even this. He knew everything would end, unless . . . unless –'

'Unless what?' Hillary interjected.

'Unless we ensured there were children,' Pip said quietly. 'Unless we protected the eternal cycle of life. Birth and death, as it has always been. That is what the ring symbolises, Richard. Not the formula to Longevity. It is Nature's eternity, the right way to live forever. Through our children, through our children's children. Through Peter, Jude, Molly and Ben, the Surpluses around the world.'

Jude tried to swallow but found he couldn't – a huge lump had appeared in his throat. Instead he turned to Pip desperately. 'I'm sorry,' he said. 'I doubted you. I thought you . . . When I saw you with Derek I thought you were on his side. I thought . . .'

'You were right to doubt me,' Pip said gently. 'You are a leader, Jude, and a leader can never trust blindly. You have helped me more than I can say. I am . . .' He looked down. 'I am very proud of you, Jude.'

Jude bit his lip. 'No,' he said miserably. 'I let you down.'

'You could never let me down,' Pip said, his voice choking slightly. Then he took a deep breath. 'I have been so hard on you, Jude. I have lied to you, I have kept the truth from you. From all of you. But I only did what I did to protect you. To protect the circle of life. Now I have done what I needed to do; now I have paid the price for what I did all those years ago.

It is time for you now. You are a leader, Jude. It is time to lead. You must inspire, you must plan, you must make the world a better place. Peter, you are a fighter. A protector.'

'No,' Peter said, shooting a look at Anna. 'No, Pip. I'm a father. That's what I should have been instead of coming to London. I'm not a fighter. Not any more.'

'Yes you are,' Anna said, her voice small but firm. 'You are a fighter, Peter. You're a father too, but you can be both. The children and I – we're not the only ones who need you.'

Peter looked at her for a few moments then nodded gratefully, as he realised that she had forgiven him, that she understood.

'Anna's right – you must be all these things,' Pip said gently. 'Fight for the future. Protect those who need protection. Be a father, Peter – to your children, to your future children, to others who have no parents of their own. And Anna?' Anna looked up, her eyes wide but resolute. 'You, Anna, must be the mother of all. You need to be the strongest of all, because you will need to lead and protect and fight. You must negotiate, you must convince, you must provide. And you must look after Sheila.'

'I'll look after Sheila,' Jude said tightly, but Sheila shook her head.

'I can look after myself,' she said calmly. She walked towards Pip, and her eyes stared into his unwaveringly. 'I don't need parents any more,' she said, her voice catching slightly. 'I don't need protectors. I'm going to be useful, Pip. I'll protect the Surpluses. I'll help.'

'Yes, you will,' Pip said, smiling gently. 'You are stronger than you know, Sheila, and I wish I could be here to watch you discover that strength.'

'You can,' Jude said uncertainly. 'You will.'

But before Pip could reply, Richard staggered up from his chair. 'Enough of these lies,' he seethed. 'Hillary, do something. Stop these lies. Guard, take them. Kill them all . . .'

Hillary looked at him with distaste. 'Guard,' she said, 'call for someone to take him away. I have heard enough of his lies. Quite enough.'

The guard nodded and seconds later, two masked men arrived. They grabbed Richard by the arms and legs and carried him out of the room.

'No!' Richard screamed as he was dragged down the corridor. 'No! Water! I just need water . . .'

Seconds later the screaming could no longer be heard and the room was filled with silence.

Hillary looked around glassy-eyed, then focused on Richard's scientist who was standing next to the door, his face as white as his lab coat.

'So there is no contamination? There's a virus? It can't be cured?' she asked.

He shook his head. 'No. Perhaps the symptoms can be alleviated with old medicine, but we've carried out hundreds of autopsies and we can't . . .' He trailed off, looking slightly ill. 'No,' he whispered. 'It can't be cured.'

'And it affects everyone?'

'Not everyone,' Pip said gravely. 'Not Opt Outs. Not Surpluses. Not those whose immune systems have been allowed to function.'

Hillary nodded slowly. 'Then we need to plan,' she said, only her shaking hands betraying her emotion. 'We must maintain order. We must organise.' She studied Pip carefully. 'How long do we have?' she asked eventually.

'Weeks. Months at most,' Pip said. 'We need to protect those who will survive. That is paramount.'

'Of course.' Hillary nodded. 'And we need to cope with the bodies . . . logistically, I mean. We have no graves. No –'

Derek moved forward. 'We've already drawn up plans for civil management too. We don't want riots. We don't want mass hysteria. But things are going to get messy. There will be a shortage of key workers, a shortage of police, of farmers, of gravediggers. There might be terrorist attacks from abroad, war even if people get really desperate.'

Hillary was nodding, as though on autopilot. 'You're talking as if the world is coming to an end,' she managed to say.

'Not an end, a new beginning,' Pip said gently. 'A beginning without Longevity. A beginning that has life because it also has death. Hillary, people have been sick for a long time now, not from disease but from their half-lives – not enough food, not enough energy, not enough things to fill the day. It's time for Longevity to end. It's time to end the sickness.'

Hillary nodded vaguely. 'The children – they must be taught. They have to understand so much if they are to . . .' She trailed off, frowning, as though her brain was trying to process too much information at once. 'The young must be taught. And quickly,' she said. Then she fell back against a chair, clutching it, her white knuckles shaking.

'Hillary,' Pip said, moving towards her and putting a hand on her shoulder. 'They understand more than you know. How to lead, how to provide for themselves, how to fight for what's right, for what they believe in.'

He looked over at Jude, at Peter, at Anna and Sheila. 'I could not be prouder of you,' he said, his voice catching. 'Of all of you. Jude, Sheila, Anna – you are all the parents of the new world. A new chance to get things right. Or at least to do things better. We have made so many mistakes, ruined so much. You are our hope.'

'We? You're talking like you won't be around to help,' Jude said awkwardly.

Albert smiled, his blue eyes twinkling. 'Exactly right, Jude, as always,' he said. 'You know, I've waited for this moment for a very long time,' he said. 'As soon as I knew the end was near, I stopped taking my Longevity. It was a release. You mustn't try to hold on to things that are past their sell-by date. None of us should, including me. Now I just need to say goodbye to you, to make sure you have all you need for the brave new world ahead of you. I have days, perhaps, but no more.'

'But . . . but we need you. The Underground needs you,' Jude said, fighting back his tears.

'No.' Pip shook his head. 'The Underground is over. There is no need for it any more. It has served its purpose. There is a new world to build, Jude, and I know that you are capable of building it.' He smiled gently. 'The truth is, I'm looking forward to a very long sleep. The longest.'

'But . . .' Peter said, shaking his head. 'You can't go. You can't.'

'We all go eventually,' Pip said softly. 'And others come in our wake. I am just a leaf, Peter. Just a leaf falling from the tree so that a new bud may grow. Look after the buds, won't you? And each other. I shall miss you.'

'And we'll miss you,' Jude said, his voice full of emotion. 'But you can depend on us. We'll be the future, Pip. We'll do it together.' He reached out to Sheila and took her hand.

'Together.' She nodded tentatively.

'Together,' Peter agreed, holding out his arm to Anna.

'Together,' she said.

''Gether,' Ben said, looking up at her uncertainly. 'Home now? Go home?'

'This *is* your home, young man,' Pip said, his eyes twinkling again. 'The whole world is.'

Epilogue

14 MARCH, AF 15

Molly lay back in her chair, letting the sun warm her face for just a few minutes more. It was early afternoon and she knew she shouldn't be wasting good daylight, but it was too delicious, too blissful just lying there, suspended in time.

'Molly?' She glanced up to see Albert, her younger brother, looking at her curiously.

'Yeah, I'm coming. I was just . . .' She trailed off as she saw him grin, his eyes twinkling, and realised that he wasn't annoyed with her, wasn't going to tell.

'I know exactly what you were doing,' he said cheerfully. 'Just don't let Dad catch you.'

She nodded, and pulled herself off the chair wearily.

'He's fixed the tractor,' Albert continued.

Molly's eyes lit up. The tractor had been out of action for days now, resulting in aching limbs and backs for all of them. 'He did? How?'

Albert shrugged and put his hands in his pockets.

'Dunno. Ben was helping him. Engine was dirty or something.'

Molly rolled her eyes. 'Dirty?' It never ceased to amaze her that her brother showed so little interest in anything of a technical nature. 'Do you know how an engine actually works, Alby?'

'No, and I don't want to,' he said, winking. Molly laughed and followed him down the dirt track towards the fields where they spent their afternoons every day. Mornings were for learning – her mother was always clear about that. Words and sums and science and questions were what mattered in Mum's eyes. 'You have to question everything,' she'd say. 'You have to always ask why, and if you don't understand the answer, you ask again.'

So Molly did. She asked questions all the time, demanding to know how things worked and why, discovering what happened when you added one thing to another, finding out how to make things and how to break them. She also asked about the past. She'd been too little to remember the Old World much – all she remembered was heated conversations and moving around a lot and staying inside because 'the hoodlums' were smashing up the high street and pillaging. She remembered her father disappearing for what felt like years to join the New Underground Army to patrol the streets and divide things up fairly, to Manage the Handover. She still wasn't sure what the Handover was, but she knew that what was being handed over was valuable and that the people who had it didn't want to give it away.

Her parents didn't talk about the Handover much – they said it was too recent, that the New Civilisation was still too fragile. But they answered Molly's questions about the Old World happily enough. What was it like to have shops instead of having to produce your own food? Was there really a time when there were too many people? What was wrong with Mrs Baker up the road, and where had Mr Baker gone?

The shops were OK, her mother told her, but you weren't always free to buy what you wanted and sometimes things were so expensive you couldn't get them even if you were allowed. That led to another question about money, which sounded very exotic and exciting to Molly, but her mother assured her it never helped anyone much.

Yes, the world was indeed too full once, her mother told her, and no children were allowed at all because no one died. Molly used to love and hate that story in equal measure. It had been her favourite bedtime tale when she'd been little – a world with no children, with Catchers and Surplus Halls and no brothers to play with, no space to play in. They had all the space in the world now, her mother would tell her. They were very lucky, even if it was cold sometimes and there weren't many other children to play with. They had each other and that was more important than anything. They had the future too.

As for Mrs Baker, her mother told her that she was one of the Old Legals. There weren't many of them left because most had died a long time ago from the Virus, but some had survived – no one really knew why. Now she was very, very old and she couldn't do much more than sit her time out, which was why they had to look after her and Molly was sent round every day to read to her, to make things more bearable until the end came. Mr Baker had already gone to the Other Side. It was good to go there, her mother told her, when it was your time. No one should outstay their welcome.

'Come on, slowcoach, or you'll have no supper before bed.'

Molly looked at Albert and raised an eyebrow. Her parents always threatened that when one of them was naughty, but they never went through with it. Mum used to be hungry a lot when she was little, Dad had told Molly once. That was why she never let them go without a meal. That was why the sight of protruding bones sent her racing into the kitchen to bake bread. Uncle Ben used to tease her sometimes, pretending to faint from hunger when he didn't like the meal she'd made, usually in the winter when stocks were running low and they were eating porridge for the fifth time in a week. But he never teased her for long because none of them could bear to see her sad.

'There you are.' Dad was waiting for them in the field and Ben was in the tractor, a dot in the distance, the reassuring hum of the machine just audible. Every time it broke Dad would say that was it – no more tractor. He would say it was a relief because it guzzled more energy than both his children put together, but somehow they always got it working again. Dad said that one day there wouldn't be any more petrol and then they'd have to do the work by hand. 'Alby, chickens. They need a run out. And Molly, clean out the pigs. OK?'

They looked at each other, Albert evidently triumphant at the division of labour. 'See ya! Wouldn't want to be ya!' he whispered under his breath as he disappeared towards the chicken coop.

'Pigs?' Molly screwed up her face in distaste. 'Really?'

Her father nodded sternly. 'Really,' he said, tousling her hair. 'Go on.'

She sighed and wandered over to the pigsty. It was large enough for fifty pigs, but they only had twenty. Dad had told her that they used to keep a hundred pigs, all penned together. That was what Molly thought the world must have been like before – people all squashed up with no space to move. Dad said that people had used too much energy and the world had been heating up, but Molly thought it was just that they didn't have enough room. Sometimes, when they were younger, Alby used to sleep in her bed when he was scared, and she always ended up throwing off the blankets.

Quickly she set about sweeping the sty, filling the troughs with food and water. Then she played with the piglets for a few minutes, being careful not to antagonise their mother. Lastly, looking around to check that no one could see her, she dug out her notebook. She carried her notebook everywhere – it had been a fourteenth birthday present from her mother.

In it, she would record interesting events such as the monthly town debates where all the grown-ups would get together and argue about things like land division and use of old stock and whether wells were the property of the community or the landowner. Once you were fourteen you were encouraged to go to the debates and learn about how things worked, and while Ben dismissed them as boring Molly like to write down everything she heard and think about it later. She also drew pictures in her notebook and listed her hopes, her fears, her desires and her views on other people.

She flicked over the pages, stopping every so often to reread a passage she was particularly proud of, like the one on Stock. Her parents had recently told her all about Stock warehouses, where things from before were kept, like petrol and watches and tissues and books. They'd been put there by the Authorities just before the Handover. You had to buy the things from the town leader, paying with food or Community Work, but her parents said one day the warehouses would be empty because no one could make those things any more. They said Uncle Jude was trying to start a training programme but no one wanted to take part. They said that the grown-ups didn't like the idea of training because it brought back bad memories of how things used to be.

She continued turning the pages until she got to her favourite picture. It was a rubbing and her mother had taught her how to do it, taking an object and putting it under the paper and rubbing the other side with a pen so that the object was revealed like a picture. She'd tried it with a few things, none of which had looked very pretty, and then her dad had given her his ring and let her rub the engraving. It was beautiful – a flower, so delicate, so beautifully drawn.

The picture was very important, Dad had told her – it represented Renewal, which meant new replacing old. Like the green leaves that come through in the spring, he'd said, and the old ones falling to the ground. Molly had nodded sagely when he'd told her, but secretly she'd thought he was wrong. It didn't represent Renewal – it represented something else, something she didn't understand yet but would figure out one day, she was sure. Because what her father didn't seem to have noticed was that the picture was made out of letters and symbols, like the ones she'd learnt about in science. She'd copied them out on the following page and stared at them until her eyes had hurt, but for now they didn't want her to know what they meant. She'd find out, though. That was what science was all about – that was what Great-great-grandpa Albert had said in his letter to her. The true scientist lets truth emerge.

'Molly? You finished with the pigs? Because Dad says we can go with him into town if you want.'

'Town?' Molly's eyes lit up. Science and butterflies forgotten, she tucked her notebook back into her pocket and jumped off the fence. 'I'm coming. Wait for me!'

Also by Gemma Malley

Find out what happens when your past
catches up with you and you don't like
what you see . . .

The Returners

Turn the page for a gripping taster . . .

I am hot. Too hot. The sun burns my skin. I'm running. The altitude is high; I catch my breath. I'm chewing something. Chocolate. No, not chocolate. Not sweet. It gives me energy. I'm thirsty, but I have nothing to drink. Up and up, like a mountain, but there are steps beneath my feet. I stumble but fear drives me forward, upward. Life or death. Survival or . . . My clothes stick to me, my shoes rub unbearably. I turn a corner, I am near the top. I must reach the top, must get far enough away. I scramble, using my hands now, flailing against the unforgiving clay. I pull, I heave, I push myself up. I am at the top. I am being pursued. I must get away from the mob. I must get away . . .

Another place – here there is a line of people ahead of me. Broken people – thin, frail, slumped, their eyes vacant, a flicker of something here and there but mostly they are looking down. For safety. They shuffle forward; no one speaks. The train behind them leaves. One or two turn to watch it go. Their faces are hollow. I reach up to feel my own face; I can feel nothing. Do I exist? Forward again, bags and children's hands clutched tightly. There are two piles. One for clothes, one for bags. Two doors – one for women and children, one for men. The line inches forward. One or two people speak, make light of the situation. It is better, no? Things will improve. Don't look like that – always so negative. A child cries; his mother pulls him to her.

It is days later. I can smell it. Death. Burning flesh. It fills my nose, fills my chest, I am choking, spluttering, it is consuming me. I am screaming, screaming, screaming . . .

I sit bolt upright, drenched in sweat; it takes me a few minutes to catch my breath, to slow my heart. I look around the room, disoriented. I was asleep. I look at my watch. It's only 9 p.m. I breathe in and out, slowly. I remember – I came up to play on the computer. Patrick's downstairs with Dad. Did I really scream? Did they hear me? Maybe they called up to me? Is that what woke me up?

I lean over the side of the bed, my head between my knees. Recovery position. Can you recover from nightmares? What is there to recover from? They're my own imagination. I do it to myself. The human brain is a scary thing when you're not in control of it.

The door opens slightly and my father's face appears around it. 'Everything all right, son?' He's drunk. I can tell from the slur in his voice. But he's happy drunk. Otherwise he wouldn't be asking if I was OK; he'd be telling me to shut up, to stop being a freak, so stop being such a bloody disappointment to him.

I nod. 'Yeah. Just . . . got carried away. With a game,' I say lamely, but he swallows it.

'We're just finishing up. Give us a few more minutes.'

'Whatever. Take as long as you want.'

I can't look at him, can't let him see my flushed face, my shaking hands. Always the same nightmares. Sometimes I get the director's cut, sometimes the edited version. Nothing different about them, though – fear, death, torture. I wonder what my old shrink would make of them.

I pull myself up heavily from the bed. Got to calm down before I go downstairs. I look out of the window. A hundred yards away or so I can see Claire's room. There's a light on. That light used to be our signal – Claire used to flash it on and off when her parents had gone to bed and I'd climb out of the window and shin up the drainpipe. We used to talk mainly. She was always very good at listening. We'd listen to CDs too – mostly hers, which were pretty rank in a cheesy kind of way. I'd bring my own round sometimes – try to educate her, try to improve her mind.

Claire was the first person I met when we moved here. I saw her immediately, as soon as I'd got out of the car. Dad told me to wait while the removal van parked, but I saw her out of the window. She was walking right towards us, dawdling like girls do.

I timed it to perfection, waiting for her to be almost next to me before I opened the car door. It nearly knocked her off her feet.

I looked down at the ground; she just looked right at me. That was the thing with Claire – she doesn't act like normal people. She never seems to have any of the hang-ups.

'You the ones moving in here?' she asked, pointing at our house.

I nodded. I was already embarrassed. I was always embarrassed.

'Are you our new neighbour?' That was my mum. 'I'm Chloe and this is William. Will.'

'I'm Claire,' Claire said, looking at my mother curiously.

A woman appeared around the corner. 'Claire!' she said, her tone exasperated. 'Here you are. I've told you before, do *not* walk away from me like that.'

'I didn't walk away,' Claire said seriously. 'You were just walking too slowly.' Even then she wasn't someone you wanted to get in an argument with.

Funny, I remember that like it happened yesterday too. I have a very good memory. Unnerving, Dad calls it. I remember whole conversations word for word, remember what someone was wearing down to the colour of their tie, remember something that happened years before. Other things I don't remember at all. There are entire weeks I can't remember. Sometimes I find myself in places and I can't remember how I got there, or even how long I've been there.

Guess that's just one more thing that makes me a freak.

Later, when Mum and Dad were unpacking, Claire appeared over the fence at the bottom of our garden and encouraged me to climb over. And that, as they say, was that.

The light thing started later on, after my Mum died. Claire knew how cut up I was, and she knew that I couldn't – wouldn't – show it. So she used to squeeze my hand secretly sometimes in school. And she said that if I was sad at night, then I could always come over. She'd flash her light every night when her parents had put her to bed and I could come over. If I wanted to. And if her light wasn't flashing and I wanted to come over anyway, I should coo like a pigeon under her window and if she was awake she'd let me in.

I didn't think I'd go – I told myself I didn't need to, didn't need anything any more. But that very night I saw her light flashing and my heart leapt and I knew I had to go. It was like I was a ship that was about to crash against something, crash really hard, and her bedroom was a lighthouse and if I could just find myself there things might be OK after all.

And she always got it. She never asked stupid questions, never told me everything would be OK, never looked awkward like everyone at school. She just listened and told me what she thought. She said that she thought losing your mother was one of the worst things that could happen, that the fact Mum killed herself made it worse because she didn't have to die, she chose to. And that was the only time I nearly cried, the whole time, when she said that, because she was right, and that was what hurt the most. My mother left me. She didn't love me enough to stay.

Claire's light goes off. Has she gone to bed? It's still early. Maybe not that early. I don't know what's early or late these days. Dad lets me stay up as late as I want so long as I don't make any noise. I watch out of my window.

There's someone there. In our garden. Down at the bottom. My heart starts to thud. It's her. It's Claire. I press up against the window, open it wide, lean down.

'Claire! Claire.' I realise how much I've longed to see the flashing light, how much I've missed it. I want Claire to bring me in, bring me home. I want to tell her about my nightmares, tell her about seeing Mr Best, about Yan. There's no one else I can talk to about that stuff.

I can see her – she's walking towards my window. Something's different about her. Her hair's longer. More straggly. Her eyes seem more . . . well, they're bigger. She looks older, her cheeks more hollow. Her clothes . . .

I feel like I've been punched. It isn't her. Not Claire. It's one of the freaks. She's staring up at me with a face full of pain, pain I don't want, don't need, can't take. I shout at her, swear, tell her to leave me alone. I shut the window and fall back on the bed. 'Leave me alone,' I sob, knowing that I'm going to have red eyes when I face Patrick, knowing that he's going to shoot a little look at Dad. 'You're in my head. You don't exist. I don't want to see you any more . . .'

I grab my pillow and punch it. I need to sort my head out. I'm losing the plot here.

I glance back at Claire's window; hoping her light would flash – that was just a moment of weakness. I haven't talked to Claire for ages. The light's not going to flash again. She's asleep. She's someone else now. I'm someone else.

OUT NOW